# CATHERINE'S PURSUIT

## MCKENNA'S DAUGHTERS
### BOOK THREE

## LENA NELSON DOOLEY

WILD HEART
BOOKS

The characters and events in this fictional work are the product of the author's imagination. Any resemblance to actual people, living or dead, is coincidental.

Unless otherwise indicated, all Scripture quotations are taken from the Holy Bible, Kings James Version.

ISBN-13:

*Dedicated to my great-grandsons - Sebastian, Holden, Hudson, Grayson, Calvin, and Henry, whose middle name is James from my beloved husband.*

*Another reason to praise the Lord, that He let James and I live long enough to know so many of our great-grands.*

And Jabez called on the God of Israel,
saying, Oh that thou wouldest bless
me indeed, and enlarge my coast, and
that thine hand might be with me,
and that thou wouldest keep me from
evil, that it may not grieve me! And
God granted him that which he
requested.

— 1 CHRONICLES 4:10

# CHAPTER 1

*September 19, 1885*

*San Francisco, California*

*C*atherine Lenora McKenna could hardly believe the long-awaited day had arrived. Her eighteenth birthday.

Now she was an adult, and her father would have to stop hovering over her as if she were a fragile china doll in one of his stores. She would be free. Holding her hands above her head like the ballerina in the music box on her bureau, she whirled in a circle that lifted the hem of her blue taffeta skirt to a scandalous height. That didn't matter, because no one was here to catch a glimpse of her ankles, anyway. Not even her personal maid, Julie, who had gone downstairs to grab Catherine a more substantial breakfast from the kitchen before she fainted dead away.

Aunt Kirstin wanted Catherine to eat very light before her party tonight, where a sumptuous banquet would precede the ball. There would be presents to open as well. Catherine hoped her father planned a spectacular gift for her birthday...maybe to send her on a tour of the Continent. Of course, Aunt Kirstin would probably accompany her, but at least she would be able to see more of the world for herself, not just read about it.

Europe should be beautiful in the autumn, or in any season of the year. Since both of her parents were born in Scotland, she wanted to visit there as well as London...Paris...Rome. She had read every book and magazine she could get her hands on, so she knew so much about Europe. A thrill of anticipation shot through her whole body. Visions of crossing London Bridge, strolling along Avenue des Champs Elysees, or touring the Colosseum danced through her head. Pictures she'd enjoyed studying with their Holmes stereopticon. She wondered if Father would accompany her or if he would allow Aunt Kirstin to be her only escort...besides a few servants, of course.

"Where is Julie with my food?" Catherine huffed out an exasperated breath. "Am I going to have to go to the kitchen myself?"

She thrust open the door and hurried down the hallway, the sound of her footsteps lost in the thick cushioning of the carpet. At the top of the front stairs, she stopped to see if she could figure out where her aunt Kirstin was before she sneaked down the backstairs.

Peering over the balcony railing, she caught a glimpse of her aunt's face through the partially opened door to the library. Her brows were knit together into a frown as she stared at someone in the room with her. Catherine had never seen such a fierce expression on her aunt's face.

Father's voice was muffled as he said something to his sister-in-law. *What is he doing home at this time of morning?* Catherine wished she could tell what they were talking about. She had never heard her father use that tone with anyone, especially not Aunt Kirstin. As if he were angry or terribly upset.

Catherine leaned farther over but kept a firm grip on the railing so she wouldn't tumble down. A drop onto a marble floor could be deadly.

Aunt Kirstin gripped each hand into a fist and planted them on her hips. "Just when are you going to tell her?"

Come to think of it, her aunt was using a harsher tone than Catherine had ever heard her use.

Father didn't answer.

Catherine quickly crept down the stairs being careful not to place her foot on the second step from the foyer, which would squeak and reveal her presence. At the bottom, she straightened and checked her reflection in the gilt-framed, oval mirror beside the front door.

When she found everything satisfactory, she tiptoed toward the library.

"I don't know." Her father's words stopped her in her tracks.

What did he not know?

"Angus." Aunt Kirstin's voice was firm and insistent. "She deserves to know the truth. And now she's old enough to understand."

Catherine didn't hesitate to enter her favorite room in the house. She pushed the door farther open, and both her aunt and her father turned startled eyes toward her. The two looked as if they had been caught in an act of mischief.

"Tell me what? What will I understand?" Her questions hovered in the air, quivering like hummingbirds without a way to escape the net of tension that bound the three of them together.

Her father glanced at her aunt, then turned his attention back to Catherine. The deep scowl on his face dissolved, and he dropped into the closest chair, dejection dragging his shoulders into a slump. Tears welled up in his eyes and rolled down his cheeks unheeded. He didn't even blink.

"I knew this day would come...eventually." Each word sounded as if it had been wrung from his throat.

Catherine had never before seen her father cry. And he had always been such a strong man. But right now, he was draped in defeat. Her heart hitched in her chest, making her breathless. Something must be terribly wrong. Was he sick with a deadly disease? About to die? How would she live without him? She wanted to grab him in a tight hug and cling with all her might to keep him close.

Aunt Kirstin dragged two chairs closer to where he sat and offered one to Catherine before settling on the other. She smoothed her skirt over her knees and clasped her hands tight enough to blanch her knuckles.

Fear swamped Catherine, trying to drown her in its depths. The strong foundation her life had been built upon shuddered, then she felt as if a crevasse opened deep within her. Tears leaked into her own eyes, blurring her vision as she stared first at her father and then at her aunt, the anchors in her life.

Her father raised red-rimmed eyes toward her, his face a pale, scary caricature of the man she'd always leaned upon. "There's so much you don't know...my precious daughter."

Such a formal way for her father to talk to her, as if they were separated in some unseen way. Trembling started in her knees. She was glad she was sitting, so she didn't sink to the floor in a swoon. The tremors rose over her whole body, and she shook as though a chill wind had swept through the room.

*Dare I ask another question?* When she tried, her tongue stayed glued to the roof of her mouth, so she waited for him to continue.

Aunt Kirstin didn't utter a single word either.

"I've brought Miss Catherine a bit of a snack." Julie

bustled through the open doorway, breaking the unbearable tension for a moment. "There's enough for all of you...and a pot of that new tea you just received from China." She set the tray on the table that stood beside Aunt Kirstin's chair, then exited the room.

Mechanically, Catherine's aunt poured three cups of the steaming liquid and added just the right amount of milk and sugar to match each person's preference. When she handed the saucer and teacup to Father, both of their hands shook, rattling the china.

Catherine received her tea and kept one hand on the cup, warming her icy fingertips.

"Would you like a sandwich or a piece of cake?" Aunt Kirstin's whispered words were only a bit louder than the clink of the dishes.

Catherine didn't think she could get a single bite down her throat that now felt like a sandy desert. She shook her head.

Father didn't glance at her aunt before he handed his cup back without even taking a sip. He turned his gaze toward Catherine and took a breath, releasing it as a soul-deep sigh. "Some things happened when you were born...that I've never shared...with you...with anyone, except your aunt."

She set her cup and saucer back on the tray and waited for him to continue.

"Would you like me to leave?" Aunt Kirstin stared at Father, a look of something akin to pity on her face. "Would that make it easier?"

"Nothing will make it easier." Father roused more than he had since Catherine entered the library, his voice slicing through the room like a sharp dagger. "And no. Since you've opened the subject, you'll sit right there until I'm finished."

Her aunt shrank back against her chair and lowered her gaze to the Aubusson carpet where she traced the intricate pattern as if she had never seen it before. Catherine doubted she noticed any of the colors or flowers right now.

If Father didn't tell her what he was talking about soon, Catherine was afraid she would scream. The atmosphere in the room hung heavy with suspense. She cleared her throat and covered the cough that ensued with one fisted hand.

"There is no easy way...to say this." Father shifted in the chair, the wooden legs creaking under his slight weight. He stared at her. "I'm going to tell you what happened. Please don't interrupt me until I'm finished. Otherwise, I might not get through the whole story. Then you can ask any questions you want."

Her nose itched, but she didn't dare rub it. She didn't want to do anything that might stop this tale from pouring forth from her father. She gritted her teeth ready to face whatever it was, no matter how grim.

"You know that your...mother and I were on a wagon train on the Oregon Trail. Lenora had some...difficulties near the end of our journey." He swallowed, his Adam's apple bobbing convulsively. "She had to ride in the back of the wagon for a couple of weeks."

Catherine knew she was born on the Oregon Trail, and she knew that her mother died in childbirth. Their family friend Odette Marshall had told her that much before Aunt Kirstin finally came to California to help her father. Even though Catherine had been only six years old when she'd heard it, the story was burned into her heart.

"When you were born, one of the women who assisted Dr. Horton brought you to me. I held you in my arms, huddled beside the campfire on that bone-chilling night." A faraway look filled his eyes, and she knew he didn't see her sitting nearby. "I loved you the moment I laid eyes on you....curly red fuzz covering your head....blue eyes."

"Blue?"

He held one palm toward her, stopping her question in midsentence. "They didn't turn green until later."

She hadn't known that. Other questions fought to escape, but she clamped her lips tightly to restrain them. The turmoil inside her made her stomach roil. She swallowed the acid that crept to her throat.

"Before long, a different woman brought another baby girl to me....curly red fuzz....blue eyes. The spittin' image of you. I cuddled both of you close to my heart and kissed each of your cheeks."

Catherine almost gasped. She couldn't remember the last time her father had held her close and kissed her cheek. She knew he loved her, but he wasn't demonstrative anymore. That was why he showered her with gifts so often, wasn't it? To show her he loved her.

"Then a few minutes later, another identical girl was brought to me. I didn't have enough arms to hold all three of you." He rubbed one hand over his chin, the rasp of unshaven stubble loud in the quiet room.

*Three of us?* How could that be? Did her two sisters die when her mother had? *Sisters!* She had always wished for siblings. Yearned for them.

Grief ripped through her. Tears streamed down her cheeks. To find out she had sisters and lose them all within a few minutes. She didn't feel like celebrating her birthday. Instead, she wanted to mourn the sisters she lost before she even knew she had them.

Catherine started formulating questions in her mind, waiting for the chance to ask them. Before they were half-formed, her father rose to his feet and walked out the door without saying another word. She waited a few minutes in a silence so heavy, it felt oppressive. She realized he wasn't coming back when the front door opened, then closed. Why hadn't he waited until she asked her questions?

~

"*M*r. McKenna wants to talk to you."

Collin Elliott straightened from behind the stack of boxes he had been checking against the bill of lading and stared at the warehouse foreman. "I'm almost finished with these. Does he want to see me right away?"

"The old man's in a strange mood. Has been all day." Howard Lane scratched his head. "Ain't never seen him like this before. Better git on up there to the office."

Collin slashed an X with a piece of chalk on the last crate he'd finished checking and laid the letter-clip board that held the forms on top of the next box. He had been working out here most of the day. Because he often shoved his fingers through his hair, he was sure he looked like a wreck.

That described him to a T. A wreck. Or at least he had been since he lost his ship at sea last spring, along with all the merchandise in the hold. It had taken him several months to recover sufficiently from the severe cuts he'd sustained to his leg, but Mr. McKenna had made sure he was taken care of, even paying him as if he were still a captain. Then the old man gave him this job in the warehouse to keep busy. Still, a dull ache in his gut wouldn't let him forget one minute of the horror he experienced that day, and the limp from his injury kept the memory fresh with each step he took.

Collin headed toward the offices at the other end of the large building. He tried to straighten his mussed hair and stuffed his shirttail farther down inside his trousers. He could try to look neater, even if he did walk like a cripple.

Mr. McKenna's secretary, Roger Amery, glanced up

as Collin entered the front office. "He's waiting for you. Just go on back."

He gave the man a distracted nod as he hurried by. The door to his boss's office stood open, so he entered.

"Close that behind you, Elliott. We need privacy." The old man didn't even look up from the paper he was writing on.

After complying, Collin dropped into the chair situated close to the front of the desk. What did the man want? Going back through the events of the last few days, Collin didn't remember anything he might have done wrong, so he slouched into a relaxed pose, hoping to give the impression that being called to the office didn't bother him. Of course, a lot of things had bothered him ever since that ghastly shipwreck, which haunted his dreams at night and his thoughts in the daytime.

Mr. McKenna laid down his newfangled, fancy pen that looked out of place on the scarred desk and clasped his hands together. Collin had never seen the old man look so bad. Haggard. Older somehow. Some calamity must have happened. He hoped it wasn't another shipwreck. Too many of those would put the business in jeopardy.

"You doin' all right, Elliott?" Even his boss's voice didn't sound as strong as it usually did.

He straightened in the chair. "Yes, sir. Better all the time."

"I'm glad. When will you be ready to go back on a

ship?" Mr. McKenna peered at him as if he could see right through to his soul.

Collin cleared his throat. *What can I say?* He might not ever be ready to go to sea again. "What did you have in mind, sir?"

"I know you feel responsible for what happened to the *Trinity Bell*, but the storm that hit her came up unexpectedly and was stronger than any we had encountered in a long time." When his employer shifted in his chair, the leather gave a familiar creak. "No one could have prevented that wreck."

Collin lowered his head and stared at his scuffed boots. "Maybe a more seasoned captain could have." He hated voicing the words that wouldn't let go of his mind.

Angus McKenna stood and walked around the desk. "I meant what I said. No one could have. And you did save every member of your crew without considering your own safety." He laid a hand on Collin's shoulder. "I'm really sorry it happened on your watch, but I knew what I was doing when I made you the youngest ship's captain in my fleet."

His words didn't change the way Collin felt one iota. If he lived to be a hundred years old, he would carry the guilt of that wreck to his grave.

Mr. McKenna folded his arms and propped himself on the edge of the massive desk. "I didn't bring you in here to rehash this. Something else is on my mind. It's about time you got back into polite society, my boy."

"I've never been accepted into 'polite society,' sir. I'm just a sailor." He clamped his mouth shut before he spewed words he would later regret. Words about rejection. About never being as good as everyone else.

"Then we'll just have to remedy that. You're a ship's captain. Captains are welcomed everywhere."

Collin stared at an odd-shaped ink stain on the blotter that covered most of the desk top. It reminded him of a half-sunken schooner. "Not anymore."

"Of course you are. And you'll command another ship soon. You have to. It's just like getting back on a horse after you've been thrown. If you don't do it, you'll forever be skittish. We can't have that." His boss went back around the desk, picked up a piece of paper, and handed it to Collin.

He recognized that the address was in a more high-class part of San Francisco than he was acquainted with. "What's this?"

"My address. Today is Catherine's eighteenth birthday. We're having a dinner party and ball for her. I want you there. You might as well start becoming acquainted with more people in the business community. Many of them are also close family friends so they'll be in attendance." He dropped back into his chair.

"I don't have anything suitable to wear to a party, sir." At least he had a good excuse not to attend. A sigh of relief escaped.

"I've thought of that. Roger will accompany you to make sure you're outfitted the way you should be. I know most of your possessions went down with the *Trinity Bell*." He picked up a piece of paper and started looking at it. "We had insurance on the ship and its contents. So we'll replace what you lost." He lifted a brass bell and gave it a swift shake.

Roger Amery hurried into the office. "How can I help you, sir?"

The way the man stood, Collin almost expected to hear the sound of his heels clicking together.

Mr. McKenna handed the sheet of paper to his secretary. "Take Elliott to town and use some of the insurance money to purchase the things I've listed."

When he gave the two of them a dismissive wave, Collin followed the other man out of the room. He couldn't think of any way to get out of this shopping trip and the subsequent party. He didn't know how he would be able to get through the excruciating evening ahead. Just how many of the people attending the festivities would look down on him? Not only was he a sailor, but he also lost the ship he captained. And his limp announced his failure and weakness to everyone he met.

# CHAPTER 2

*P*icking nervously at her cuticles until they were sore, Catherine paced across her room. It had been several hours since her father rushed from the library leaving her reeling from the shocking news he shared. Before she could even voice any of the questions bouncing around inside her head, he was gone, and she sat staring at Aunt Kirstin. Catherine didn't want to talk to anyone right then, so she retreated to the sanctuary of her own room. Her heart felt like a boulder in her chest, and her thoughts were as scrambled as the eggs she usually ate for breakfast.

All the ideas that assaulted her mind led nowhere except to a deep pain in her heart. She had missed having a mother, but Odette Marshall, and then Aunt Kirstin, did a good job of filling that void in her life. But finding out she had two identical sisters created a hole so large inside her, she knew nothing could ever fill it.

Why hadn't Father stayed and let her ask questions? He'd said he would. Whatever changed his mind?

When Julie came to the door earlier bringing her usual light lunch, Catherine sent her away without opening the door. She was too distraught to eat or do anything besides grieve. A cascade of tears had coursed down her cheeks and saturated half a dozen hankies. Now all she felt was cold, her heart a lump of ice. She couldn't stop the tremor that shook her.

A light knock sounded on her closed door.

"Go away, Julie." She knew her tone was too sharp, but she didn't care. "I told you I don't want anything to eat."

Even though she couldn't see her maid, she knew Julie hadn't left. Her presence hovered outside the room like a heavy cloud.

"I'll use the bell pull if I need anything." Catherine tried to sound calm and collected. No need to mistreat her maid.

"Yes, ma'am." The swishing of a skirt and the tinkle of silverware on glass accompanied Julie as she started back down the hallway.

Catherine slumped into the pink satin balloon chair and leaned back. Like a lost little girl, she pulled her feet up onto the seat. Very unladylike, but she couldn't even care about that. If her sisters hadn't died soon after they were born, she would be sharing life with them right now. They would be planning how they would enjoy their eighteenth birthday party. Dressing each other's hair and helping choose accessories for matching evening gowns. Or would they have dressed exactly alike? Could they have developed differing personalities?

A feeling of isolation and loss flashed through her, bringing with it the memory of the first emotion she could remember experiencing, that something vital was missing from her life. As if something precious was gone. Several times during the intervening years, the same feeling overcame her. Now she knew what it was. *Her sisters.* She missed her sisters.

"Catherine?" A soft knock accompanied Aunt Kirstin's voice. "May I come in?"

For a moment, she couldn't decide whether she wanted to see her or anyone else, for that matter. But maybe Aunt Kirstin could give her more insight into what happened. She needed to know where her sisters were buried. She had never seen where their mother was buried either. Perhaps she should beg her father to take her there so she could find some peace.

"I know you're in your room, dear." Tenderness wove through her aunt's tone the way Julie wove ribbons through Catherine's flaming curls. "Please let me come in and talk to you."

She glanced at the window and noticed the sun sinking toward the horizon. Far too soon, the time for her birthday ball would arrive, and she had nothing to celebrate. Only deaths to mourn.

She slowly opened the door, then stepped back to admit her aunt.

Kirstin gathered Catherine into her arms, smoothing her hands across Catherine's back in slow comforting circles. "You poor dear. I wanted to give you time to consider what you learned today. I hoped you'd come down for lunch. And Julie tells me you haven't let her in either."

Catherine slowly pulled away and closed the door. "I didn't want to see anyone."

Her aunt nodded as if she agreed.

Taking a deep breath, Catherine stiffened her spine. "Is Father home yet?"

Aunt Kirstin frowned. "No...but he should be soon."

"I have questions." Catherine dropped back into her favorite chair. "Do you want to answer them, or shall I wait for him?"

The older woman sat on the cushioned cedar chest at the foot of the bed. "I only know what I've been told. It might be better if you ask him. Do you want a little bite to eat before you start dressing for your ball?"

Catherine leapt to her feet. "You can't be serious. Surely, we're calling off the party."

Aunt Kirstin rose slowly. "No, we are not."

"And why not?" She huffed out an angry breath. "I don't care if I have a birthday party now...or ever."

Clasping her hands in front of her waist, her aunt gave her a stern look. "I know it will be hard, but sometimes we have to do things that aren't easy. All the plans have been made and a number of people received invitations. You will go to the party and hold your head high. Then later you and your father can have a heart-to-heart discussion."

For the first time in a long time, Catherine wished she *was* a little girl and could stomp her foot and insist on getting what she wanted. But if this was how they wanted it, she would go to the party. But she wouldn't enjoy a minute of it. She might never enjoy anything...ever again.

⁓

*D*uring the awkward shopping trip with Roger Emery to rig him out like some dandy, Collin decided to stay home from the party if given the chance. *No such luck.* Evidently, the old man's secretary understood the nature of other men better than Collin realized. He had stayed until he made sure Collin was trussed up like a Christmas goose in a black formal suit and waistcoat. The stiff-winged collar attached to the snowy shirt jabbed his chin, and a white bow tie almost choked him.

Growing up on the ship his father captained, Collin was used to loose clothing. Even after he became a ship's captain himself, his uniform left plenty of room for him to maneuver however he needed to run the vessel. This long-tailed coat fit his muscular physique, but with very little breathing space. He flexed his shoulders to test the stitching. It held. *Thank goodness.* He wouldn't want a disaster at the banquet. But he still hoped to slip out after the meal.

Standing at the front window of the parlor of the boardinghouse where he'd lived since recovering from his extensive injuries, Collin raked the street with troubled eyes. He watched for his transportation while Roger Emery lounged on the sofa reading the newspaper as if he had all the time in the world.

Mr. McKenna's brougham pulled up in front of the boardinghouse, and the driver started tying off the reins. Collin hurried out the door and down the front steps before the driver could climb from his perch. The fewer people who saw him decked out like this, the better. Collin had never worn full evening dress. Wouldn't his crew get a hoot out of this if they could see him now? At least the men were on other ships, where he wished he was as well. Out of this booming city and on the open seas where he could breathe fresh air.

An unwelcome, but familiar, feeling swept over him just as the saltwater had completely swamped him during that fateful storm. Bad enough that his dreams were filled with the sinking unsteadiness and crashing waves, but when they overwhelmed him in broad daylight, or twilight as it was now, he had no way to escape. No way to awaken from the daytime terror.

Sweat popped out on his forehead and his hands felt clammy. He pulled a handkerchief from the pocket of his trousers and mopped his face.

He hurried to the boardwalk in front. "No need to climb down." He doffed his top hat and settled it more firmly on his head.

"Thank ya, Gov'ner."

*Now why would a driver in San Francisco have an English accent?* The world seemed to shrink more all the time, making San Francisco a real melting pot.

During the ride, Collin stewed about what to expect when he arrived. He'd only caught occasional glimpses of Mr. McKenna's daughter, and she always looked like a haughty little thing. Not someone he'd choose to spend time with.

And what about the others? He felt as if he was about to jump off a pier into unknown waters, and he knew no more about swimming in those murky waters than he had about staying afloat in the deep Pacific in a storm. In the McKenna mansion, there would be no broken debris from a sinking ship to help him keep his head above the swirling waves. *Is it too late to have the driver turn around and take me back to my boardinghouse?* He pulled back the curtain and peeked out just as the brougham took its place in a line of other carriages moving slowly up a long, steep driveway. His fate was sealed for this night.

"Captain Collin Elliott." An English butler solemnly

intoned his name as he entered the largest room he'd ever seen in a private home.

Across the vast crowd, numerous people—both men and women—turned to stare at him. Collin wanted to sink right through the marble floor, but there was no convenient hatch.

His host left a group of men at the side of the room and approached with a smile. "There you are, Elliott."

Mr. McKenna wore similar clothing to Collin's. If he met the man on the street dressed like that, he wouldn't even recognize him. "Yes, sir."

"Just call me Angus." His employer clapped him on the shoulder. "Come along. I want to introduce you."

As they worked their way around the room, Collin studied each person, quickly learning how to conduct himself in this situation. New clothes weren't enough to change him. With the men clustered on one side of the vast room, he felt as if he were approaching a colony of penguins like the ones he saw on his way around the Horn.

Angus led him straight to a stocky man with *pince-nez* spectacles perched on the bridge of his nose. "I want you to meet Leonard Melby, the manager of Wells, Fargo bank on Montgomery Street."

The man stared at Collin. Probably wondering where he came from. The banker gave a new meaning to the phrase *a stuffed shirt*. The businessman turned toward Angus and finally gave a tight smile.

Collin's employer stood with his hands behind his

back. "I've been banking with him since we first met in the gold fields. That's where I had my first store, in Placerville near the gold fields. Figured we could make more money selling things to the miners than we would digging for gold."

That was news to Collin. He never realized that Angus had been at the gold fields. His employer must have been wise even as a young man. Collin had heard many a tale told on a long night at sea by men who'd worked hard digging through solid rock while others struck the golden vein in the claim right beside theirs. Lady Luck was fickle. He knew that all too well.

"Leonard, the man is one of my ship captains."

The banker gave Collin a critical onceover. "Kind of young for that, isn't he?"

Angus nodded. "But he's got a lot of experience under his belt. His father was a captain, and Elliott started as a cabin boy on his ship and worked his way up. He's even sailed around Cape Horn and navigated through the Strait of Magellan north of Tierra del Fuego."

"I've heard sailing is rough in that area. Lots of ships haven't made it." A grimace glinted in the banker's shrewd eyes.

"That's true, but this young man was up to the challenge. Weren't you, Elliott?"

The banker's frown deepened. "Elliott? Surely, not Collin Elliott. Isn't he the one that lost your ship in a storm several months ago?"

Collin cringed inside. *I knew I shouldn't have come here.* He turned away, not wanting to continue as a part of this conversation. His gaze roved over the crowd looking for even one familiar, or friendly, face. Then his eyes alighted on a gorgeous woman standing in the doorway. Curly red hair caught up on top of her head in an elaborate style had shiny decorations woven in. Her beauty stole his breath and held it captive before he realized this sophisticated woman had to be the pampered McKenna daughter. The green ball gown nearly swept the floor and nipped her waist, showcasing a figure with curves in all the right places. Must have been a while since he saw her because she looked much older than he remembered. *Is she just now arriving at her own birthday party?*Catherine McKenna was shadowed by a woman who had to be at least a decade older than she was. With her show of deference, she must be her lady's maid. Of course, she would have one. Another woman hurried toward them. She was even older, her smile wide as she grasped the guest of honor's gloved hands. No smile of welcome graced the younger woman's lips.

*Haughty.* That was his impression of her. Holding her head high, she stepped farther into the room, but she didn't look as if she expected to enjoy her ball. Icicles dripped from her demeanor. He could feel the chill from where he stood across the room. Like an iceberg that was too close to a ship.

Collin had to find a way to leave the party soon after

dinner. He had no desire to spend time with the Ice Princess. Especially not to dance with her as he assumed all the men would be expected to do. *No siree!* He would jump ship when the opportunity first presented itself.

# CHAPTER 3

*C*atherine stared into the mirror, wondering what her sisters would have looked like if they had lived. Would their hair be the same bright, coppery red that formed corkscrew curls around their faces if not tamed into a more severe style? And their eyes. Would green eyes stare back at them as hers did now? Or maybe they only looked identical when they were born and by the time they reached eighteen years of age, they could be entirely different.

The dull, throbbing pain in her heart hadn't left since she heard about losing her sisters. Even the banquet and ball last night didn't loosen its grip. At least the agony of feigning pleasantness for hours on end was over. She wouldn't let herself suffer that way ever again.

Nothing could take her back to the naïveté of her existence before her father made his bombshell announcement yesterday morning. Since then, the hours had dragged like a sloth in the treetops of a tropical jungle, making the passage of time feel like a decade instead of only a matter of hours.

"Catherine, may I come in?" Even Aunt Kirstin's kind voice wasn't welcome this morning.

She glanced at the door trying to decide whether to admit her. Catherine might as well get this over with. Maybe, just maybe, she could convince her aunt that she should stay home this morning. She didn't feel up to facing so many people.

"Yes?" To help lay the groundwork for her excuse, she made her voice sound as scratchy as she could.

Aunt Kirstin frowned at her. "Catherine, why aren't you getting dressed for church?"

"I have a headache." She puckered her brows and squinted, rubbing her forehead for added emphasis.

The older woman gave a quick shake of her head. "What you need right now *is* to go to church. It often helps rid me of headaches. When we're singing praises to God, somehow all my burdens lift."

Catherine swallowed a groan that almost choked her. She coughed it away. She couldn't imagine anything that could remove the weight from her heart.

Without another word, Aunt Kirstin wrapped her arms around Catherine as she used to. For a moment, she sank into the familiar comfort before tugging herself away from her aunt's embrace.

"Wasn't last night bad enough? Do I really have to

go out today?" Hating the whiny sound of her own voice, she stood straighter and tried to stare the older woman down.

For a brief moment, she thought her aunt was about to relent, but that wasn't the case. "Angus said we would be leaving in half an hour. We have much to do to get you ready." Aunt Kirstin scanned the room as if she were looking for something. "Where's Julie?"

"Did you want me, Mrs. MacPherson?"

Catherine had been so involved with their emotional battle that she hadn't even noticed her maid come through the door.

Aunt Kirstin turned a tight smile toward Catherine's closest ally. "Yes, you need to help Catherine get ready for church. Her father wants to leave shortly."

After those terse words, her aunt quickly exited, leaving Catherine feeling weepy. She turned away from the doorway and swiped the tears trembling on her lashes with the palms of her hands. "I'll choose what to wear." She scurried toward her armoire without even glancing at her maid.

Catherine felt so devastated she wished she owned widow's weeds and could hide behind a heavy veil. She dug through her dresses trying to find something dark and drab enough to depict her feelings. When her fingers encountered the steel gray taffeta trimmed with black, she recalled wearing it to the only funeral she had ever attended. *Perfect!* Julie helped her quickly pull the dress over her unmentionables.

Opening her mother's jewelry box, which occupied a place of honor on her dresser, Catherine lifted the black, hardstone cameo brooch, surrounded with tiny pearls in a gold setting and attached to a velvet ribbon, and eardrops made of gold with black jet beads. Aunt Kirstin had told her several years ago that Mother had worn them to funerals. They added the perfect touch to her somber costume. Knowing these had been worn by her mother might help her keep the tears at bay.

She added a chic black chapeau that perched on the top of her upswept curls. A veil covered her chin and was pulled up and attached to the hat on the side to help mask the moisture that might venture down her cheeks while they were gone from home. If only she could have met her dear mother and sisters, her heart would not grieve so deeply.

When Catherine, Julie, and Aunt Kirstin stepped into the cool September morning, Father waited beside the carriage. He didn't say a single word as he helped the women into the coach and joined them. Of course, he had been a man of few words for as long as Catherine could remember.

She felt isolated even though people shared the ride with her. Her father never even glanced at her face as they rode to the church or when he helped them out of the conveyance.

The darkness of isolation captured her...as if she were completely alone.

A single tear crept over her lower eyelid. She didn't

even bother wiping it away. Clenching her teeth to keep her chin from trembling, she held her head high as she ascended the steps leading to the ornate front door. She could be just as aloof as he was.

Not a word of the pastor's sermon breached the protective barrier she'd placed around her heart and mind. She stared at the stained glass window high in the wall behind the pulpit. Jesus as a shepherd holding out his arms for his lambs. Today, she wished she could run into His embrace, since she felt no comfort here on earth.

After the silent ride home, Julie left for her half day off. Only when the door closed behind the maid did any of them utter a word.

"Angus."

How could Aunt Kirstin address him with such a kind voice? Didn't she realize how unfeeling he had been to his own daughter?

Catherine headed toward the wide staircase, pulling off her gloves as she went.

"Don't go, Catherine."

Turning around, she glanced first at her aunt, then at her father. His face so blank and Aunt Kirstin's filled with worry lines.

"You have questions for your father, don't you, Catherine?"

He looked almost like a marionette whose strings had come loose. As though he could topple to the floor at any second.

Catherine nodded. "I'll be back down in a moment."

Her father silently followed her aunt into the parlor.

As Catherine walked up the stairs, she counted them as she used to when she was learning her numbers. With each one, she took a deep breath and released it. Anything to get her mind off the coming confrontation.

After depositing her hat and gloves on her bed and grabbing a hanky, Catherine returned to the foyer. She stopped and stood on the cold marble, postponing the inevitable for a little longer. Even though she didn't want an uncomfortable situation, she needed to know as many details as she could get her reticent father to share.

As she entered the room, Aunt Kirstin glanced up from her needlepoint and flashed an encouraging smile at Catherine. Her father stood beside the fireplace with one arm leaning on the mantel, his face blanched almost as white as the flour that Cook used. He looked as if he were standing in front of a firing squad and had just heard the cock of the guns. For a moment, her heart melted. She loved her father, but she couldn't let that emotion keep her from learning the whole truth about her sisters and mother.

She went to her favorite wingback chair and perched on the seat, her back ramrod straight. Clasping her hands with interlocking fingers, she paused to let her heartbeat slow down.

"I want to know where my... mother and...sisters are

buried." She pushed each word out with great difficulty. "I have to see the place and spend a little time with all three of them. When can you take me?"

Aunt Kirstin gasped. A look of horror veiled her face.

Catherine hadn't thought her father could look any paler than when she entered, but his face turned ashen, and he grabbed the mantel with both hands. "Whatever...made you think your sisters are dead?" His voice cracked on the last word.

None of this made any sense to Catherine. Her stomach felt as if it were tumbling over and over inside her, and she was glad they hadn't eaten yet. "If they didn't die, then where are they?"

Her aunt quickly jumped up and went to where her father stood. She put her arm around his waist indicating she thought he might fall. Even to Catherine's eyes, he looked older and more frail than she had ever seen him. Aunt Kirstin helped him move to the sofa.

After he was settled, he leaned back and closed his eyes. "I never dreamed it would be so hard to tell you all this."

"Tell me what?" Catherine knew her question sounded shrill, but she needed to know what was going on. She could not imagine any situation where her sisters could possibly be alive without her ever seeing them.

"Speaking the words is almost as hard as the decision I had to make the day all of you were born." His shoulders sagged, and he pinched the bridge of his nose.

"What decision?" A pounding headache fulfilled the prophetic words she'd spoken when she had tried to get out of attending church.

He clasped his hands between his knees. "I didn't know what to do....My precious Lenora...was gone. I thought my life had ended. I loved her so much." Tears streamed down his wrinkled cheeks. "The only thing I had to live for was our daughters." He lifted his eyes toward her face. "What was I going to do? Grief tore through me leaving nothing but devastation in its path."

Catherine heard every tearful word, knowing each one was ripping him apart. She leaned back in the chair and tried to relax. She decided that this time, he wouldn't stop until she had the whole story.

"We had been so happy, knowing our family was growing. We wanted to fill a house with children we could love and nurture. Bring them up knowing our God." He took out his handkerchief and mopped his face. "But we thought we were expecting one baby we would rear together. Lenora knew about caring for infants. I didn't."

Catherine didn't like the direction this conversation was turning. Biting the inside of her cheek to keep from interrupting, she waited.

"There were...other women...on the wagon train, who knew how to care for newborns." His expression begged her to understand. "I understood the tiny babies would be better off with two parents, instead of one shell of a man who had no idea what he was doing. I had little idea of how I would feed one baby, much less three."

Catherine could no longer restrain herself. "Other women?"

"I really prayed about it, crying out to God in my anguish. I believe He helped me see the best way to handle it." Once again, he gripped his hands, but harder this time, making his knuckles whiten.

"Handle it?" Her voice was shrill. Tears streamed down her face. She dabbed at them with her hanky, not knowing if she was happy that her sisters were alive or angry that they'd had so many years together stolen from them, never to be reclaimed.

"I asked two different couples to adopt each of the other babies. And they were glad to have a child. Joshua and Florence Caine had been married several years with no children. She was so good helping with the babies, I could see she would make a wonderful mother for Margaret Lenora." He stared at the wall behind Catherine as if he were seeing a vision there. And maybe he was—a vision of the distant past. "Kenneth and Melody Murray agreed to adopt Mary Lenora. They had lost a young baby a short while before you three were born. Another woman on the wagon train needed someone to feed her baby, because she couldn't. So Melody was still nursing a baby while grieving her own loss. I talked to Kenneth, and he agreed that it would benefit both Melody and one of my daughters.... Watching her cuddle Mary Lenora after we came to an agreement, I knew I had chosen wisely." Tears still trickled from his eyes.

Catherine didn't know what to say. Her thoughts were in turmoil. "Why did you keep *me*?" The question escaped before she could stop it.

Her father studied her face a moment. "I couldn't let you all go. I needed to keep a part of what Lenora and I...conceived...in our great love for each other."

Captured by his gaze, she couldn't move. Couldn't breathe.

"And you were my firstborn child." The tender emphasis on that word reached her heart. He broke the connection between their eyes and shifted on the sofa. "I'm tired. I'm going upstairs to rest."

When he stood, so did Aunt Kirstin. "Aren't you going to eat dinner with us?"

He shook his head. "Not right now."

Catherine's gaze followed her aunt as she walked beside her father, watching his every move. He might be too tired to talk anymore right now, but this wasn't over. She still had too many questions he would have to answer...no matter how long it took.

# CHAPTER 4

*C*ollin awoke to a blinding sunrise on Monday, feeling as if he'd fought a shipload of pirates. An all-night bender couldn't have made him feel worse, but those days were far behind him. Besides, nothing would've been able to take his mind off the Saturday evening festivities. All of his mental scheming to make a quick escape had been for naught. It hadn't freed him from the McKenna daughter's party.

When they were seated at the long banquet table in the dining room, his name card rested above the place setting on Mr. McKenna's left. The Ice Princess sat on her father's right, across the white linen expanse from Collin.

He shouldn't have worried over what to talk to her about. The woman hadn't said a dozen words during the two-hour meal. Collin wondered what other people thought about the guest of honor's behavior. Or maybe they were just there for Angus, because most of the guests were of his generation, not his daughter's.

At least the food had been excellent, some of the best Collin could remember. Some kind of creamy lobster soup was the first course. Followed by the best-tasting, most tender steak he'd ever eaten, along with so many other dishes Collin couldn't remember them all. He was full long before dessert. Thankfully, they waited until an interlude in the dancing before cutting the enormous cake—a baker's masterpiece of chocolate cake that towered several layers high with fluffy, snow-white icing.

His stomach rumbled at the memory of the sumptuous fare. Breakfast would taste mundane in comparison.

Too bad the rest of the festive night hadn't lived up to the quality of the food. Angus McKenna kept Collin close to his side for much of the party. And eventually, like every other man in attendance, his turn came to dance with the Ice Princess. If he could have ignored her aloof demeanor, he would have enjoyed the waltz.

The woman danced with the grace of a swan, looking as if her feet were hardly touching the floor. And he had to admit that holding her gloved hand in his and swirling around the dance floor messed up his equilibrium more than walking the decks of a ship in a storm. The lilting music combined with rhythmic movement made him desire the beautiful woman with curly red hair and stormy green eyes. If only she'd come down off her high horse, he would've counted himself lucky. Funny how he could ignore the pain in his leg and danced without the limp.

Ever since Saturday night, he hadn't been able to swab her from his thoughts. She kept popping up in at the most inconvenient times. So Sunday was almost wasted. After reading the newspaper, he went for a walk before stopping at one of the eateries on Fisherman's Wharf for lunch, Sunday being the only day of the week that Mrs. Molloy didn't provide meals. He put a couple of hard rolls in his pocket for supper to go with the hunk of cheese he kept stowed in his room.

Even through his breakfast of sausage and eggs, his mind kept wandering to his boss's enigmatic daughter. He wondered what it would take to get through the defenses the woman wore like a coat of armor. Somehow, he had pictured her as being vivacious and maybe a little bit daring. But nothing like that revealed itself at her party, where she should have been the belle of the ball. Maybe she wanted something more than what they planned. Just as he thought, she was so spoiled she didn't care how much she hurt the people who loved her.

Collin had noted Angus McKenna's face when he thought no one was looking. Some kind of deep sorrow drained his color and added even more wrinkles to his weathered skin.

A brisk walk to work in the nippy morning air did nothing to clear Collin's headache or the memories. At least now he could bury himself in the invoices, cartons, and numbers, pushing the troubling thoughts into an isolated compartment in his head.

The morning was far gone when Howard Lane approached, accompanied by Roger Amery. The two men were a study in contrasts. Lane's tall, burly frame was topped by hair needing a good cut and a beard at least three days old. Stains covered his rumpled clothing. But working in a warehouse would do that to a man.

Mr. McKenna's secretary stood erect, careful not to brush his immaculate clothing against any of the large, soiled crates. Trimmed hair and a clean-shaven face looked out of place in the jumbled mess of the barnlike structure.

"Good job, Elliott. I thought it would take you all day to get this far along." Lane's face wreathed in a smile as he looked at all Collin had accomplished. He turned toward Amery. "This man is the hardest worker in the whole place."

"I'm sure that's why Mr. McKenna wants to see him." After the clipped words, Amery quickly turned and headed back toward the front of the cavernous room. "Come along, Elliott." The echo of the words wove between the staccato of his footsteps.

Collin wondered what was so important that his employer sent his personal secretary into territory where he was clearly uncomfortable. He took off his work gloves and laid them beside his letter-clip board. After nodding to the warehouse foreman, Collin hurried toward the front door as well. As he walked, he brushed some of the dust off his pants and shirt. He couldn't do anything else for his unkempt appearance.

Roger ushered him straight into Angus's office. "Will there be anything else, Mr. McKenna?"

"No, just close the door behind you." The older man slowly rose to his feet and waved toward the chair where Collin had sat two days earlier. "Glad you could come so quickly."

*Did I have a choice?* Of course not. Especially since Amery was sent to get him. The air hung heavy with questions.

Collin studied the man standing before him. He seemed to have shrunk an inch or two since Saturday night. And his sallow complexion didn't appear healthy. He hoped the old man wasn't seriously ill.

His employer stood with his hands clasped behind his back and looked as if he were on the deck of a ship on a choppy sea, swaying backward and forward on the balls of his feet. Should Collin go help him or stay seated? If something was wrong with Angus, all kinds of problems would cast a pall over the man's business.

*And where would that leave me?* He didn't welcome that selfish thought, but he knew he'd have a hard time getting as good a job as he enjoyed here, especially with his new limitations.

"I'm sure you're wondering why I wanted to see you twice in only three days." Angus peered at Collin from under bushy brows that looked far too large for his face.

"The question did enter my mind." Collin tried to appear nonchalant, but he didn't think he pulled it off.

Finally, Angus dropped back into his leather chair. He leaned his elbows on the desktop and steepled his fingertips. "A lot of things have been weighing heavy on my mind lately." He stopped and took a deep breath. "I'm not going to live forever, and I don't have a son to take over the business." He leaned closer to Collin and continued studying him as if he was looking for something in particular.

Collin couldn't even speculate what that might be. What did the man's health and longevity have to do with him?

"It occurred to me that I should be training someone to take over the business if that became necessary. I must see that my daughter is adequately cared for...as long as she lives."

The words seemed to drain the man's strength. More evidence that his employer wasn't well.

Maybe Angus planned to move Lane from warehouse foreman into the office and move Collin up to foreman. An increase in pay, and even more responsibilities, would be nice. Maybe soon he could afford his own house. Something modest and comfortable. A cottage by the sea where he could be lulled to sleep by the sound of the waves lapping the shore. He had always loved that aspect of the ocean.

"I saw how well you fit in with other business people at the party Saturday night."

*Sure I did.* The irony made him want to laugh. And that banker who had to bring up his sunken ship made him extremely uncomfortable. He didn't think he ever wanted to go into that kind of environment again...even if he did have the right clothes for it. What a waste of his, and his employer's, money. Maybe he could sell them to help pay for a small house.

Angus clasped his hands on the desk and studied Collin as if he were trying to read his mind. "I want you to be that person. Eventually, you could become a partner in the business."

"A partner? In the business?" Incredulity laced his tone, but he couldn't help it.

Angus nodded. "Unless you'd rather have another ship to captain."

What a turnaround! The exact opposite of what Collin expected. What could he say? He'd be crazy to turn down an offer like that, but would he be able to learn the business and do the work? His limp slowed him down more than he liked.

"You do read, don't you? I saw several books in your cabin on the *Trinity Bell*."

Angus glanced toward the polished, mahogany shelves lining one wall of his own office. The largest number of books Collin had seen outside a bookstore or library.

"My father encouraged me to read while we were at sea. It made the long days pass more quickly."

And the characters in the books became his friends. He had gained a fairly complete education through those volumes.

"I'm sure it would. What do you think about my idea so far?"

"Actually, I wasn't expecting it." Collin cleared his throat. "I'm not sure what to think."

Angus stood and came around the desk, then crossed his arms and leaned against the edge. "I haven't come to this decision lightly. You're the only employee I have who could handle what I'm offering."

Collin straightened in his chair. "I'm honored that you think that...and a little surprised. After all, I did lose one of your ships."

His employer huffed out a deep breath. "I've tried to make you understand you're not responsible for the weather. I doubt any of my ship captains, or any one else's, could've prevented that disaster."

*Maybe someday I'll agree with you, but not right now.* Collin could only stare.

Angus walked back around his desk and dropped into his chair. "You probably need some time to think about it. Since the offer was so unexpected."

"Yes, sir, it's a lot to consider."

"How about you going on home now? I want you to

think about it...pray about it...then come back tomorrow ready to discuss the matter." His words carried definite dismissal with them.

"Yes, sir." Collin arose and headed out the door, wiping his sweaty hands on his trousers as he went.

He did have a lot to think about. If he didn't agree with this new proposal, would Mr. McKenna fire him from the job he had? Did he want to risk that?

# CHAPTER 5

*T*he past week had been enlightening for Angus. He was now convinced he'd made the right decision about Collin Elliott. The morning after he presented the idea to him, the young man, dressed in a suit, waited outside his office when Angus arrived at work. After thanking him for the offer and accepting it, Elliott proved an eager and able student of business. His quick mind would be a real asset to the company. Already he had shared ideas that piqued Angus's interest. New ways to handle some of the tougher situations.

Relieved of the worry about the business and the future, Angus had nothing to keep his mind off his other worry. Unfortunately, Collin Elliott couldn't be the answer to what weighed so heavily on his mind. The need to make Catherine understand about what happened so long ago. He couldn't move into a brighter future until he'd taken care of the sorrows from the past. Sorrows he hadn't even faced for himself until now.

Each morning this week, he had gotten up early and headed to work before his precious daughter came downstairs, and he lingered at the office long into the night. Of course, after everyone else left the building, Angus had spent a lot of time in prayer. Finally, today he felt strong enough to face her and tell her everything she wanted to know. He didn't know what he would've done if he hadn't had the strength of the Lord in his life.

Although he told himself he had good reasons for what he had done...and better reasons to keep the secret, he now realized his solution had robbed both him and Catherine of so much. He stepped into his carriage with purpose in his heart and a rod of steel in his backbone.

As he approached the house, his palms started to sweat, but he wiped them with his handkerchief and whispered another prayer. He alit from the buggy and squared his shoulders, taking a deep breath and slowly letting it out before climbing the steps to the wide front porch. Before he could grasp the doorknob, the door flew open.

Catherine looked so pretty standing there wide-eyed.

*Thank you, Lord, for giving this precious gift to me.*

"Papa, what are you doing here at this time of day?"

He chuckled. "Can't a man come home without it being a surprise?"

"I'm sorry." She stepped back, opening the door even wider. "I haven't even seen you for several days."

*Was that longing he heard in her voice?* Or was it the echo of the desire of his own heart?

He took off his hat and laid it on the marble-topped table in the foyer. "I know, and that's my fault. I've been working hard, training Collin Elliott to work in the office with me."

Confusion wrinkled his daughter's brows. "Is Mr. Amery leaving?"

"No, he's still my secretary." Angus laid his coat and gloves beside his hat and headed into the parlor.

Catherine trailed behind him. "So what will Mr. Elliott be doing? I thought he was a ship's captain...at least until his wreck."

Angus relaxed into his favorite wingback chair near the fireplace, welcoming the warmth. "He was. But he's a very good employee. I've never had anyone work as hard as he does. I'm getting older, and I want to be sure someone will be trained to take over the business...if something happens to me."

Her eyes homed in on his face, revealing concern in their green depths. "Are you ill? I thought that might be what Aunt Kirstin was talking about when I overheard your conversation last week."

Her concern caused him to pause. He had only wanted to protect his last precious daughter. But now that she was growing more mature, her questions were hard to answer without distressing her. He didn't want her to make too much of his desire to train young Elliott. Angus knew he had caused too much damage already by keeping secrets from her.

"No, but I won't live forever. That's why I wanted to take care of the matter." He waved her toward the chair across from him. "Sit with me. We can finish the discussion we were having when I rushed out last time."

She sat demurely on the chair and clasped her hands in her lap. He read the expressions that chased each other across her pretty face. Surprise, fear, even eagerness to hear what he had to tell her. His little girl was much too transparent with her feelings. He hoped no one would ever take advantage of her.

"First, I want to apologize to you." He strengthened his tone.

She started to speak, but he held up his hand to stop her.

"I never imagined you'd think your sisters were dead."

His own words caused his stomach muscles to tighten like the winch that hefted the loads onto the deck of his ships. He deserved any pain these words caused him. Why had he been so callous? So concentrated on his own loss without considering how adversely it would affect the daughter he had kept close to his own bosom, trying to protect her from the realities of life.

"You can ask me anything you want to." He uttered these words with trepidation, hoping she wouldn't hit him with a landslide of hard questions.

Catherine stared at her hands. "Aunt Kirstin has tried to help me understand a little about what you went through the day we were born."

She turned those eyes the color of the fields of his beloved Scottish highlands toward him, reminding him so much of his sweet wife. He blinked to hold back a few tears.

"And I can understand how bad your situation was." Her voice had softened to almost a whisper. "I just need to know when I can meet my sisters."

Her tone sounded so final, but her request could not be fulfilled by him. He leaned forward with his hands on his achy knees and shook his head. This was the thorny question he had expected and avoided, because he knew his answer wouldn't satisfy Catherine. He hadn't wanted to inflict more pain on his dear child.

"We really can't go."

For a moment, an expression of horror flickered in her eyes. "What do you mean, we can't go? Didn't you just tell me that Mr. Elliott was learning how to run the business? If you can trust him to run the business after you're...not with us, you could trust him to take care of things while we're gone a few weeks."

In her eagerness, she leaned toward him, just the way Lenora had done when she wanted something desperately. He didn't want to destroy the hope shining in Catherine's eyes. "That's not the problem, Katie."

~

*C*atherine slid back against the upholstered chair. She really hated when her father called her Katie. When she was a child, she liked it, but now it was evidence that he didn't recognize she was a woman, instead of a young girl. She blew out an exasperated breath.

"So what exactly is the problem?" She placed too much emphasis on the last word, but she didn't care.

"A lot goes into a decision to adopt a baby." Her father stood, leaned one arm on the mantel, and stared into the dancing flames. "No one wants to take a baby to love when there is a danger of someone else reclaiming that child. Since your sisters had a living parent, I wanted to give their new parents assurance that I wouldn't someday come and rip them from their new families."

But he thought it was all right for him to rip from her the possibility of knowing her sisters while they grew up. How could he make a decision like that so soon after they were born? Couldn't he take the time to really think through all the ramifications?

Quickly rising from her chair, she stood facing him with hands on her hips. "What kind of assurance?"

"I'll show you." He straightened and headed down the hallway toward his study.

Catherine didn't know whether she should follow or wait until he returned. Then she decided to make him come back to her. She wouldn't trail behind him like an eager child. While she waited, she wondered what kind of assurance he could have given the families. They had to have been on the trail. And probably the area wasn't even settled then. There couldn't have been laws governing adoptions out there in the wilderness, could there?

Of course, Catherine hadn't ever thought about the legalities of adoptions even in these modern times, but she knew there had to be some. What could possibly keep a loving father from his own children? And she could tell from the sorrow in her father's eyes that staying away had caused severe pain in his heart. One she doubted she'd ever be able to erase.

When he returned, he carried two folded sheets of paper yellowed with age. He unfolded one and handed it to her, then dropped back into his chair.

*September 19, 1867*

*I, Angus McKenna, do hereby give my daughter, Margaret Lenora, to Joshua and Florence Caine to adopt and raise as their own child. I promise not to ever try to contact Margaret Lenora.*

*Signed,*

*Angus McKenna*
*Joshua Caine*
*Florence Caine*

*Witnessed,*
*John Overton*
*Matthias Horton, MD*

When she finished reading the first paper, he handed her the other one. The wording was exactly the same with only three of the names changed. She held back tears that blurred her vision as she reread every word. How could he have made a promise to never see them again? Could he have done the same thing to her? That question pierced her heart like a dagger.

Holding back her tears, she turned her attention to her father, watching his expression as she asked the next question. "So who was John Overton?"

"The wagon master."

She nodded. "I know that man and woman who signed after you are the couple who adopted each of my sisters."

He stared across the room as if he were seeing the distant past. "I'm certain the Lord led me to the right people to care for my other daughters."

She jumped up and paced across the floor. "But you can't be sure of that. What if something bad happened to them?"

As she turned back toward him, his shoulders

slumped. "You're right. I can't. All I can do is pray for their well-being. And I've done that every single day since they were born...as I've prayed for you as well."

Catherine waved the papers in her hand. "How can these papers keep you away? Are these legal documents?"

He got up from the chair and stood straighter than he had in a long time. "I gave my word as an honorable Christian. A man's word is his bond. If it's not, this world would be in chaos. When I signed my name on those documents, I was making a sacred pledge to the parents. I won't break that pledge...No matter how much I wish I could."

The last words surprised Catherine, because they opposed the other things he'd asserted. What a dilemma her father had faced ever since her mother died. She knew there was no way he would go against his principles, even though he had paid a hefty emotional price. So she had to think of another way to find her sisters.

She sat back down, still clutching the papers. After a moment, she raised her head. "You really haven't told me a lot about the journey to Oregon. Where exactly was the end of the trail?"

Once again, her father stood close to the fireplace. This time he held his hands toward the multicolored flames. "When we left Independence, Missouri, we were headed to Fort Vancouver. Because Lenora was having so much trouble, the wagon master decided to take the Barlow Cutoff, which is an easier trail, instead of going through the Dalles. He assured us there was plenty of land near Oregon City."

Catherine closed her eyes and committed that information to her memory. "How long were you in Oregon City?" She wished she had a tablet and pencil to take notes, but somehow she believed these were details that would be permanently seared into her brain. She would have plenty of time to write them down as soon as she went to her room.

"Since I wanted to open a store for the gold miners near Sutter's Mill in California, we only stayed long enough to replenish the supplies we needed to get us there." Finally, her father looked more relaxed.

"You mean you and the Marshalls?" She relaxed her grip on the papers and placed them on the pie crust table beside her chair.

"Yes. Lenora and I asked them to accompany us to California. I don't know what I would have done without their help."

"Do you know if the other two families settled at Oregon City? The ones who adopted my sisters?" She hoped she sounded casual, but she felt wound up as tight as an eight-day clock, making plans in her mind as she went along.

"They were there when we left the area, but it's been eighteen years. They could be anywhere by now." He turned his back to the fire and clasped his hands behind him. "I know you may question my ability to love someone I gave away, but I've often wondered where my other two daughters are."

Another thought suddenly entered Catherine's mind. "Do you think they know they're adopted?"

He pondered her question for a moment. "I'm not sure. If Lenora and I couldn't have had children, and someone gave us the opportunity to adopt a baby, I'm not sure what we would have done about it. We'd probably tell the child when he or she was old enough to truly understand."

"And how old is that?"

He looked perplexed. "I really don't know. It might depend on how mature the young person was."

Was he judging her level of maturity? Ideas jumped around in Catherine's head. What if her sisters didn't know? They would never try to find her. Well, she knew about them, and she would do everything in her power to track them down.

Her heart ached to hug each of them. Had they also felt that something was missing from their lives as they grew up just as she had? Did they miss her as much as she missed them? If they knew, surely, they would have tried to find the other two, so she would have to go on the assumption that they didn't know the truth of their birth. Somehow, she had to find them.

# CHAPTER 6

*C*atherine awoke Saturday morning with new hope in her heart. Ever since she heard about having sisters, all she could think about was finding them. Before she learned why her father wouldn't help her, she had considered ways she could look for them in case he didn't agree to take her. Because of what her father shared with her about his vow, she knew she must find her sisters on her own. Well, with the help of her personal maid, Julie.

Eager to share her plans, Catherine jumped out of bed and quickly finished her ablutions. As she went through the dresses in her wardrobe, trying to decide what to wear, her thoughts explored ideas for accomplishing what she desired most in life.

The door opened, then closed behind Julie. "I like that green dress on you."

"Thank you."

Ten years older than Catherine, Julie had been a gift from God when Catherine didn't even know she needed one. When she was younger, Catherine had hoped to be as tall and slim as Julie, but she never reached her height. And Catherine would never be able to tame her unruly curls into the smooth chignon like Julie's dark auburn hair. Even though they had different stations in life, Julie was the closest thing to a friend that she had. Now that Catherine knew about her own sisters, she wondered how Julie could be so serene after losing so many of her own family members. Julie had come to live with them five years ago after losing her family in a house fire. Angus had hired her in part to guide Catherine through her adolescence and coming out.

Hoping to please her closest ally, Catherine pulled out the garment and laid it on the bed. She wanted to be as agreeable as she could with her lady's maid. Maybe that way, she wouldn't have any trouble from Julie when she asked her help with the plans. Catherine knew she wouldn't be able to do all of it by herself.

Julie helped her into the dress and fastened the long line of buttons down the back. Then Julie unfastened the ribbon around the end of Catherine's braid and started brushing out her hair. Catherine stared into the cheval looking-glass above her dresser. No wonder her maid liked this garment. The way the dress followed the contours of her body made Catherine look like a woman, something she needed right now. Besides, at eighteen years old, she had reached that designation, even if her short stature often belied her age. If only she could always remember to act like a lady instead of a spoiled child.

"Are you ready to go down to breakfast?" Julie began styling Catherine's hair.

"I thought we could eat here in my room today. You can go for a tray while I put the finishing touches on my hairstyle."

Without another question, the older woman exited the room. Julie was easy to get along with, so Catherine didn't see any roadblocks to gaining her compliance.

After securing the curls in a cluster at the top of her head, she dropped into her balloon chair and relaxed against the cushions, letting it wrap her in comfort. As the chair gently swayed, she considered alternatives that might help her get what she wanted. Her thoughts took her several places—the bank, the train station, and even to other stores in town besides the one owned by her father. No need for him to wonder why she was buying some of the things they would need for the journey. Excitement bubbled inside her like one of the natural springs in the hillsides of San Francisco.

"Catherine." The sound of Julie's voice penetrated the closed door.

Arising from her perch, Catherine opened the door, then helped Julie place all the items from the tray she carried on the round table in the sitting area of her bed chamber. She hadn't realized how hungry she was until she caught the enticing aroma of bacon and biscuits, the perfect accompaniment to the poached egg swimming in melted butter in the dainty china bowl she placed on her own plate.

"Oh, good. You brought tea as well." She lifted the cozy-covered teapot and set it in the center of the table. "I don't know how you can carry so much at once. I'd probably let all of it slide off on the floor."

Julie placed the empty tray aside and stood next to the laden table.

Catherine dropped into her chair. "Sit down. We need to talk while we eat."

She didn't know if Julie had noticed the difference in Catherine's disposition. But how could she miss the change from the last several days? Her maid could read her moods, and Catherine knew she had been gloomy ever since finding out the truth about her sisters.

Julie catered to Catherine's needs without probing too much into things Catherine wanted to keep to herself. Julie waited patiently until she was ready to share with her. Sometimes, Catherine did. Sometimes, she didn't. Today, she must. There was no other way to reach her goal. And not finding her sisters was not an option Catherine would ever consider.

They shared their repast accompanied by small talk, while Catherine planned ways to present her ideas to the other woman.

When they finished eating and Julie started to stand up, Catherine clasped one of her hands. "Please stay. I need to talk to you about something important."

Julie stiffened, staring at her hands then up at her face. Interest and questioning fought for dominance in her expression. "All...right."

Her pause carried a load of hesitation. Catherine recognized this, knowing she would have to overcome the objections Julie was sure to present.

"We've known each other for a long time, and you are more to me than just my lady's maid. I know at first my father hired you as a companion who would be closer to my age than he and Aunt Kirstin were."

Julie's eyes widened. "And how do you know that?"

"You remember what a brat I was when you arrived, don't you?"

Her maid nodded.

"I was very good at creeping about the house without making noise. I overheard the two of them discuss hiring a companion for me." Catherine flashed a warm smile at Julie. "I'm so glad you are that person. Later, when I needed a lady's maid, I talked them into keeping you here."

"I'm glad you did."

"I know you can keep any confidence I share with you. And I have something really important to tell you today." Her heartbeat accelerated, and her hands felt damp.

She got up and nervously moved around the room. Talking about the journey was harder than she imagined it would be. She stopped to straighten the porcelain figurines on her bureau then turned back toward Julie.

"I recently discovered I'm a triplet." She clasped her hands together, trying to keep them from shaking. "I assumed my two sisters died when mother did."

She could tell the exact moment Julie realized the implication of her statement. At first, her eyes widened with surprise, then they sparked with excitement. She gave a wide smile and reached a hand toward Catherine before pulling it back and clasping her hands in front of her waist.

"So where are they now? Will you be going to meet them?"

Catherine released a pent-up breath. "Yes...with your help."

"My help? Where are they living?" Julie got up from her chair and moved closer to Catherine.

"That's the problem. I don't know."

The excitement melted from Julie's face like butter off the hot biscuits they had just eaten. "How can we find them?"

Her maid's question brought hope that she would provide the help Catherine needed.

*Here comes the hardest part.* "I know where to start looking. Oregon City."

Julie mulled over Catherine's words for a moment. "Have you asked your father to take you?"

"Yes."

"And he refused?"

Catherine had seen that expression on her maid's face many times in her younger years. Although they had become friends, she felt Julie withdrawing into what she considered her *proper place* in their relationship. Catherine knew she had to convince the maid quickly or the opportunity would disappear like the early morning fog over the bay.

"He gave his word to the people who adopted them that he wouldn't try to contact Margaret or Mary." Tears burned the back of her eyes. *My idea has to work.* "All my life, I've felt as if something essential was missing from my heart and life. Now I know it was my sisters. I have to find them."

Julie tapped her foot against the carpet. "Have you asked your father if you may try to contact them on your own?"

Catherine shook her head. "He would likely object. I would prefer he not know until I'm gone."

Julie took a moment to absorb that information. "Do you have any idea how long this will take or how much money you'll need?"

Catherine gave a dismissive wave, as if batting away this objection. "No, but that's not important to me."

"It is to me. I would be remiss if I didn't try to stop you." Julie's grave expression cast a pall over Catherine's excitement. "And I could lose my job for helping you. You do realize that, don't you?"

"I can make my father understand that it's not your fault. Besides, I have an inheritance from my maternal grandparents. I would make sure you still had a job, even if I have to hire you myself." Catherine didn't want to cry again, especially in front of Julie, but tears drew near to the surface. She hoped to appear mature enough for such an enormous undertaking.

"I'm not worried about myself as much as I am about you." Julie stood her ground, crossing her arms over her chest and clasping her upper arms in a tight grip. "Even if I were to help you get everything you'll need, you can't travel alone. A woman alone is in danger from all kinds of things...especially men who would take advantage of you."

Catherine began to pace. "I know that. I want you to go with me."

Julie stared out the window before answering. "Two women would be better than one...but it still wouldn't be completely safe."

"Is anything in this world ever truly safe?" Catherine wasn't going to give up now that her maid had moved past a definite *no*. "I could hire someone to accompany us."

"You have no way to find a suitable male escort who could be gone for an indefinite amount of time." Julie frowned. "You don't want someone who will take your money and maybe leave us stranded somewhere."

"I've seen two women arrive on a train without a male escort. In these modern times, travel is much safer than it was when my mother and father came west."

Catherine knew she was grasping at straws, but she wouldn't let go of the idea.

Julie rubbed her forehead as if she had a headache.

"You do know if you don't agree to accompany me, I'll go, anyway." This was the last thing she could think of to try to sway her maid. She hoped it wasn't a bluff Julie would call her on, because she doubted she could make it by herself.

"What's to keep me from telling your aunt and father of your plans? They're the ones who hired me. I've never given them any reason not to trust me, and I don't want to start now."

The strength of her words cut Catherine, but she couldn't back down yet. She hated to say the words that came to mind, but she must. "Then you really would be out of a job."

Her life wouldn't be complete until she found her sisters. Catherine stood and stared the other woman down.

Consternation crept across Julie's features, followed by an expression akin to defeat. "Let me take the tray back down to the kitchen while I think about what you've told me. I can't make a hasty decision that could change the course of both our lives."

Catherine didn't want to let her go, but she knew there was no other way. She could not coerce her maid into going with her. Julie must make the decision on her own.

After the other woman closed the door behind her,

Catherine massaged her temples. She didn't want the throbbing to turn into a full-blown headache. She would need her wits about her when Julie returned.

Her maid didn't take as long as Catherine anticipated she would, but every minute felt like an hour to her. Her feet beat a path in the Persian rug covering her bedroom floor, as she tried to come up with other ways to plead her case if need be.

Without knocking, Julie came in empty-handed. "How soon do you plan on this trip?"

Catherine stared at her intently before answering. Relief rushed though her like rain pouring down the hills of her dear city. "As soon as we possibly can. The yearning to find Margaret and Mary is compelling. I won't be able to rest until we're on our way."

# CHAPTER 7

*I*n the five days since he'd had his talk with Catherine, Angus felt better than he had in a long time. Getting all the secrets out in the open freed him from a burden he hadn't realized he'd shouldered. Of course, he still missed Lenora so much it hurt, and thinking about his other two daughters brought an additional ache to his heart. But now he was free of the great weight he'd carried alone his whole life.

He'd been surprised when she backed off about wanting him to take her to find her sisters. Seeing them again had long been a desire of his heart, but the people who agreed to take care of his other daughters needed him to remain true to his word. Plenty of times he'd wished he'd never added that phrase to the document, but he understood the significance of the words for the other parents. If he hadn't been so distraught, he probably wouldn't have made such a drastic decision. Why didn't he wait before doing something so final?

He dared to allow his thoughts to drift to Margaret and Mary. Did they both have personalities like Catherine's? Or were they three distinct individuals? Their homes would be full of activity and noise if they were like their sister. A grin slipped across his lips. For a moment, he imagined his three beautiful daughters chattering away here in this house. But that was never to be. And his heart ached for all he had missed.

He had to believe their lives were happy and full of good things. Anything less was unbearable.

Opening a ledger, he glanced down the column of figures, his gaze stopping at the final number. This year had been profitable. And with Collin shouldering more of the responsibilities, Angus could relax. Maybe plan a vacation for him, Kirstin, and Catherine. He could take them to Europe. They could visit Scotland, the land of their ancestors. Perhaps that would take his daughter's mind off what she had missed by not knowing her sisters.

They could take the train across the vast continent to New York City. Along the way, they could see the amazing sights of this country. Then they'd set sail across the Atlantic, but that would have to wait until next summer when the weather would be better for an ocean voyage. When he got home tonight, he'd tell Catherine and Kirstin what he was planning. They could even take his daughter's maid along. She was used to having Julie to help her with everything. Maybe he'd spoiled Catherine, but lavishing things on her eased the ache of missing his other two daughters...at least a little.

With a full smile, he picked up the bills of lading from the latest ship to return to San Francisco. Customers were waiting for their merchandise, and the rest would go into town for McKenna's Mercantile.

"I'm sorry, ma'am. You'll have to wait until I announce you." Roger Amery's raised voice carried through the closed door.

The knob turned and the door was thrust wide. Kirstin entered in a flurry, followed by his exasperated secretary.

"I must see Angus right away."

Roger peered over her shoulder at him.

"It's all right, Amery. I always have time for my sister." Angus stood and glanced at her face. Something had her very upset.

He hurried around the desk while Roger left the office, pulling the door closed behind him.

"Has something happened?" He took her trembling hands in his.

"Yes." She dropped onto one of the chairs in front of his desk.

He maneuvered the other one closer, then sat so he could look her straight in the eyes. "What?"

It had to be momentous to bring Kirstin here. No matter what it was, he would make sure it was quickly taken care of. He'd always looked out for his wife's younger sister before she married...and after she was widowed.

She took a couple of deep breaths, pulling one hand free and flattening it against her chest as if she needed to calm her heart. "I don't know how to tell you."

Fear shot through him like a bullet from an assassin's gun. *Catherine!* "What has happened to Catherine?" What else could have her in such a tizzy?

"She's not been injured...or anything like that."

"Then what is it?"

She pulled her other hand free and dug into the handbag she carried on her arm. "I spent most of the day helping at the church." Her fingers continued to shuffle through the contents. "We were preparing baskets to take to the shut-ins tomorrow. And I didn't get home until just a few minutes ago."

He wished she would just get to the point. Why did women always need to explain every detail?

"Oh, here it is." She pulled an envelope from her bag and clutched it in her hand, wrinkling it. "Neither Catherine nor Julie was downstairs, so I went up to her room and knocked on the door. There was no answer, so I opened the door and peeked inside."

Tapping a pencil on his desk, he wished Kirstin would cut some of this extraneous information out.

"No one was there, but this was on her pillow. Although it's addressed to you, I opened it. I didn't mean to be so presumptuous, but..."

He snatched the letter from her fingers and pulled the stationery out.

"I'm so sorry." Her last word held a hitch in it.

"It's all right." He unfolded the sheet and scanned the words.

*Dear Papa...* His daughter had stopped calling him that a couple years ago. Seeing the words on the paper, he remembered how much he missed the sound of the endearment.

> *I respect you because you are an honorable man, and I understand why you can't take me to find my sisters. However, something compels me to seek them out. I really can't wait any longer, so Julie and I carefully planned our trip. I knew you would probably stop us if I told you before we left. And please don't get angry at Julie. I practically forced her to accompany me, but we'll be safer traveling together.*
>
> *We'll start looking in Oregon City. According to what we find there, we'll search farther or come home. I will write letters to you and Aunt Kirstin so you'll know we are fine.*
>
> *Until we meet again, I love you so much.*
>
> *Catherine Lenora*

His fist tensed as he stared at the final words. Anger tried to surge through him, but he kept a tight grip on his emotions. *What's done is done.* Indeed, it was.

He'd known Catherine felt passionate about finding

Margaret and Mary, but he hadn't realized she'd take the matter into her own hands. And even if he wanted to, he couldn't stop her now. All he could do was make sure she and Julie were safe.

Laying the letter on his desk, he pulled Kirstin into a hug, patting her back to comfort her. "I don't blame you, and you shouldn't blame yourself."

"But I do. I should have been home for her." Kirstin's tears trembled on her lashes. "If I'd imagined she would do something so drastic..."

He gave a dry chuckle. "You know how Catherine is when she gets a wild hare in her head. Nothing, and no one, could stop her."

Kirstin pulled away and took a deep breath. "Don't you fear for their safety?"

"A little." He could agree with her without actually letting on just how strong his fear was. "But I have an idea." He led her to the door. "Have Clarence drive you home. I'll see what I can do, then come tell you."

After Kirstin exited the outer office, Angus turned to his secretary. "Please have Mr. Elliott come to my office immediately."

By the time Angus sat back in the chair behind his desk, Collin opened the door and stuck his head in. "Roger said you wanted to see me right away."

"Yes." Angus beckoned him inside the office. "We need to talk."

*T*he tone of urgency in his boss's voice made Collin's gut clench. He glanced back over the last few days in his mind, trying to see if he'd done something Angus wouldn't approve of. He couldn't think of a single thing. "So what's going on?"

He relaxed into one of the chairs across the desk. Angus looked more worried than angry.

"A situation has developed, and I need your help." His boss steepled his hands the way Collin had observed when Angus was pondering something important.

"What kind of help?"

This man had given him more opportunities than anyone else ever had. He'd enjoy repaying Angus for trusting in his abilities.

"It's a delicate situation that requires discretion." Angus leaned forward. "And it really doesn't have anything to do with the business."

That aroused Collin's curiosity more than ever. "All right." He waited expectantly for more information.

"I know I can trust you, Elliott, with my life." Angus picked up a pencil and wrote a few words on the paper before him. "Now I'm going to have to trust you with my daughter's life."

*The Ice Princess?* Collin bit back the words. "How is her life in danger?"

"This is a private, family matter that I can't do anything about."

A curious choice of words. He waited for Angus to continue.

"My daughter and her maid have embarked on a journey, and I need you to protect them." A frown marred Angus's face. "I don't think they realize they are in an unsafe situation."

Just what kind of trouble was his daughter in now?

Angus arose and came around the desk, then sat in the chair beside Collin. "They left sometime today for Oregon City, and I want you to follow them. Don't let them know you're following them. Just keep them under observation, and be prepared to step in if they need assistance."

None of this made any sense to him. "How will I find them?"

Angus cleared his throat. "I'm not really sure how they left. You'll need to check to see if they are on the train or if they booked passage on a ship. Then catch up to them as soon as you can. I'll advance you plenty of money to fund your journey, and you can telegraph me if you need any more.... Actually, I want to receive regular reports from you as well."

Collin hadn't expected anything like this. He had just been working in the office for a short time. Now he was going who knew where to shadow two women who should have more sense than to strike out on a long journey unaccompanied by a man to protect them. He didn't doubt he would be successful, but this would be an expensive undertaking just to support the whims of a spoiled young woman.

After Angus explained all the details of the situation, Collin's thoughts tumbled around. He could understand why the Ice Princess made the choice she did, but he knew she didn't have any idea how much danger she and her maid would probably encounter. He hoped he would be able to find the two women before they got themselves into serious trouble.

# CHAPTER 8

$\mathcal{C}$atherine stared out the soot-stained train window as the huge steam engine huffed its way toward the passenger station in Oregon City. "I'm really tired." She turned toward Julie. "Aren't you?"

"Yes." Weariness emphasized every line of her maid's face.

The journey from San Francisco, which should have taken less than twenty-four hours, had stretched across one day, all night, and into the early afternoon of the next day. Two separate times, they had to stop in some godforsaken place, while the track in front of them was mended by Chinese workers. The overseers treated the men with such disdain that Catherine questioned her own choice, almost forgetting why she insisted on coming all this way. Her normal life, the one before she knew she had sisters, had sheltered her from some of the brutality of everyday life for others. But thoughts of her sisters and a dawning realization of the difficult lives they may be living returned the urgency to her pursuit.

"This town seems to be a nice size. Lots of homes, businesses, hotels...and just look at the river with the bubbling rapids and short waterfalls." Catherine hoped this was the place where her sisters had settled. "At least it's civilized."

Julie gave a wan smile. "Let's pray we can quickly find adequate accommodations."

Catherine wondered if Julie's idea of adequate was the same as her own. Somehow, she doubted it, since Julie was reared in an atmosphere far removed from the mansion in San Francisco where she now lived. As the engine slowed, the conductor made another trip through their passenger car. Catherine held up her hand to get his attention.

"Anything I can help you with, miss?" This smiling man had shown them the utmost courtesy throughout the whole journey.

"I'm just wondering where we might find lodging here in Oregon City." She tried to sound as if she knew what she was doing. Always in the past when she traveled with Father, someone else took care of all the minute details.

"For nice ladies such as the two of you, I recommend the Barlow House. It's a hotel that's owned by the man who built the Barlow road." He doffed his uniform cap and headed toward the back of the car.

Julie's gaze followed him. "That Mr. Wilson is a nice man."

Catherine smiled. "His stories about how he wanted to be a conductor just like his father helped the time pass while we were stopped for rail repairs."

"There wasn't much else to do besides listen to them." Julie didn't turn back toward Catherine until the conductor closed the door behind him as he exited.

With a lot of hissing and screeching of metal, the train came to a full stop. Catherine stood and pressed her skirt with her palms, trying to get some of the wrinkles to disappear. She couldn't remember the last time she'd been so unkempt. This was not the way to make a good first impression. Of course, at this point, she had no one to impress, so she wondered why she cared so much.

"I wonder how we'll get to the Barlow House." If they were arriving in San Francisco, her father's driver would be waiting with the carriage.

Julie glanced toward the open door at the end of the car. "A town this large should have cabs available." She picked up her handbag and bandbox then reached toward Catherine's.

"Remember...on this trip, you are my friend. We really don't want anyone to think of you as a servant." Catherine picked up her own bandbox and nodded for Julie to walk in front of her.

Catherine knew it was hard to change from years of their previous relationship. But she needed to continue their act, so no one would try to take advantage of them. She really wanted them to appear as seasoned travelers...and friends.

During much of their journey through Oregon, rain had accompanied them. She stepped into welcome October sunshine, which brought a smile to her face. The man she assumed was the station master stood beside the baggage car with the side door opened. Julie was already headed toward where he waited. Catherine hurried to catch up with her, but the tighter skirt of her traveling suit kept her from walking very fast.

"We each have a padded, wooden trunk." Julie was talking to the station master when she arrived.

"And we need to know where to find transportation to the Barlow House," Catherine added.

An appreciative glance sparkled in the man's eyes, but he didn't make her feel uncomfortable the way the leers from some men on the train had. "Glad to help, ma'am. I'm Laurence Greene, and my brother Henry owns the livery. He always sends a few of his cabs when a train is expected." He waved toward an area at the north end of the station where several of the horse-drawn conveyances waited. "They're over there."

When one of the drivers saw Mr. Greene's hand signal, he jumped down from his perch on the back of the vehicle and headed toward them.

"Now what kind of trunks do you have?" The station master peered into the shadowy interior.

Julie stared at the piles of baggage. "Our trunks are

new, and they're just alike, covered with dark red leather. I think I see them toward the end near the caboose."

The man climbed into the car and started moving pieces of luggage to get to their trunks. Julie kept her eyes trained on his every move.

"Ma'am?"

Catherine turned toward the man who stood near her. "Yes."

"Will you ladies be needing a ride?" He grabbed his cap from his head and held it in front of him.

"We certainly will." Catherine liked the respect she saw in his eyes, because it bolstered her confidence. "Can you take us to the Barlow House?"

"Yes, ma'am."

With a nod the driver joined Mr. Greene, helping the man unload the two trunks. Catherine appreciated the way both men took great care when handling their luggage. After the driver helped Julie and then her into the vehicle, he hopped back up on the driver's seat, which was behind the roof of the cab.

Even though she was tired, Catherine tried to take in all the scenery, constantly on the lookout for anyone who might be one of her sisters. Although she wasn't sure what they would look like, she felt certain she would immediately recognize them. A quieter, more sedate town than San Francisco, Oregon City had its own unique charm.

Julie pulled back the curtain on the window beside

her. "When you first told me where we were going, I pictured a much smaller place.... It's lovely."

"I just hope we can easily obtain the information we need to find my sisters." Uncertainty and fear lay like a lump of unformed clay in Catherine's stomach, chasing away her hunger.

The availability of food on the train trip had been sketchy at best, and until that moment, she had felt ravenous. Eating lunch had been foremost in her thoughts, but not now.

Julie let the fabric drop back to drape across the upper part of the window. "From all you've told me, we should be able to find someone who knows about the other people who traveled on the wagon train with your parents." She leaned closer and clasped Catherine's hand. "Don't give up yet. We've only just begun. I'm sure you'll feel more hopeful after we're able to clean up and rest a bit."

The cab stopped in front of the Barlow House. The driver jumped down and opened the door for them. Catherine thanked him as she alit.

"My pleasure, ma'am. I'll wait here until you get checked in, so I'll know which room to deliver your trunks to." He closed the door after Julie and crossed his arms and smiled.

The hotel was more rustic than any hotel Catherine had seen in San Francisco. And yet, it held a certain charm. Evidently, many others felt the same way, because a number of people appeared to be coming or going through the lobby. She headed toward the front desk.

A tall man with a snow-white droopy mustache glanced over his spectacles at her. "Can I help you, young lady?"

She held her head high and tossed him her most beguiling smile. "My...friend and I would like a room, or even a suite, if you have one."

His laugh pealed across the room. "Don't have a suite. Don't even have a single empty room. One of the other hotels burned down awhile ago. They're rebuilding it, but until it's finished, we're booked solid. Lots of workers at the mills spend their week nights here, then go home on the weekends."

That was the last straw. Catherine gritted her teeth and fought to keep tears from spilling down her cheeks. She didn't want the man to think she was somehow weak.

Julie stopped beside her. "Do you know where two gentlewomen can find lodging?"

He scratched at a spot under his thinning hair. "Well, now. Let me see. Seems I heard that the widow Davis has started renting out rooms in her large home since her husband died. She doesn't rent to the mill workers and such. You should be safe and cozy over there."

"And where exactly is this home?" Catherine pushed the words past the lump in her throat.

He grabbed a scrap of paper and scribbled the

address with the stub of a pencil. "Did you ladies come alone, or do you have a driver?"

Catherine glanced back over her shoulder, noticing the number of eyes trained on them as if they were the entertainment for the day. Gooseflesh skittered up her spine. "Our cab is waiting for us."

The hotel clerk looked past her shoulder, studying the street. "Just give this to the driver. He'll know where to take you."

As they walked back out the door, she felt the weight of the stares. Her bravado had all but disappeared. Whispered tales she had overheard in the last few years of women being kidnapped or robbed flocked to her head, crowding out other thoughts. What if these two men were conspiring to commit some crime against her and Julie? Had she been too precipitous when she practically forced her maid to help her?

She took a deep breath and stepped into the bright sunlight. Out here, she was able to gain a little control over her emotions...and fears.

Perhaps she hadn't hidden her tears well enough, because their driver had a look of deep concern on his face. "Is something wrong?"

Julie stepped between them. "The hotel is full. They don't have a room for us."

"The desk clerk gave me the name of a widow who is renting rooms. Here's the address." Catherine held out the paper she had crumpled in her fist.

He smoothed it out and stared at it. "He's right. This

would be a good place for you to stay." He held the door open and assisted them inside. "Only thing is, Mrs. Davis's cook is sick, so there won't be any meals until she gets well."

On the way, Catherine leaned her head against the cushioned back of the seat. Could anything else go wrong today? She hoped not.

"I think you'll feel better if we get something to eat after we acquire a room." Julie used the tone she always did when she was trying to cheer Catherine up.

She raised her head. "Didn't you hear what he said? We'll not get any meals until the cook comes back."

"We'll manage. I'm sure a town this size will have restaurants or a café or some place to eat."

Why did she have to sound so chipper? Catherine felt as if she could just melt into a puddle of despondency and stay there.

The driver stopped the cab in front of a beautiful, three-story house that looked as if it sported a new coat of paint. The various colors harmonized, and all the curlicues that decorated the roof line and porch gave the impression of comfort and a real home.

The women climbed down from the coach and started up the steps. Catherine gave the door a soft knock.

"Come in," a reedy, feminine voice called out. "The door is open."

The area must be safe if Mrs. Davis let strangers just walk into her house. Catherine opened the door and peeked around it. A tiny woman sat in a rocking chair with a partial garment in her lap, her wooden needles clacking against each other.

"Do I know you?" The woman stopped knitting and stared. "You look so familiar. Remind me what your name is."

Catherine walked over to her. "No, you don't know me. I'm Catherine McKenna from San Francisco, and this is my friend Julie Myers. It's the first time either of us has been to Oregon City."

"You sure do remind me of someone then. I never forget a face." She started working on her needlework project again. "Names, I forget all the time, but not a face. And yours is so lovely...and memorable."

"The Barlow House is full right now, and the desk clerk told us you rent rooms. We need two, if you have them." Catherine was intrigued by all the knickknacks in the room. The top of each piece of furniture and the mantel held crocheted doilies with figurines scattered in pleasing arrangements across every surface.

Once again, Mrs. Davis's hands lay idle in her lap. "Right now, I don't have any renters, so I'd love to have you ladies." She studied both Catherine and Julie from head to toe. "Your clothes are beautiful. Maybe you can tell me all about the fashions from the big city. San Francisco, such a lovely place."

The door opened again, and their driver stepped inside and stopped. "Does Mrs. Davis have space for you?"

"I surely do, young man. Aren't you Eldon's oldest son?" The sparkle in Mrs. Davis's eyes lit the whole room.

"Sure am, ma'am. Tell me where you want their trunks."

"Put one of them in the room to the right at the top of the stairs on the second floor. The other one can have the adjoining room." The older woman started rocking again. "I'm sure they want to be close to each other."

After everything was unloaded, he returned to the parlor. "I can take you ladies to a good place to eat and even wait for you and bring you back."

"How far away is this place?" Julie sounded eager to get there.

"Not very far."

Catherine's stomach gave a very unladylike growl. She felt a blush rush into her cheeks. "That would be nice, but since it's only a short distance, we'll walk back after we eat and enjoy the sunshine. We've been cooped up in a train far too long."

# CHAPTER 9

*C*arrying his leather Gladstone bag containing everything he needed for his journey, Collin stepped down from the train in Oregon City. It had taken him longer than he would've liked for him to discover the Ice Princess and her maid left San Francisco by rail. After fearing he might not ever find them, he'd boarded the next train headed toward Oregon City with relief, confident he would be successful.

The fates seemed to be smiling on him, because the train carrying the women lost a lot of time on the way. The friendly conductor on his train kept him apprised of all the problems slowing the other one. Consequently, he arrived only an hour or two behind the women, if his information proved correct. But of course, they weren't waiting at the passenger station. He'd obtained a list of the finer hotels in Oregon City from that same conductor. In a place as small as this, he should be able to find where they were staying and keep an eye on them without them knowing he was even there.

He'd been told the most likely hotel was the Barlow House. He quickly arrived and strode across the pleasant lobby. He could imagine the two women being comfortable in these surroundings.

The desk clerk didn't even look up when Collin set his bag on the counter. He cleared his throat. Finally, the man's face came up, and Collin stared into the eyes of a youth wearing wire-framed spectacles.

The boy put his finger in the book he was reading. "How can I help you? Oh, you want a room, don't you?" He tore a corner off the newspaper lying on the counter and slipped it between the pages. "I'm afraid you're out of luck today. We're full up."

Collin frowned. Surely, he should've known it wouldn't be this easy. But he could find a room somewhere else and still keep this building under surveillance, even if he had to sit in the lobby. "Actually, I'm looking for two friends of mine. Do you have a Catherine McKenna and Julie Myers registered here?"

The clerk opened the ledger and ran his finger down the last two pages. "No, sir, I don't see those names. Would they be registered any other way?" Curiosity lit the youth's eyes.

"I don't think so." Collin started toward the front

door then turned back. "Maybe they came in here looking for a room and were turned away. One of the ladies is tiny, with curly red hair. The other one is taller and...older." How could he describe a person he'd never seen? He had no idea what the maid looked like, but he assumed she wouldn't be as short at the Ice Princess.

"I've been here for about two hours, and no women came in for a room during that time." The youth picked up his book and settled down as if dismissing him.

The other train should have arrived within that time period, so this clerk probably would've been here if they came in. Collin pulled his list out of his pocket as he headed toward the front door. One down and five more to go. The conductor said the Cliff House would be his second choice. He stopped a man on the street and asked where it was located. He stared at the high bluff where the man pointed as he gave the directions.

Collin would have to climb more than one long set of wooden steps up the side of the hill to get to the place, and he was at least a mile from the bottom of those stairs. He hoped all the walking wouldn't aggravate his limp. He might have to stop and rent a horse if the women weren't there. In his estimation, the Ice Princess was much more trouble than she was worth...no matter what Angus said.

The climb up the wooden stairs was arduous. By the time he was halfway, his leg throbbed with a deep ache. His limp became more pronounced, and that bothered him even more than the pain. He hated to look like a cripple.

But at least no one here in Oregon City should know about his ship sinking.

A quick trip to the front desk of the hotel revealed that the women were not registered here either. He went back outside and dropped into a rocking chair on the front porch. This would be a pleasant place to spend an afternoon if he was so inclined, but he had too much on his mind to enjoy the view. Was he destined to disappoint Angus once again? Not only did he lose the ship he captained, but he very well might've lost Mr. McKenna's daughter. And he realized the girl was more important to Angus than the ship ever could be. Losing her was not an option for Collin. He had to find her.

He hoped none of the passersby could tell how hot and overwrought he was. By the time he caught his breath, a carriage had stopped in front of the hotel, and the passengers went inside.

After the driver finished unloading the baggage and returned from taking it into the lobby, Collin approached him. "Are you from the livery?"

"Yes, sir. How can I help you?" The man wiped his brow with a rumpled red bandana.

"I'd like a ride to the livery so I can rent a horse." He hoped he didn't sound as desperate as he felt, but he couldn't face going back down those steps. It would be much harder than the climb up had been.

"Of course." The driver popped his cap back on his head. "The ride's two bits."

That seemed a bit excessive, but at this point, Collin would've paid even more. He pulled himself into the cab and leaned back, thankful no one could see him wince. When the vehicle started rolling, he massaged the cramping muscles in his bum leg.

The ride was over before he really relaxed. After flipping a coin to the driver, he entered the shadowy stable while the cab headed back into town.

"How can I help you?" The voice came from the other side of a horse, two stalls down.

Collin approached the bay. The animal leaned its neck over the gate and gave a soft whicker. Without thinking, Collin scratched it under the neck and spoke a few soft words into its ear.

A head with shaggy hair popped up from the other side, and the man started currying the animal's back. "You like horses?"

"Always have, but I've never owned one." Collin promised himself that one day he would have a home with a stable and a horse much like this one.

"This here's Dream Girl. We call her that because she never gets excited. She's an easy ride." The man patted the mare's withers.

Collin ran his hand down the horse's jaw, patting her and whispering a few more words in her ear. He turned to the man. "That's what I'm looking for, an easy horse to ride."

"That's Dream Girl, all right."

"How much to rent her for awhile?"

The two men worked out the details, and Collin paid him for one week. He watched the man saddle the mare, memorizing every move and in what order they occurred. He'd have to do it by himself after he and his mount left the stable, and he didn't want to risk making a mistake.

He hadn't thought about mounting the horse. At least the bad leg was the one he would sling over the animal's back. He hoped gripping the horse's side while he rode wouldn't tire the leg too much.

He rode out of the livery yard and on toward the next hotel....And the next...and the last two. With each negative response, he became more convinced this search was a lost cause. What if the women got off the train before it reached Oregon City? He would have no way of knowing where.

When he was younger, he liked to drink whiskey, but when he became the captain of his own ship, he stopped. He never wanted to go back to that life in saloons, but right now medicating himself with a bottle of the strong drink was sounding better all the time. Finally, he slid from Dream Girl's back, tied the reins to the hitching rail, and walked into a saloon, taking his place at the bar.

"Bring me a shot of whiskey, barkeep." He couldn't even look himself in the eye in the murky mirror behind the liquor bottles, so he hung his head and waited for the glass to be set in front of him.

~

*A*lthough the food was just roast beef with potatoes and carrots, Catherine felt as if she had dined at a banquet. The plain fare was far better than anything she and Julie had eaten since they left San Francisco in such a hurry. She actually ate three hot rolls slathered with butter. If she were to continue eating like this, she would soon outgrow her fashionable clothing. But today, she had been extremely hungry.

After they were both satiated, they paid their bill and stepped into the late afternoon sunlight. Even though the season of autumn was upon them, the day had an almost spring-like feel. Perhaps the nearby Willamette River helped produce this feeling. She had read about this area having frequent rain, and that must be what kept the area so fresh and green looking.

Julie unfurled her parasol and laid the handle across her shoulder. "The sun is really bright today."

"Yes, but you can tell by the puddles, it hasn't been too long since it rained." Catherine glanced down the street one way, then the other. Her weariness drained some of her enthusiasm for their quest. *Where are we? Why couldn't this have been easier?* "I almost wish we hadn't told the driver not to return for us. I'm not exactly sure which direction to go." Tears gathered into a pool in her throat, making her voice scratchy.

"Things do look different from what I remember." Julie looked one direction then the opposite way.

"I guess we were so intent on a good meal we didn't pay close attention." Catherine moved her handbag from her left arm to the right. Even her elbow ached from where the drawstrings had pulled with the added weight of the money she carried. If they weren't on the boardwalk, she might just crumple into a heap and sob. Was their search doomed before they even got started? "We told the man a walk would do us good after being on a train so long, and that's still true."

Julie's brow wrinkled as she glanced once more to their right. "I remember seeing the building on the corner of the next block, don't you?"

Catherine stared at the edifice that looked so much like the others surrounding it. "It might be familiar." She turned that direction, and they strolled along, their steps lagging.

There weren't very many people around, and they were all intent on getting somewhere fast. The two women reached the corner and stopped to look around.

"Do you remember which block we turned onto this street?" Catherine tried to keep her voice strong. She didn't. The food she'd eaten began to curdle in her stomach.

She couldn't imagine asking any of the men she saw for directions. Walking up to a stranger and starting a conversation wasn't anything she had ever done, and now wasn't the time to start. Her previous bravado leaked from her like water through a kitchen sieve.

"I think we should go one more block this direction." Julie ventured from the boardwalk to cross the empty, but muddy, street.

Catherine quickly followed. Standing alone wasn't an option. "What will we do when we reach the next block?"

"If I remember right, we need to turn to the left, go three blocks, then turn right. That should take us to Mrs. Davis's home."

Julie sounded so sure that Catherine followed along, hoping her maid was right. After changing one direction, then the next, she began to wonder if Julie knew what she was doing. Nothing on this street looked remotely familiar. Actually, it looked a little seedy, a place Catherine would have never approached alone and walking without a male escort.

Her heart beat faster, and her gaze darted about. The people who were out on the boardwalk were not anyone she would ever speak to. On the next building, a lop-sided sign proclaimed *Golden Slipper Saloon* in garish, faded-gold letters on a red background. Her father would have apoplexy if he could see her now. She felt the way she imagined a woman felt when the vapors came upon them. But Catherine had never fainted in her life, and she didn't want to start now.

Catherine latched onto her maid's arm. "We have to

get away from here, Julie, but I have no idea which direction." She knew her voice held an accusatory tone, but Julie had brought them to this place, so she didn't care if her words were harsh. She no longer felt safe.

Before Julie could answer, a man staggered through the swinging doors of the establishment and lurched toward them. Catherine looked for a place they could hide before he saw them.

"Well, whatta we have here?" His breath reeking of alcohol, the man grabbed his hat and swooped it in a low bow, almost losing his balance. He teetered before righting himself. "Shome...pretty..." He hiccuped, emitting more of the sour smell. "...ladiesh."

He glanced toward Catherine then stopped and stared. "Sho, Mary, whatter you doing down her? Shlumming?" He lurched toward her again.

Horrified, she backed away, but he grabbed her arm.

Now Catherine was closer to fainting than ever before. The man was repulsive. She didn't want his grimy hands touching her in any way, but he had a tight grip.

Julie stood her ground. "Get your hands..."

"Unhand me!" Catherine sounded as firm as she could manage while quaking inside. She tried to pull away, but the man was strong even though he had a hard time keeping his balance.

Almost as if he had a glass of cold water thrown in his face, he changed. "Now don't go gettin' all high 'n' mighty with me, Mary. Jush 'cause yer engaged to

Daniel Winthrop don' make you better'n me. We ushta go to shchool together. You liked me jush fine then."

"I said, unhand me!" Catherine yelled and once again tried to yank her arm away from the man, but he tightened his hold on her.

"The woman said to unhand her." With a tone of authority, a vaguely familiar masculine voice spoke close behind her.

The drunk stared over her shoulder. "Shtay outa thish."

A strong arm, clad in a dark wool jacket, reached around her and took the drunk by the front of his shirt, lifting him from the ground. "I said let her go!" This time the words bit the air, like bullets flying.

The drunk released his grip, and Catherine quickly moved away from him. Julie placed her arm protectively around her.

"Thank you for your help." Catherine finally looked at her rescuer, and surprise flooded through her, chasing her fear. "Mr. Elliott, what are you doing here?"

"Mr. Elliott?" The drunk looked even more sober than before. A sneer filled his face. "Does your fiancé know you're meeting another man on saloon row, Mary Murray?"

"I'm not—"

"Leave the ladies—"

Catherine and Mr. Elliott spoke at the same time.

"—alone. You shouldn't be accosting women in the

street." Mr. Elliott appeared to be upset. "If you wouldn't spend so much time in a bar—"

The drunk stood much straighter. "Who d' you think you are? You were belly-up to the bar right beshide me a while ago."

Mr. Elliott's face turned red. "How dare you?"

Then it hit Catherine. *Mary Murray.* The drunken man had called her Mary Murray!

# CHAPTER 10

*C*ollin could hardly believe his good fortune. About the time he'd been ready to give up, the Ice Princess and her maid had appeared right in front of him. So what if the ladies were somewhere they shouldn't have been, At least he hadn't lost them completely. Relief flooded through him.

"What are you doing down here, Miss McKenna?" He knew he sounded as if he were scolding a child.

"That, Mr. Elliott, is none of your business." She lifted her haughty little head as if she owned the world. "What exactly are *you* doing here?" Her fists came to rest on her waist, and she had a fighting gleam in her eyes.

"Your father sent me to Oregon City." He resented having to answer to this pint-sized spitfire. And he resented having to drop everything to come rescue her from dangers she hadn't even considered.

"Did my father send you to a saloon as well?"

Her scorn burned another streak of regret all the way through him for not being better prepared for this encounter.

"I didn't drink anything." Pride filled his tone.

Yes, he'd been tempted. And yes, he'd ordered something, but he just sat there and stared at the amber liquid in the shiny glass while the ache in his leg tried to convince him to take a gulp. It would've been so easy...but the consequences would've devastated him.

"I shaw a jigger o' whishkey sittin' in front o' you when I got there."

Why couldn't the drunk keep his mouth shut and move on? Collin had enough trouble today without having to deal with him as well. "You were so drunk, you didn't know—"

"Leave him alone." Now Miss McKenna turned her wrath on him instead of the man who accosted her.

*Does the woman have no sense?*

"I need to ask him something." Her softened voice almost purred.

Why in the world would she want to talk to the stinky, filthy man?

Her maid stood beside her as if she were protecting the girl. If she wanted to do that, why had the woman let her come to this part of town? Surely, they realized what this area was. Suddenly another thought pierced his brain. They couldn't be staying anywhere near here, could they? A gasp escaped his lips, but no one seemed to notice.

"Mr. I-don't-know-what-your-name-is." Miss McKenna jabbed her forefinger toward the drunk's chest, but didn't quite connect. "Why did you call me Mary Murray?" The gleam of interest in Miss McKenna's eyes seemed to light a bonfire inside her.

"'Cause that's who you are. Are you crazy or somethin'?" The man was emerging from his alcohol-induced stupor.

Miss McKenna crossed her arms over her chest. "I am not Mary Murray. I'm her sister, Catherine McKenna, and I'm searching for her."

Now the man looked almost as confused as he had when he was completely drunk. And Collin couldn't blame him. The story did sound farfetched, even though he knew it to be true.

"Can you tell me where to find her?" The eagerness of the woman's face struck Collin somewhere in the vicinity of his heart. How could she be so naive? She shouldn't trust a man like this.

After what Angus shared with him, he finally understood why Catherine McKenna had seemed so aloof and cold at her party. Angus said she'd only found out about being a triplet that day. And Collin wanted to help her find her sister...sisters, actually. Maybe meeting the one that lived in Oregon City would open the door to helping them find the other sister as well. He crossed his arms and listened intently.

"Mary livesh out o' town a few miles on a farm with her sister...and two brothers. Heard they had a Chinaman out there too. Wouldn't put it pasht her." The man from the bar grimaced, but he was making perfect sense now. "And she's engaged to Daniel Winthrop. He useta be one of my best friends. Thinks he's better'n me now." Bitterness laced his words. There had to be a story there, not that Collin wanted to hear it.

He stepped between the two women and the other man. "Where can we find either this Daniel Winthrop or Mary Murray?"

The man stared at him, then turned his attention toward Catherine. "You know this man?"

She flashed a kind look at the drunk. "Yes, he works for my father, Mr....uh? You still haven't told me your name."

"Bowen...Gary Bowen. You can find Daniel Winthrop at Winthrop's Wool Emporium." He glanced around and pointed. "It's a few streets thataway in the same block as the Clyde Huntley Drug and Books store. You can't miss the sign across the top of Huntley's."

Catherine held out her hand to the man. When he took it, she gave his a quick shake. Collin want to jerk her back from having any kind of contact with the degenerate, but instead he just moved closer to her, stressing to Gary Bowen that she was under his protection.

"Thank you." She turned away from the man, and

the drunkard lurched on down the street. "Julie, we need to look for this wool store."

"I think we should have a little discussion, Miss McKenna." Collin couldn't let the women go there alone. He knew he'd have to place all his cards on the table before they would trust him.

When Catherine turned her gaze toward him, her face held the same scorn he'd seen earlier when she looked at the degenerate. He wasn't even sure she would listen to him now.

"I can't imagine anything we have to discuss, Mr. Elliott." She turned away, and her maid moved with her.

"Your father sent me to find you." He hadn't planned to blurt it out like that, but they needed to talk as soon as possible. He wasn't going to let these women get away from him again.

She turned back, disbelief clouding her face. "If he did, I'm sure he didn't know you were given to strong drink."

As the sun lowered in the western sky, more people drifted down this street, searching for a place to anchor and imbibe. He needed to get these two gentlewomen away from this area before night fell.

"Do you really want to have this conversation out here on the street? Some people have noticed our confrontation with Mr. Bowen. I don't want to give them another show." He didn't think she would want that to happen either.

"Catherine, perhaps we should go back to the restaurant and get a quiet table and listen to what Mr. Elliott has to say." Finally, her maid was considering Catherine's best interests.

Angus's daughter stared at her maid for a moment. "Perhaps you're right." She looked back toward the intersection. "Do you remember how we got here?"

"Come this way." The maid took her mistress's arm and the two women hurried away.

Collin had to stretch his legs to keep up. *As if my leg hasn't had enough punishment today.* For two women, they traveled fast. He followed them around a corner, then up a ways where they turned and crossed the street. Finally, they stopped in front of an eating establishment. The aromas coming from the building enticed his stomach to growl, but he'd have to wait to get a meal until they were finished with their discussion.

~

When they entered the restaurant, Catherine glanced around. The room was only about half full. She noticed an empty table off to the side. She hurried toward it without even looking to see if that man followed. If he didn't, she and Julie could just have a cup of hot tea and then return to Mrs. Davis's. As late in the afternoon as it was, the wool store might be closed. They could start looking for Mary tomorrow after they had rested. She was long past exhausted.

When she stopped beside one of the four chairs, two masculine hands grasped the back and pulled it out for her. Someone must have taught Mr. Elliott manners. A picture flashed through her mind of the man, elegantly dressed and holding her while they waltzed at her birthday ball. Even though she was reeling from the news she learned that day, she had realized how handsome and accomplished he was as a dancer. And she felt safe in his arms.

Why did that image have to appear right now? If he was a drinker of strong spirits, she didn't want anything to do with him...on a personal level or otherwise.

"Thank you, Mr. Elliott." She tried to keep her tone cool and aloof.

The same grandmotherly woman who had served her and Julie earlier in the afternoon approached the table. "So you ladies came back and brought a gentleman friend."

Catherine started to set her right, but Julie answered her more quickly. "Yes, we would like two cups of tea, so we can visit with our acquaintance in peace." Her tone didn't leave any room for misinterpretation.

"I'll have a cup of coffee if you have any." Mr. Elliott flashed the woman a charming smile. "And this will be my treat."

The older woman nodded and bustled off toward the kitchen.

Was the man just trying to show off for her? Catherine wondered how often he used that charm to his own advantage. It wouldn't work with her. She was immune, especially now that she knew he frequented bars.

"We can take care of our own bill." Catherine clenched her handbag in her lap.

"I'm sure you can, Miss McKenna, but it'll be my pleasure." He leaned his forearms on the table. "I'm very glad I saw you when I did...in front of that saloon."

"I am too." Julie nodded.

"So why did you want to talk to us?" The sooner they finished their little tête-á-tête, the better. She didn't want to spend a single moment with the man that she didn't have to. How dare he force his presence on them? Maybe his manners weren't as refined as they seemed when he politely held her chair.

He clasped his hands and stared across the table at her. "Your little escapade really upset your father. He was frantic when he found out you'd left San Francisco without saying a word."

This infuriating man didn't need to tell her she'd upset her father. She hadn't wanted to, but she felt it was important enough to find her sisters that she took that chance. "That is none of your business, Mr. Elliott." She felt like jumping up and storming out, but they had made too much of a spectacle already today. She would hear him out.

"Get down off your high horse. Mr. McKenna gave

me a better job than anyone else would have, and even after I lost his ship, he believed in me." He leaned even closer across the table. "I care a great deal about your father. Evidently, even more than you do."

Julie's eyebrows shot up like two signal flags, but she didn't say a word.

"What gives you the right to speak to me like this?" Catherine forced the words through a fake smile. It was the only way she could keep from letting everyone in the restaurant know they were in a major disagreement.

"You're spoiled, Miss McKenna." His tone carried a thread of steel. "If you care about your father as much as you do for yourself, you wouldn't have left the way you did. He loves you enough to send me to watch over you and make sure you don't come to harm. After what just happened out there, I know he did the right thing."

Julie breathed out a deep sigh, and she leaned back in her chair just as their waitress returned with their beverages. As soon as everyone had been served, the woman went to help another group sitting near the windows.

Shock at the man's words made Catherine speechless. Unfortunately, she realized he was right. She shuddered to think what could have happened if he hadn't come along when he did.

"You may be right. Did you come here to lecture me as if I were a child?" He still raised her hackles.

He released the tight grip he had in his hands and leaned back in the chair. "I didn't come to argue. Your father told me everything. He wants me to help you with your quest...and make sure you're safe."

"Oh, Mr. Elliott, I'm glad you agreed." Julie relaxed as if the man saved them from great harm. "I tried to talk her out of coming, but she was adamant. I felt I should accompany her to protect her."

*Traitor.* Why did her maid have to be so effusive with her comments?

Maybe he did rescue them, and Catherine realized he would be a great help in protecting them. She would just have to keep him so busy he wouldn't have time to visit another saloon.

"What do you have in mind?" She tried not to look down her nose at him, but it was a strong temptation.

His gaze slid from her to Julie and back again. "I need your cooperation to be able to fulfill my promise to your father. I went to every hotel the conductor told me about, but couldn't find you."

"Were you on the same train we were?" Evidently, Julie was ready to overlook his faults.

He shook his head. "No, but I was on the next one. You would've reached here a long time before I did if you hadn't had so much trouble. My train arrived an hour or two after yours did."

Relief rushed through her. What if he hadn't come? Would they have been harmed down in that seedy part of town? They were foolish to try to find their way in a strange place. *I won't make that mistake again.*

Julie stirred a little milk into her tea and took a sip. "We tried the Barlow House, but it was full."

"Someone told us about a widow who had started renting rooms in her house." Catherine watched Mr. Elliott closely for a reaction.

Did relief flit across his face? Maybe he had worried about their safety. She hoped so.

"We are going to stay there until we check out the information we received this afternoon." She picked up her spoon and twirled it, wondering just where he was staying.

"I'll help you." He put three heaping spoonfuls of sugar in his coffee and started stirring.

Catherine made a face. The stuff would be like syrup. *Coffee syrup.* She couldn't imagine anything tasting worse than that...except alcohol. But then, evidently he liked the taste of that as well.

"Mary Lenora Murray, why are you dressed like that, and who are those people?"

A man of medium height with dark blond, wavy hair stood staring down at her. Catherine flinched. *Did he just call me Mary?*

# CHAPTER 11

*C*ollin hadn't noticed the man approach their table until the demanding voice interrupted their conversation. He cut his eyes toward Catherine. Her eyes widened and for once she seemed at a loss for words.

The man couldn't get away with talking to her in that tone. Collin rose and faced the stranger, towering over him. Maybe he looked menacing enough to scare the intruder off, but with this bum leg, he'd have a hard time staying on his feet in a fray, should one ensue.

Confusion clouded the hazel eyes staring at Catherine. "You're not Mary." He shook his head is if clearing his brain. "But you look like her...only slightly different." He tipped his head to the side and rubbed his chin with one hand. "Same kind of hair. Same eyes. But she wouldn't be wearing that color right now. She's still in mourning."

The man was babbling. Was he insane? Collin didn't want to tangle with someone who was unbalanced in the head. No telling what he would do.

Catherine quickly stood, almost knocking her chair over. "How do you know Mary Lenora Murray?" Her words were barely above a whisper.

Collin glanced back at her. So much hope filled her face that he wished the man did know Mary...wait, Mary Murray was one of her sisters, wasn't she? He swung his attention back to the stupefied stranger.

"We are to be married in October...a month from today, actually." He continued to stare at Catherine.

Collin didn't like the way the man looked at her, his expression halfway between admiration and confusion. So he went around the table to stand beside her, lending her any support she might need. Physical...emotional, whatever. For a brief moment, he wished he could put his arm around her and comfort her. Thank goodness that absurd idea swiftly took wings.

"Won't you join us?" Catherine gave the gracious invitation as if she were welcoming someone into her parlor in San Francisco.

He wasn't sure it was such a good idea. "Maybe Mr. uh...Winthrop needs to be going." He'd like to give him a shove right out the door. The man's presence made Collin uncomfortable. The way he looked at Catherine just wasn't right, especially if he was going to marry another woman so soon.

"No, I can stay a little while." Winthrop pulled out the chair across from Julie and sat down, never removing his gaze from Catherine.

The waitress arrived immediately. "Can I get you something, Daniel?"

"I'll just have a cup of coffee. Thanks, Millie." He only gave a quick glance at the woman before returning his attention to Catherine.

Collin couldn't think of anything to do except go back to his own chair without taking his eyes off the interloper. Why was Winthrop here? What did he want from Catherine?

"Mr. Winthrop." She plunged right into a conversation. "We were going to look for you tomorrow, anyway."

"What gave you the idea to look for me?" From his expression, Winthrop still hadn't overcome his confusion.

Catherine grimaced. "Earlier in the day, I was accosted by a rather disgusting, drunken man." A frown puckered her eyebrows. "He said something about you having been a friend of his and that I was being too stuck up because we were engaged.... And he called me Mary." Her tone softened when she spoke her sister's name.

"That had to be Gary Bowen." Now Winthrop frowned as well. "We were friends most of our lives, but Gary has started spending too much time in saloons. I'm sorry you had to meet him that way." Finally, the man smiled. "Are you one of Mary's sisters?" His voice held a note of wonder. "She has wanted to find her sisters ever since she found out about them."

Evidently, Mary knew about the other girls. Collin wondered why she hadn't tried to find them sooner. He hoped that fact didn't hurt Catherine.

"Yes, I am Catherine Lenora McKenna. What do you mean 'as soon as she found out about them'? Did she not know about us either?"

Winthrop shook his head. "No. She only found out after her father's death this summer. I promised I would help her find the two of you sometime after we're married. I've been pondering just how to start the search."

A bright smile spread across her face like the sun coming up over the ocean on a summer day, bathing the surroundings in a golden glow. Collin had never glimpsed that smile before. She was beautiful. Breathtaking. In that instant, he wanted to be able to keep her smiling every day of her life. The thought wouldn't let go of him.

*This is the Ice Princess.* He'd just have to keep reminding himself of that fact. He wouldn't be in her life that long. A sudden feeling of losing something valuable overwhelmed him.

Winthrop returned her smile. "Mary will be so pleased you're here."

The waitress arrived with his cup of coffee. She also carried a coffeepot with a wadded-up piece of fabric around the granite handle. "Do you want a warmup?" She looked straight at Collin when she spoke.

He covered the top of his cup with one hand while he continued eyeing Winthrop. "No, thanks."

The woman headed toward another table full of customers.

"I have so many questions." Catherine's voice took on a lilting tone, like a meadowlark. "To think, we're close to one of my sisters."

Tears gave her eyes the glitter of the polished emeralds that he'd unpacked and sent to the store from their last shipment. For the first time, he didn't think of her eyes as cold and unfeeling. Maybe the Ice Princess was melting.

Collin peered around the area. "Do we really want to do this here?" The room was filling up, and soon people would be sitting at the next table.

Julie patted Catherine's arm. "I'm sure Mrs. Davis would allow us to use her parlor for a private visit."

Maybe the maid had more sense than Collin gave her credit for.

"Mrs. Davis?" Winthrop glanced toward Julie. "She's one of Winthrop Wool's best customers here in Oregon City. How do you know her?"

"We were told she's a widow who rents out rooms. We had a hard time finding a suitable place to stay, so we're staying with her." Catherine cut her eyes toward Julie. "My ma—my friend, Julie Myers, is traveling with me."

Winthrop dipped his head. "Glad to meet you, Miss Myers." Then he turned toward Collin. "And how do you know these ladies?"

The man was being presumptuous. What business was it of his? Collin wanted to put him in his place. Instead he took a deep breath before replying.

"My father sent his employee, Collin Elliott, to protect us." Catherine's musical laugh stopped Collin before his own harsh comments spilled forth. "He's doing such a good job."

*A good job, my eye.* The woman was full of surprises. He crossed his arms and waited to see what would happen next.

"I've been out of town today, and as I drove down the street I saw what I thought was Mary through the window. She is supposed to be in Portland with my mother, shopping for her trousseau. So my driver and carriage are right outside. If you'll allow me, we can all ride to Mrs. Davis's house together."

Maybe Winthrop wasn't such a bad fellow. After the day he'd endured, Collin would welcome not having to walk to their destination. The ache had made its way up and down his calf. The throbbing intensified until his limp was very pronounced. While he was at this widow's house, he would inquire about taking a room at Mrs. Davis's as well. That way he could indeed watch over the two women.

~

*S*oon they were seated in a cozy parlor with another pot of tea in front of them. Catherine wasn't interest in the hot beverage, even though it came with delicious-smelling cookies. All her senses were overcome by the possibility of actually meeting Mary Lenora. When they set out on their journey, she had been sure it would take a long time to find either sister. God must be smiling on their endeavor. Her heart felt lighter than it had since she first found out she had sisters.

"Mr....Winthrop..." Catherine wasn't sure how to word her question.

"Please call me Daniel. You'll soon be my sister-in-law."

*Sister-in-law.* That was a new thought, but it would be true. All these years she had felt so lonely, wishing for a sister or brother. Now she would have all that...and more. Daniel was a pleasant man. She only hoped Mary wouldn't be disappointed in her when they finally met.

"And you should call me Catherine." Her eyelids felt heavy, but her heart soared. "We'd planned to search tomorrow, but perhaps we should see Mary this evening."

"I'm not sure..."

"Maybe not..."

Both men spoke at once, and Catherine's muddled thoughts couldn't separate their words. It sounded as though Mr. Elliott didn't think that was a good idea and

Daniel agreed with him. The men stared at each other as if they were opponents in one of those savage boxing matches she'd heard about.

Collin nodded to defer to Daniel.

"I know Mary will be deliriously happy." Daniel leaned forward, staring at her.

She wasn't completely comfortable with this turn of events. Why did the two men have to be so bristly? Without having brothers, her experience with males had been limited to elementary school and church. As she got older, she had tutors and Julie to help her learn. Never had she experienced this kind of tension between two strangers. And that's what they were really...strangers. Feeling a wayward lock of hair tickle her cheek, she quickly tucked it behind her ear.

"I'm sorry I keep staring. I just can't get over how much you look like Mary. Even some of your mannerisms are just like hers. She often tucks her hair behind her ears, the same way you just did." He huffed out a breath. "Mary has been looking forward to meeting her sisters so long that I don't want to just spring you on her as a surprise. Perhaps I should talk to her this evening and tell her what has happened. Then she can be rested and ready to meet with you on the morrow. The anticipation will be good for her. She's had so many disappointments in her life. Looking forward to a fulfilled dream would lift anyone's spirits."

Disappointments? Whatever did the man mean? The hope that her sisters were probably happy as she was had sustained her in the last few days. Hearing that Mary had numerous disappointments made her feel melancholy, or perhaps the long trip had taken a heavy toll on her.

Collin arose from his chair and stood with his arms crossed over his chest. "That's a good idea. I believe these ladies are weary from their travels as well. Everyone can have a fresh start in the morning."

Catherine frowned up at him. Yes, he was right. She was so tired she could hardly see straight, but he was interfering in her life. Not something she really wanted right now, and she would let him know her objections in no uncertain terms.

Julie smiled at the man. "That's a good idea, Mr. Elliott. I know how exhausted I am, and I'm sure Catherine is as well. The journey was arduous. Although we are eager to learn more about your fiancée, perhaps it would be better if we finished this conversation at another time."

She looked to Catherine for agreement, with a hint of concern in her eyes. Catherine nodded numbly.

Daniel rose and bowed slightly. "Till tomorrow, then."

Catherine expected Collin to leave at the same time Daniel did. However, he escorted the other man to the door, but stayed inside.

Mrs. Davis came from her private parlor. A smile wreathed her face. "Did I hear the young men leave?"

Before Catherine could say a word, Collin headed

toward the tiny woman. "I've been wanting to meet you, Mrs. Davis. I'm Collin Elliott from San Francisco. I need a room while I'm in Oregon City."

*Oh, no.* The man wanted to stay here. She would never get away from him. How could she prevent it?

"I'm pretty careful who I rent rooms to, and I don't know if these young women would feel comfortable with you in the house." She glanced toward Catherine.

Julie stepped forward. "We know Mr. Elliott. Actually, Catherine's father sent him to help us. We feel perfectly safe with him, don't we, Catherine?" Her tone dared Catherine to disagree.

*Almost*...she almost took the dare, but thought better of it.

"Good." Mrs. Davis clasped her hands in front of her waist. "Since the young women are on the second floor, I have just the room for you on the third floor."

Catherine would never have guessed there was another floor above theirs. She started to object, but Julie must have realized what was on her mind. A slight shake of her maid's head gave Catherine something else to think about.

Perhaps having Collin in the house would be a good thing. Only time would tell. But if he interfered with her one more time, she'd send him back to her father.

# CHAPTER 12

*D*aniel told Garrett Henry, his driver, to take him to his parents' house. Since it was so late in the day, he felt sure Mary and his mother had returned from Portland by now.

*Did I make a mistake?* Should he have arranged for Mary and her sister to meet tonight? Knowing how Mary was trying to overcome her previous insecurities, he couldn't help feeling his decision was the correct one. He wanted to break the news to her privately. Let her get used to the idea before the two girls met. That way, their time could be free from the element of surprise and all it brought with it.

He bounded up the front steps and stopped in the doorway to the parlor. Mother sat on one of the loveseats while his beloved Mary rested in the wing-back chair across from her. Mary noticed him first.

"Oh, look." She flashed a bright smile. "Daniel's home." She started to rise.

"Don't get up." He entered the room and sat beside his mother.

Mary was so beautiful, but he recognized the slight droop around her eyes. A long day of shopping had drained her as he'd feared it would. Mother had her heart set on finding everything Mary would need after they married, and she probably didn't slow down one time during their search. She dove into shopping with the passion that pushed many men as they hunted game or rode fast horses.

"So...how was your day?" He never took his eyes from Mary, and her gaze connected with his, almost blocking out everything else.

"It was wonderful, wasn't it, dear?" Mother's words broke their complete connection.

Mary gave her a quick glance. "Your mother had so many ideas about what I would need. I've never had so many new clothes at one time."

Daniel patted his mother's shoulder. "She really knows what she's doing."

"Since I never had a daughter of my own, I'm thrilled to have you, Mary dear." She set her china cup and saucer on the table that divided the area between them. "But it was a long day, and I am a little tired."

She arose and straightened her skirt. "I'll just give you a little time together before dinner." After dropping a kiss on his brow, she left.

"Are you staying for dinner?" He hoped Mary would, but he was about to burst with his news.

"I probably shouldn't." Mary got up, and he followed suit.

After circumventing the table, he gathered her into a hug. She laid her head against his chest. He was sure she could hear his heartbeat accelerate. The fingers of one of her hands made lazy circles on the front of his shirt, and they felt like exquisite torture. Their wedding couldn't come soon enough for him. He yearned for the day when he and Mary wouldn't have to be separated at night. Already she always invaded his dreams.

"I've been away from my siblings a long time today. I should head home." Even as she made the assertion, she sounded reluctant.

He grasped her fingertips in his hand. "I'll drive you." He finally noticed all the parcels stacked here and there around the room. "Do you want to take all this?"

"Your mother told me I could leave everything here until tomorrow. I'm sure she knew I couldn't rest without unpacking things before I go to bed." Her warm breath against his cheek added to the heat building inside him.

He stepped back. "Since it stopped raining earlier today, I'll take you home in the buggy. That way we won't need a driver."

She stared up into his eyes with a Mona Lisa smile. "I'd like that."

He knew just the spot on the road to her house

where he'd stop and kiss her the way he wanted to right now.

Daniel sent Garrett to get the horse and buggy ready and bring it around to the front of the house. Then he and Mary went to tell his mother they would be heading out to the Murray farm. She was disappointed Mary wasn't staying for dinner, but she gave them her blessings and sent them on their way.

After helping Mary up into the velvet-covered seat of the vehicle, he joined her. Even though twilight had fallen, and it was late autumn, the night wasn't too cold. He did tuck a blanket around Mary before flicking the reins to start the horse down the road. As the lingering glow that followed the sunset faded, he put his arm around Mary and pulled her close to his side.

"Did you enjoy today?" He whispered against her hair, inhaling the hint of lilacs that meant Mary to him. He was thrilled that he'd be cuddling her for the rest of his life. *I am so blessed, God.*

"Yes." Her eyes drifted closed, a leisurely smile gracing her lips. "You make me feel so safe, Daniel."

Basking in the tenderness of her last declaration, he continued down the road to the farm, almost forgetting his previous plan. Just in time, he remembered and slowed the horse to a stop.

She lifted her head from his shoulder. "Why are we stopping, Daniel? Is something wrong?"

He tied the reins to the dashboard rail, then turned to face her. "I've been wanting to do this all day."

He lowered his head slowly, and their breaths mixed just before their lips met. The feel of her soft mouth against his made everything in his life take on a deeper meaning. He poured out his love and received hers at the same time...until they were both breathless. Finally, he slowly pulled away.

"Just think, soon we won't have to be separated again." The words whispered between her luscious lips.

"Only a few more days." He dropped another quick kiss on her mouth, then picked up the reins.

As they pulled into the lane that led to the house, he heard Bobby yell. "Someone's coming. I think it's Daniel and Mary."

A welcoming party waited anxiously on the porch. The next couple of hours were spent greeting each other and sharing the meal Frances had prepared for all of them. That girl had changed a lot since he first met her. The food was good, but her helpful, cooperative spirit was even better.

Finally, the boys were in bed, and Frances sat in the parlor reading the latest copy of *Harper's Bazar*.

Daniel and Mary sat in the swing on the front porch. "I have something exciting to tell you." He hoped Frances couldn't hear what he was saying.

Mary leaned away from him and stared. "If it's so exciting, why did you wait to tell me?"

He shook his head. "I wanted us to be alone and have enough time for you to really think about it."

Confusion puckered her brows. He'd seen that cute

expression before. After he shared the news with her, he hoped she would understand why he waited.

~

*M*ary's life had changed so much since Daniel asked her to marry him. What could he possibly have to tell her that was more exciting than that? She rested against the back of the swing and waited.

Stopping the slight swaying of the swing, he leaned forward and stared at the floorboards of the porch. "Remember when you told me how much you want to find your sisters."

Her heart skipped a beat. Of course, she remembered. She lived every day with the ache where two sister-shaped holes lay inside her chest. "Yes."

"A strange thing happened in town this afternoon. It's the reason I was so late getting home." He glanced up at her, then back at his clasped hands.

Something fluttered inside her. Was it hope? Had he heard something that might help her in her quest? Maybe she wouldn't have to wait too long to begin the search.

He leaned back and started the swing again. "I thought I saw you in a restaurant with strangers, another woman and a man."

She gasped. How could he think something like that

about her? She'd never be with another man when she'd given her heart to him.

"I even went in and confronted them."

Mary turned to look him straight in the eyes. "And what happened?"

"When we were face-to-face, I knew she wasn't you. Oh, she looked just like you...only different. Same hair, same eyes, even some of the same mannerisms, but there were subtle differences."

Her eyes widened. Did he mean what she thought he did? She was afraid to even hope he did. If not, she'd be so disappointed. "So who was this woman?"

"She's one of your sisters...Catherine McKenna." He grasped her hand and held it tight.

"Catherine...McKenna?" That could mean only one thing. This woman was the sister their father kept. Once again the question entered her mind. *Why her and not me?* But that wasn't really important right now. One of her sisters was in Oregon City.

"Yes." He scooted even closer to her and put his arm around her. "She's on a journey to find her sisters. She's looking for you, Mary."

Warmth grew inside her, filling every hollow place until she could hardly breathe. "Where did she come from? Who was she traveling with? Our..." She nearly choked on the word. "...father?"

"She came from San Francisco on the train with a female friend. Her father sent a young man to watch over them as well. But we really didn't get to talk very much. Quite frankly, we were all a bit stunned by the situation, I think."

"How does she appear? What is she like?"

"She was wearing stylish clothing and appeared to be well educated. She was a little haughty." He stared into her eyes, and she wondered what he was thinking. "She looks a lot like you, but it didn't take me but a minute to know she wasn't. I'd recognize you anywhere."

His words warmed her heart. "Where is she? Why didn't she come out here today?"

He rested his cheek on the top of her hair. "It's my fault she didn't." His warm breath disarranged her curls, but she didn't care.

"How is it your fault?" Mary tried to keep disappointment from her tone, but it crept in.

"I didn't want to just spring her on you. She and her friends had just arrived in town and were very tired. And I knew you would be exhausted after your trip to Portland with Mother. I wanted to give both of you a chance to rest and prepare yourselves for your first meeting." He raised his head then pushed an errant lock of hair behind her ear. "I wanted you to have plenty of time to get to know each other at leisure. I hope you don't think that was wrong."

For a moment, she wanted to say he made a mistake, but she could understand his thinking. She wanted to find her sisters, but she had thought of it being something they would do later...probably much later. To have it thrust upon her without time to realize what was happening might have been too much.

"No, you weren't wrong." She leaned up and kissed his cheek. "Thank you for being so careful of my feelings."

"I thought maybe your first meeting could be at my parents' house. I could pick you up and take you into town about nine o'clock in the morning. Then I would send Garrett to pick her up as well. Mother could have refreshments to serve, and we could give you all the privacy you want, but we'd be close by if you need us." He pressed his lips against her temple. "Mary, I love you and want what's best for you."

"I know you do." Mary had always followed his lead in their embraces, but this time she initiated a kiss and poured all her love into it.

The night sounds slipped from her consciousness. Only Daniel and their intimate connection mattered to her. The kiss took on a deeper meaning that swept her away on the wings of their love.

When she finally pulled away, he breathed out a contented sigh. "Wow! You can do that anytime you want."

"I'll remember that after we're married," she whispered into his ear.

"It's a good idea not to tempt me like that anymore before the wedding." A laugh rumbled up from deep within his chest.

Mary could hardly wait for that day.

He stood and pulled her to her feet. "I'll be going back to town now."

After another quick kiss, he loped out to the buggy. Her heart followed his every move, and her love for him overwhelmed her once again. With her fingers against her tingling lips, she watched him until he was out of sight on the road.

*Catherine McKenna.* She wondered about her sister.

*Will she even like me? Maybe I'll appear to be a country bumpkin beside her.*

# CHAPTER 13

*B*efore the first light of dawn crept across the Willamette River, Catherine awoke completely refreshed. A feeling of contentment glowed in her heart. She had been so exhausted yesterday that much of the time was a blur. Standing out in crisp bas relief against the muddy background was Daniel Winthrop, her sister's fiancé.

Mary Lenora Murray lived so close to where she and Julie spent last night that sometime today, they would meet for the first time. Excitement pulsed through her. She climbed from the warm cocoon of covers, pulled on her quilted robe, and walked to the window, staring into the dark void outside.

If both of them lived in San Francisco, Catherine could probably call Mary on the telephone, but here in Oregon City, Catherine hadn't seen any evidence of that technology being available. How she longed to hear her sister's voice. Would they sound alike? Evidently, they looked alike, since Mr. Winthrop had mistaken her for Mary. At least, at first.

The chilly air finally penetrated her layers of clothing. She wrapped her arms across her chest and gripped her upper arms. *When will I hear from Mr. Winthrop?* She hoped it would be very soon. Like a little girl on Christmas morning, she couldn't wait to unwrap the most important gift she'd ever received. And hopefully, there would be another one following in the near future. Margaret Lenora Caine. *Thank You, God, that we connected with Mary so quickly.* Perhaps someone here in Oregon City could provide information that would point them toward their other sister. There was no doubt in Catherine's mind that Mary would join her in the pursuit of Margaret.

Hearing the slight clanging in the walls, she turned from the window and moved to stand beside the warm air register in the baseboard. The warmth bathed Catherine's feet and ankles, but didn't rise much farther into the room.

Footsteps sounded on the stairs that were right outside her door. They came down from the third floor. Mr. Elliott must have awakened as early as she had. She leaned her ear against the door for a moment and listened to him continue down the lower flight of steps, then the front door opened and closed. He couldn't very well protect them if he was gallivanting all over town, could he? *Where is he going this early in the morning?* It would serve him right if she and Julie were well on their way to meet Mary before the man returned. During all the time they spent together yesterday, she got the feeling that he wished he were anywhere else besides accompanying her. *What was my father thinking, sending him along?*

She was so lost in thought she didn't hear Julie's approach until she tapped on the door. "Miss Catherine, may I come in?"

Catherine hoped no one heard her greeting. She'd have to remind her maid again that she was her friend on this trip, not her servant. She opened the door.

Julie was fully dressed. "I didn't know if you were awake." She stepped into the room. "I'm here to help you prepare for the morning."

Catherine couldn't stay upset with Julie for very long. And this morning, she did want her assistance. She wanted to look her best when she first met Mary.

By the time they were both satisfied with what she wore and the way her hair was dressed, Mr. Elliot had returned. When they went down the stairs, he waited in the parlor for them.

"I can take you to the restaurant for breakfast." He stood with his hands thrust into the front pockets of his trousers, looking totally in command of things. His stance irked her. She wanted to take him down a peg.

Mrs. Davis followed Catherine and Julie into the parlor. "I'm not feeding my boarders right now, but I did cook a lovely breakfast for the three of you. It will be just like feeding family members. Mr. Davis and I weren't blessed with children, but I'm sure they would be lovely people just like all of you."

Catherine didn't want to disappoint the woman, since she had taken the time to prepare the food. "How kind of you. We'd love to eat here." She glanced from Julie to Mr. Elliot. "Wouldn't we?"

He shrugged. "It sounds like a good idea."

Julie didn't make a comment, but she followed Catherine as they headed down the hallway.

Just as they finished eating the delicious meal, a knock sounded on the front door. Mrs. Davis excused herself and went to answer the summons.

Catherine heard a male voice as well as the older woman's, but she couldn't understand what they were saying. She glanced up and caught Mr. Elliot's intent stare at her. He quickly averted his gaze.

"Do you have any idea what's happening when today?" His tone conveyed that he didn't like not knowing what was going on.

A grin crept across her lips. "Not really." She wiped her hands on her napkin and arose. "I assume we'll have to wait here until we hear from Mr. Winthrop."

Mrs. Davis bustled back into the dining room with more energy than she exhibited yesterday. "That nice Henry boy stopped by with a message. He'll be picking you up just before ten o'clock to take you to the Winthrop house." She stopped and stared at Catherine. "Now I remember why you look familiar. Daniel Winthrop will soon be married to Mary Murray. You look a lot like her." She started gathering the dirty dishes together. "It's so sad all the heartaches that poor girl has endured. But he'll take good care of her." She went out the other door, carrying the stack of plates with her.

*Heartaches? What heartaches?* To even imagine them living less than ideal lives when she had been so cherished and cared for was an idea she had considered but quickly discarded, not wanting to picture them as unhappy or suffering. Now she worried what she would find when she met Mary.

True to his word, Daniel Winthrop's driver arrived right on time. Catherine and Julie were in the parlor visiting, and Collin Elliott stood on the front porch, leaning against a column, staring across the river. Catherine sat where she could see him through the window, wondering if he was going to just hang around here while they were gone. He straightened as the carriage came to a stop in front of the house.

Catherine and Julie pulled on their gloves and stepped outside. "So what are you going to do today, Mr. Elliott?"

"I'm coming with you." His voice held a determined edge.

"I don't think so." She wanted to go down the steps, but he moved in front of her, blocking them.

"Miss McKenna, your father instructed me to telegraph updates to him. I sent him one yesterday. This morning he sent one telling me to stay with you, so everyone would know you're under my protection." His tone sounded smug to her.

Maybe she couldn't stop him from coming without causing a scene, but she could just ignore him the rest of the day. "Fine. You can sit with Julie."

Her maid quirked one eyebrow.

All right, so she was being bossy, but sometimes that man set her teeth on edge. She wasn't sure exactly what it was about him, but she wasn't entirely comfortable with his presence. Just because he worked for her father didn't give him the right to know every intimate detail of her life.

Mr. Elliott hurried down the steps and waited beside the carriage. When she reached the vehicle, he assisted her into the seat that faced forward. Then he treated Julie the same way, but she sat in the seat facing backward. He hopped up beside the maid.

As soon as he was seated, the driver pulled away. The journey to the Winthrop house was silent. Catherine kept her attention on their surroundings. They left the neighborhood of homes and followed a street that took them through the area where stores, hotels, and other businesses lined every street. Then the street led up onto a higher bluff to a neighborhood with more houses. Soon they stopped in front of a three-story mansion that was much larger than Mrs. Davis's, but not as large as Catherine's home in San Francisco. She stared at the façade of the abode.

Lacy panels hung in the windows, screening the rooms from prying eyes on the street. *Is Mary living here?* Or was she coming here from her home? Catherine's heart beat with anticipation. Her palms became sweaty inside her gloves. *What if Mary doesn't like me?* But Mr. Winthrop had said Mary wanted to find her sisters. She took a deep breath just as the front door opened.

Daniel Winthrop stepped outside. "Welcome."

Mr. Elliott jumped down and offered her his hand. She reached for it, but tripped on the step at the side of the carriage. His arms closed around her as he kept her from falling on her face. Not a very graceful way to arrive.

Without removing his arms, he let her slip down the front of his muscled body until her feet touched solid ground. As her shoes connected with the surface, Catherine tried to stand, but she wavered. He slid one arm across her back and steadied her with a hand on her waist. *The cad!* No man had ever handled her this way. And she didn't like it...did she? Somehow, feelings she'd never experienced warred inside her. She didn't need a distraction like this right now.

Meeting Mary was uppermost in her mind. She

looked up into Mr. Elliott's face and shot him her most ferocious frown.

He leaned toward her and whispered against her ear. "I'm sorry, your highness. I was just trying to keep you from falling on your face."

Removing his hands from her person, he stepped back. For just a moment, she felt as if she were teetering again. She steeled her backbone and straightened her ruffled peplum, then made sure her skirt wasn't twisted or pulled up far enough to reveal a glimpse of her limbs.

"In the future..." She kept her eyes averted and spoke low enough that his ears were the only ones that could hear her words. "...keep your hands to yourself."

The low chuckle that emitted from between his smiling lips added fuel to her flaming indignation. She sashayed around him and started up the front steps. Her face burned with what she knew was a bright blush. What a way for Mary's fiancé to see her.

She didn't look back to see if Mr. Elliott was also helping Julie from the carriage. Now Catherine regretted not slapping his face when she had the opportunity.

"Welcome, Catherine." Daniel held the door open for her.

"Thank you." She entered and her gaze roved around the wide foyer filled with tasteful decorations, but her mind still dwelt on the humiliation...and something else, she didn't know what...she felt. "You have a beautiful home."

"You'll have to tell my mother that. My house is a couple of blocks down the street, and I haven't done any decorating there. I want Mary to make it the kind of home she desires." When Daniel uttered her sister's name, his tone softened, revealing longing and love.

She heard Julie and Mr. Elliott come in behind her, but she was still ignoring the man, so she didn't turn around. "Is Mary here?" She couldn't have kept the eagerness from her tone if she had wanted to...which she didn't.

"Yes, but first let me introduce you to my mother." Daniel ushered them into the parlor. "Mother, I want you to meet Catherine McKenna, her friend Julie Myers, and Collin Elliott."

Mrs. Winthrop sat on a sofa upholstered in a fabric that matched the floral design in the carpet, and the table in front of her held a silver service with steam coming from the spout of the teapot and dainty sandwiches on another silver tray. Another dish held several kinds of cookies. "Won't you sit down and have tea with us?"

Catherine searched the far reaches of the beautiful room, but didn't see her sister. She glanced at Daniel.

"Perhaps Miss Myers and Mr. Elliot can visit with Mother while I take you back to the sitting room where Mary is waiting." He crooked his elbow. "I thought you and she might like your first meeting to be completely private."

Catherine gladly slipped her hand inside his waiting arm. They walked toward the back of the first floor.

"That was discerning of you. I feel more comfortable already."

He stopped beside an open door and ushered her through. "Here's your sister, Mary." After those words, he left.

Excitement coursed through Catherine like the Willamette River rushing over the falls. Should she run to her sister or wait for her to approach?

Mary stood facing long windows with the draperies opened, letting in the sunshine. Outlined by the golden light, she did, indeed, have the same very curly, red hair that Catherine saw each morning. Her green dress hugged a figure that appeared to be a match to Catherine's own body. For an extended moment, she didn't move.

Was Mary as nervous as Catherine was? Did she think Catherine might not like her?

*What should I do?*

Mary slowly turned with her gaze on the floor. When she raised her head, Catherine stared into eyes the same color and shape that looked back at her from her own mirror every day. A connection sizzled between them with all the power of the electricity produced by California Electric Company in San

Francisco, but here there was no need for the wires. They were drawn together by an entirely different source. Without thinking about it, Catherine took a hesitant step. So did Mary. With only a few quick steps, they entered an embrace that carried all the love that had been missing from their lives for eighteen long years.

Catherine felt it. She knew without asking that Mary did too. Once they hugged, they couldn't let go.

Tears streamed down Catherine's face and onto the shoulder of her sister's gown. "Oh, Mary. I feel a part of me that has been missing has come back into my heart."

"Me too." Mary's voice was husky with tears, but it was the same timbre as Catherine's.

Finally, they moved from each other's embrace. Catherine pulled her reticule from hanging on her elbow, dug through the contents for her hanky, and started dabbing the tears from her own face.

Mary slipped her handkerchief from her sleeve and followed suit. "We're a mess."

"I don't care, do you?" Catherine wanted to laugh through her tears. All her emotions were out of control.

"I almost didn't believe you had really come." Mary sniffled. "Even though I knew Daniel wouldn't lie to me about it."

"How long have you—"

"When did you—"

They started together.

They stopped at the same time and stared at each other.

Mary took Catherine's hand and led her over to the couch upholstered in flowered chintz. They sat down and both turned to face the other one at the same time.

"We have so much to talk about." Mary's smile looked so familiar.

"We certainly do." Catherine didn't know where to start.

# CHAPTER 14

*W*hen Catherine fell into Collin's arms, he was so startled he stood there far too long, clasping her against him. She was closer than she'd ever been when they danced the waltz at her birthday party. And heaven help him, but the warmth and soft contours of her body awakened a desire to never let her go. Protect her at all costs. Befuddled, he lowered her too quickly, almost making her lose her footing.

Knowing she wasn't happy about what happened felt like the thrust of a sword in his gut. How could he have forgotten himself to the degree that he made a spectacle of both of them? His unwelcome desires aside, no woman would ever want to be close to him. Or intimate. Especially, not a woman like Catherine McKenna. Not with the unsightly scars on his leg and the limp he hadn't been able to get rid of, no matter how hard he tried.

He'd watched her ramrod-straight back as she walked from him toward the house. The proud tilt of her head told him she couldn't get away quickly enough. The skin above her collar shone a deep red. He knew she probably felt his stare boring a hole into her back, but she never turned around. If she had he would've given her his most apologetic smile.

When Julie cleared her throat, he'd turned back and helped her alight from the carriage without a mishap. As he followed the maid up the steps to the Winthrop mansion, his world tipped on its axis. He wondered if it would ever right itself again. He almost felt as if he were once again walking the unsteady deck of a ship at sea, and storm clouds advanced toward him.

Daniel's mother was a gracious hostess. Collin tried to keep up with the conversation after Catherine went to meet with her sister. But his mind wasn't on the group in the parlor. He couldn't keep from wondering what was going on with the two women in the room down the hall. Something deep inside him wished he had the right to be there with her. But nothing like that would ever happen in his lifetime. With her...or any other woman. The dark cloud in his mind obliterated the bright sunlight of the day.

"Miss Myers..." Mrs. Winthrop's voice cut through his brooding thoughts. "How long have you known Catherine?"

Julie looked uncomfortable and took a sip of tea before she answered. "Several years." Her teacup rattled when she set it on the saucer.

Collin wondered if Catherine even cared that her maid might have to answer uncomfortable questions when they decided to travel as friends instead of a woman with her servant. No matter how drawn he was to the beautiful Miss McKenna, he wouldn't have agreed to their deception. Too bad he hadn't had any say in what they were doing.

"And you, Mr. Elliott..." Mrs. Winthrop turned her charm his way. "Have you known Catherine long?"

He wasn't going to start telling lies for the Ice Princess. *Whoa.* The woman he'd held in his arms a short time ago was anything but cold. "No. Actually, I work for her father. He sent me to protect the women."

No need to tell her that they didn't arrive in Oregon City at the same time. He would just answer the questions she asked without offering any extra information.

"Yes, Angus. I remember him." Mrs. Winthrop stared at the table in front of her, but she looked as though she were seeing something in the distant past. "It's too bad about Lenora. We came on the same wagon train with them. I remember when the baby girls were born. I enjoyed holding them, since I only had a son." She quickly shook her head and turned her attention back toward Collin. "Did Angus make it to the gold fields?"

He didn't like gossiping about his boss. "I did hear

something like that from my father. Now Mr. McKenna owns several businesses in San Francisco."

Mrs. Winthrop took a dainty sandwich and placed it on her plate. "Does he own stores? That's what he and Lenora planned. To establish a store selling quality products to the miners. They even brought a wagon loaded with merchandise across the country on the wagon train."

Collin shifted in his chair. He hoped this inquisition wouldn't last very long. He didn't want to inadvertently share something that went against whatever Catherine was telling people. "He has a department store, but he also owns an import and export business with a number of freighters in his shipping line."

She gave a bright smile. "I'm so glad he is so successful. When he and the Marshalls left Oregon City, he was a broken man. Such a sad time."

Daniel had been leaning against the doorframe. Now he straightened. "I don't know how long Mary and Catherine will be. Mother, will you and Miss Myers keep watching for them. I'll take Mr. Elliott out to the stables to see our horses."

Collin welcomed the reprieve. He didn't know how many more questions he could field and not give his hostess more information than he should. He wished he was back in his snug office at McKenna Shipping. He disliked being under this much scrutiny.

He stood. "I'd like that."

Daniel led the way toward the back door. "Do you ride?"

"Only when necessary." Collin tried to see if he could hear the sisters talking, but couldn't. He and Daniel did pass several closed doors. "I've spent more time on the deck of a ship than on a horse."

After crossing a large back lawn, Daniel led the way through a break in a tall hedge. On the other side, paddocks held several horses and connected to a rather large stable. When he reached the door, he stopped and turned toward Collin.

"Is that where you picked up the limp, on board a ship?"

Collin couldn't believe the man had the audacity to ask such a question on such a short acquaintance. Maybe people in smaller towns took more interest in the personal matters of the strangers they met.

"Not exactly." The words sounded harsh, but he wasn't going to apologize for his tone.

Daniel opened the door and led the way down the center of the neat barn. He stopped beside a stall with a large stallion inside. The horse came over and nudged the man's shoulder. He patted the horse's neck. "This is Sultan."

"He's a beautiful animal." Collin didn't come too close to the powerful horse. He wasn't exactly scared, but he didn't want to risk an injury in case the horse wasn't friendly.

Sultan nudged his muzzle near Daniel's shirt pocket. "I usually bring him an apple or a carrot, but I forgot to pick one up in the kitchen before we left the house."

He whispered something into the horse's ear and scratched his forelock. The animal tapped the floor with one front hoof. Evidently, Daniel and his stallion had their own way to communicate, just the same way a captain learned the creakings of a ship to tell if everything was all right.

Daniel led Collin out the door and toward the fence around the paddock. "I've been wondering about something." He stopped and leaned backward with his arms on the top railing while placing one booted foot against the bottom rail. "This Angus McKenna you work for, does he own the McKenna Shipping company in San Francisco?"

Collin had no idea where this discussion was going, and he didn't want to give any more information than absolutely necessary. "Yes."

Daniel let out a slow breath. "I can't believe it. I've known where Mary's father was for several months, and I didn't even realize it."

This information interested Collin. "What are you talking about?"

"In the spring, I went to San Francisco to meet with Mr. McKenna about shipping our wool products. I had no idea he had any connection to Mary. Of course, we weren't engaged at that time." Daniel studied the hedge they had come through.

"What difference does that make?" Collin leaned the arm from the same side as his scarred leg on the top rail, taking some of the pressure off his injuries.

Daniel turned toward him. "After Mary's father died, she found the adoption paper. I knew I had met a Mr. McKenna, but he seemed far too old to be her father, so I didn't think anything about it when she told me she wanted to find her sisters. I assumed the man I met wasn't any kin."

"That's some turn of events." If Daniel and Mary had contacted Angus at that time, Collin wouldn't have had to come on this wild chase after Catherine and her maid.

"I almost didn't recommend to my father that we use McKenna Shipping. Not too long before I went there, one of their ships had gone down in a storm." Daniel stood up straight and hung his thumbs in the front pockets of his trousers. "Heard the captain was a real hero, saving every man in his crew even though he couldn't swim himself."

Without thinking, Collin shook his head. "He wasn't a hero."

"Do you know the man? I'd like to meet him."

*Why didn't I keep my mouth shut?* Collin clamped his jaw tight and gritted his teeth. "You have." He spat the words as if they tasted vile.

He turned and clomped off toward the house, hating his uneven gait, wishing he'd never left San

Francisco. His inglorious past had followed him. He'd never escape its shadow.

~

Catherine studied Mary's face, noticing subtle differences. Her sister's skin had a slight tan with a sprinkling of freckles, where her own had always been protected from the sun, at least since she had been old enough to wear her hair up. Perhaps Mary's cheeks were slightly fuller, but a person would really have to look hard to notice. And her hands weren't quite as smooth as Catherine's. Her nails were much shorter, and evidently Mary didn't buff hers to the soft shine Catherine always worked for.

No wonder Daniel could tell she wasn't Mary as soon as he arrived at the table in the restaurant. But no one could deny how much they looked alike. Father had said they were identical when they were born. Perhaps Margaret looked just like them...wherever she was.

Catherine took hold of Mary's hand. "I didn't know about you and Margaret until our eighteenth birthday."

"I found out a few days after my father died this past summer. I knew I was adopted. They always told me about it. Mother called me God's Blessing." More tears glistened in Mary's eyes.

Catherine gripped her hand even harder, trying to

comfort her. "Why didn't your parents tell you about your sisters?"

Mary swiped at the corners of her eyes with the sodden hanky. "My mother might have, but she died when I was eleven."

"But you still had your father." This wasn't making any sense to Catherine, but maybe it should, since Father never mentioned the others to her.

Mary nodded. "He loved Mother very much. They had lost one baby on the wagon train. That's why our fa —Angus McKenna...gave me to them. And when my mother died of diphtheria, so did my two older sisters, Carrie and Annette."

Catherine noticed how Mary refused to call Angus their father. In a way, she couldn't blame her. "You had sisters?" She felt a stab of jealousy. "I always wanted siblings. I was so alone while I grew up."

Mary patted her shoulder. "I still have Frances, my sister, and my two brothers, George and Bobby. You'll have to meet them while you are here. How long do you plan to stay in Oregon City?"

Catherine hadn't thought about that. Just how long did she want to stay? She really wanted time to get to know Mary, but she also wanted to rush back to San Francisco and talk to Father.

"You have to stay until the wedding. It's October 28, which is about a month away. Please." Mary's tender tone touched Catherine's heart.

How could she deny her sister's request? But

Catherine knew she would have to contact her father and let him know she had found Mary. Maybe if she agreed to stay awhile, Mary would come visit her in San Francisco and meet their father. Surely, her father would want to reunite with his daughter now that Mary's adoptive parents were deceased. Perhaps seeing her would bring him joy and relieve him of some of the pain he had carried all these years.

"I'll see if we can work that out. I do want to meet your siblings. But I still don't understand why your father never told you about us."

Mary gently tugged her hand free and leaned back on the sofa. "When Ma and the girls died, I think Pa wished he'd died with them. He hurt so much he pulled away from the rest of us emotionally. He worked the farm and took care of us, but he wasn't the same man he had been before. He had dark moods. He stopped going to church. So many things were different."

Catherine's heart broke for her sister. "So who took care of you and the others?"

"I did."

Those words hung in the air between them like a stone wall, revealing the disparity in their lives more than anything else had. Her sister had a so much harder life than Catherine had. She couldn't help wondering if Margaret did too.

"How could you? You were just a child yourself."

"Oh, Catherine. You do what you have to do. Bobby

was two years old, George was three, and Francie was seven, old enough to help me. Ma had taught us girls a lot about cooking and cleaning the house, and we got along. It was all we could do. This year, Pa finally changed. He apologized to us and became more like the Pa I remembered. Then so many things happened...and he...died."

Catherine could tell there was more to the story than what Mary revealed. Staying until the wedding might give them time to explore the rest of each other's lives. She had to give Mary that chance...and she needed the opportunity to really get to know her sister.

"But you still have our father." Catherine thought Mary would be glad.

Almost like a dark veil covering her face, Mary's lips thinned and her jaw muscles tightened. She pulled away and leaned hard against the back of the sofa. "No, I don't." She spoke with a finality that shocked Catherine.

"Why do you say that?" Catherine said. "I'm sure he will want to meet you."

"I'm not ready for that. Not yet." Mary's tone said she would brook no argument. At least not now.

Catherine wanted to create a connection between Mary and their father. But she could sense the rawness in Mary's emotions. Right now, Mary didn't really want anything to do with him, and Catherine knew better than to press her. Somehow she had to bridge the gap between father and daughter, but she had no idea how to bring that about. Maybe staying a little longer would open the door to her sister's heart.

# CHAPTER 15

After Collin's inglorious exit from the conversation with Winthrop, he didn't know where he was headed, except away from his personal torment. But the other man quickly caught up with him before he reached the house.

"How long will you be staying in Oregon City?" At least the man had the sense not to pursue their previous subject.

Wishing their discussion had never entered those old murky waters, Collin gladly grabbed on to the new question. "I'm not sure." He stopped walking and turned toward Winthrop. "Catherine will probably make the decision about how long we'll stay. I'm sure Angus wouldn't want me to leave her here, even though she should be safe with Mary and your family. She and Miss Myers will need an escort home."

"That's a pleasant thing to look forward to." Daniel

laughed. "Escorting two lovely women on a journey." He deliberately bumped his elbow against Collin's and winked.

Collin moved farther from him. "Catherine really has a mind of her own." He joined with Winthrop's laughter.

"Then that's another way the girls are alike." Daniel thrust his hands into his front trouser pockets. "When Mary gets an idea in her head, she doesn't often let it go. I only found that out after I started courting her. And I got myself into real trouble quickly enough."

Collin fell into step with Winthrop as they headed toward the house. "How long ago has that been?"

"Since April." Daniel opened the back door and followed Collin inside.

Catherine and Mary came out of the sitting room just before the men reached the open doorway. Collin studied both women, wondering what exactly they talked about. At least they were smiling right now. Actually, Catherine looked more at peace than he'd ever seen her, and her face had a special glow about it.

"Where have you two been?" Mary sidled up to Winthrop and slid her hand inside his crooked elbow.

The look of adoration she gave him proclaimed her feelings. For some reason, lately Collin had noticed emotional things like that more than ever. Before, he hadn't given a thought to what he'd missed in his life. His own mother had died when he was so young he hardly remembered her, and his father raised him. Mostly on the decks of ships, without a woman anywhere around. But watching this couple express their love in every expression and each gesture brought an ache to his heart. He shot a glance toward Catherine and caught her gaze trained on him. He hoped she had no idea of what he was thinking.

"Let's go join Mother and Miss Myers." Daniel's words broke the tension.

In a move to hurry their progress, Collin held out his elbow toward Catherine. At first, she hesitated, and he wished he hadn't offered. Then she slipped her hand through the opening and gently rested her fingers on his forearm. Even through the woolen suit, each slender finger left an indelible impression on him, and he relished the tender touch.

He must be losing his mind. With the way he'd reacted to Winthrop's conversation, and now being so drawn to Catherine. The sooner he returned to San Francisco and his office work, the better.

Mrs. Winthrop welcomed them into the parlor. She requested that they sit with her. Daniel and Mary scooted close together on one of the short loveseats, and Catherine perched in a wingback chair. Although Daniel's mother waved for Collin to approach the group, he held back. Instead, he leaned against the flocked wallpaper near the doorway, crossed his ankles and his arms, and tried to look nonchalant. A good place to observe all that went on.

He didn't really have any place in this conversation. Today was Catherine's day...with Mary.

~

*A* feeling of wellbeing infused Catherine. To have found one of her sisters so soon, and to know that they loved each other, brought sunshine to her day, whatever the weather. Outside the windows, clouds were scudding across the sky and a gentle rain now fell. But nothing could mar the wonderful event that had transpired inside this home.

"Mary, you look so happy." Their hostess smiled at her future daughter-in-law.

Her sister nodded. "Of course, I am." She glanced toward Catherine. "To have one of my sisters arrive here before I even started looking for them is beyond my wildest dreams." Then her gaze turned toward Daniel. "And knowing I'm soon to be married to the love of my life, how could things get any better?"

Catherine was almost jealous of the love Mary had for Daniel. She was pleased for them, of course, but it revealed to her that something else was missing from her life besides Margaret Lenora. Of their own volition, her eyes were drawn toward Collin Elliott. Why would they go there? The man meant nothing to her. And he didn't even like her...did he? Of course not. He barely tolerated her...and that only because her father told him to protect her. She wondered exactly what the man did think of her personally. She had no indication he even thought about her in a personal way, except for that embarrassing moment in the street when they were leaving the coach.

Just thinking about the moment brought the memory of his strong arms once again. She couldn't deny enjoying the feel of them even in her embarrassment. Once again, warmth stole up her neck and across her cheeks. Wouldn't he laugh if he knew what she was thinking? She turned her attention back toward their hostess and tried to ignore the man's presence, no matter how hard it was to forget him.

"How long will you be staying in Oregon City?"

Glad she had started listening to the conversation at the right moment, Catherine leaned forward in her chair. "I'm really not sure."

"I've asked her to stay at least until after the wedding." Mary once again gave Catherine a wistful smile.

Mrs. Winthrop clasped her hands. "That's a wonderful idea. Please say you will."

"If she stays, I want her to be my bridesmaid."

That was news to Catherine. And she really wanted to be involved in her sister's life that way. "I'd like to, but I must send a telegram to my father and ask him." She hoped that soon her sister would extend an invitation to the wedding to him as well. "I don't think he'll mind us staying. Do you, Julie?"

Her maid had been sitting quietly watching everything that was going on. "I'm sure your father will agree with whatever you really want. He doesn't often deny you anything."

For a moment those words cut through Catherine, even though their tone didn't contain malice. Why in the world would Julie say that? She made Catherine sound spoiled.

Mrs. Winthrop's eyes widened. She stared at Julie for a moment. "Perhaps he only wants her to be happy."

Julie clamped her lips tight and looked as if she were wilting.

"Daniel said you arrived in Oregon City yesterday. Where did you stay last night?" Mrs. Winthrop's voice sounded the way Catherine had always imagined her mother would sound, her tone soft...and loving.

Finally, an easy question for Catherine to answer. "With a widow named Mrs. Davis."

"She is a sweet woman." Daniel's mother shook her head. "It's really too bad she had to start taking in boarders when her husband died. Before that, she was active with so many other things in the city. The garden club and the orphanage. Even helped to build the library book collection."

"We enjoy her lovely home." Catherine studied Julie. Something was really bothering her. She couldn't imagine what, but as soon as they were alone, she'd find out.

Mrs. Winthrop glanced over Catherine's shoulder

toward the place where Mr. Elliott stood. "And did you stay there as well, Mr. Elliott?"

Catherine heard the man shift his position. She was too aware of his every move, even if she wasn't looking at him.

"I had been to all the decent hotels, and none of them had any available rooms. So, yes, I booked a room with Mrs. Davis."

"I have an idea." Their hostess's cheery voice captured everyone's attention again, including Julie's.

Catherine knew how her maid felt about their deception. If she had it to do all over again, she wouldn't have insisted they lie to people. Every time the words left her own mouth, a twinge of conscience gripped her. She wished she could somehow undo the damage. Making Julie take the role of a friend drove a wedge between them that Catherine never expected. She hadn't even considered her maid would be uncomfortable in that position.

"Having to pay for a place to stay will get expensive if you're here a month." The words lilted from Mrs. Winthrop's mouth. "When Edward and I built this house, we wanted to fill it with children. Evidently, that wasn't God's plan for us. But we love sharing our home with others. With you and your friend here, it'll be easy for you and Mary to spend a lot of time together."

Catherine didn't miss Julie's slight flinch when Mrs. Winthrop called them friends. Even if it changed the way the others saw them, she had to confess to fabricating the deception. Then Julie could go back to being her maid. Perhaps they could also become the kind of friends they were before the journey.

What words could she use to explain what she did? "That's an interesting proposition. We'll need to wait until I hear back from Daddy, but I'd love to accept your kind invitation."

The frown on Julie's face deepened, and she kept her face tilted down a little as her unseeing gaze roved over the pattern in the beautiful carpet.

Catherine cleared her throat. Revealing her dishonesty wasn't as easy as she had supposed it would be. She didn't really want these people to condemn her, even though she deserved it. "I cannot move into your home, even for this short time, without telling you what I've done. Something I'm not very proud of."

All eyes turned toward her, making her more uncomfortable. She even felt Collin's unforgiving stare bore into her back. She didn't like the feeling.

"Julie is my lady's maid." She felt the unspoken gasp that should have gone up. "We've become friends, but not the kind I've led you to believe." Now she couldn't get the words out fast enough. "Julie never wanted us to deceive people. It was all my idea. I thought we would be safer traveling as two women friends, instead of a young woman and her maid."

Mrs. Winthrop's gaze flew toward where Collin stood behind Catherine. "Wasn't Mr. Elliott traveling with you?"

Catherine had no way to explain what happened without telling the whole story. She lowered her head, not wanting to see their expressions while she finished. The room remained so quiet during the telling that she could hear the soft rain fall against the windows.

"And so you see, all of this was my fault. The running away without telling my father. Forcing Julie to come with me. Making up this story in the mistaken idea that it would protect us. I understand if you want to withdraw your invitation. I've never liked being around anyone who wasn't completely truthful." Her last few words came out as a whisper, and she felt totally drained.

Tears streamed down her cheeks, but she didn't try to wipe them off. She couldn't have looked up if she had wanted to.

Catherine felt more than saw Mrs. Winthrop come and stand beside her. "My dear child. Although what you did wasn't right, I totally understand your strong desire to find your sisters."

The precious woman wrapped her arms around Catherine and pulled her into a motherly hug. One the likes of which Catherine had never felt. All she could do was lean her head on Mrs. Winthrop's shoulder and sob.

The room remained silent, and no one else moved. Catherine had never asked another person for forgiveness. She had never totally understood why she needed God's forgiveness, but Mrs. Winthrop's open heart helped release strong ties inside her. She hadn't realized until that moment that they had bound her.

She needed to learn to forgive her father for the things he had taken from her. And staying in this home with these people would help her understand even more what God had done for her. She was sure of that, even if other things in her life weren't so certain.

# CHAPTER 16

*C*atherine wasn't sure what to wear to go to the Murray farm to meet Mary's siblings. She knew she shouldn't wear one of her traveling suits with coordinating hat. Wouldn't going to the farm be almost like a picnic? Well, she hadn't been to many of those either.

A soft knock at the door preceded Julie's entry into the lovely bedroom at the Winthrops' where Catherine slept last night. "I'm here to help you dress. How do you want to wear your hair?"

"I'm not sure. What do you think?" Catherine worked her fingers through her hair releasing it from its sleeping braid.

"I've been downstairs in the kitchen, visiting with that nice Mrs. Shelton. She has cooked for the Winthrops for many years. Since Mr. Daniel was a boy." Julie picked up Catherine's silver-backed hairbrush and started pulling the bristles through the tight, red ringlets. "She said Mary often just pulls her hair back and ties it with a ribbon at the nape of her neck."

Catherine knew that her own curls wouldn't stay pulled back very long. The shorter hairs would gather around her face, framing it with a very red halo, which emphasized the light freckles she tried to hide. "Maybe we should do that with mine. But what shall I wear? I want to make a good impression on her family, but I don't want to be so formal that I seem haughty or unapproachable."

Julie stopped brushing and went to the armoire where she had placed Catherine's clothing after she ironed them late yesterday. She pulled out a forest green serge skirt that fit tight at the waist, but the rest of the garment was bell-shaped, without a bustle. "This skirt always looks good on you, and it if should become soiled at the farm, it will be easy to wash."

Catherine agreed. This was so much nicer...having Julie serve as her lady's maid again. And she could tell Julie was more comfortable than she had been at any point on their journey. Life felt more settled now.

Julie stuck her head back inside the armoire and came away with the white, long-sleeved waist with vertical stripes formed by tiny, yellow embroidered flowers with green leaves. A ruffled jabot, trimmed with lace, ran from the neat collar all the way down to where her waistband would rest. "With this, you'll look really nice, but not intimidating."

When Catherine started down the stairs to go to breakfast, Daniel came in from outside. He glanced up and a huge grin spread across his face. Then he stopped still as a statue.

She didn't know what just happened, but she kept descending toward him.

"I'm sorry I was staring." He finally relaxed. "For just a moment, I thought Mary was here. With your hair fixed like that"—he drew a circular wave toward his head—"you look just like her. But then I realized you had to be...you." He cleared his throat. "This is embarrassing."

"After meeting Mary, I understand your confusion." She stopped beside him. When she looked up at his face, she didn't have to tip her head as far back as she did with Collin. "How do you think I feel? It's like looking in a mirror...but not quite."

With a shared laugh, they went into the dining room.

Collin rose from where he sat at the table. "What's so funny?"

His eyes roved over her, making Catherine uncomfortable. Why did the man always do that? She hoped he would stay here at the house while she accompanied Daniel to the farm. That way, she would feel more relaxed with Mary's family.

"I made a mistake." Daniel pulled out her chair for her before going to sit on the side of the table beside

Collin. "When I saw Catherine coming down the stairs, for just a minute, I thought she was Mary."

Collin's stare moved from one of them to the other, finally alighting on Catherine and remaining.

"And I told him that I feel funny when I look at Mary. I can see how confusing this is." She shook the folds out of her napkin and placed it daintily on her lap.

"Funny." Collin's tone was intense. "I don't have any problem telling you apart, even though you're dressed more like your sister today. I'd know you anywhere."

The words took her aback. Maybe he wasn't as indifferent to her as he appeared. She wished he wasn't so hard to understand. Strong and silent most of the time, but when he did say something, the words mattered.

Mrs. Shelton entered followed by a younger servant Catherine hadn't seen yesterday. They both carried dishes filled with delicious-smelling food. Lots of it. After their hit-or-miss mealtimes since they left San Francisco, Catherine looked forward to regular eating times.

The meal progressed with pleasant, inconsequential conversation until they were finished eating. Catherine folded her napkin and laid it beside her plate. "I was surprised your parents didn't join us for breakfast."

"They ate earlier. Father went to open the store, and this is the day Mother volunteers at the orphanage." Daniel took his final bite of a large biscuit filled with butter and strawberry jam.

She turned her attention toward Collin, who hadn't

said much during the meal. "What are you going to do today?" Even though they had only been together for less than two days, she would breathe easier while they were apart.

He took a drink of his black coffee before he glanced at her. "I'm going to the farm too."

She cut her gaze toward Daniel, and he nodded.

Before she could formulate a reasonable objection, Collin smiled at her. "In your father's telegram to me, he stressed the importance of my accompanying you everywhere you go. I can't really let him down now, can I?"

Somehow his tone didn't sound enthusiastic about their time together. *Is that an insult?* She hoped that wasn't what he meant.

"I'll be with Daniel and Mary. You don't have to go. Father will never know." There, that should settle it.

Collin frowned. "But I would." He arose from his chair and hurried out of the dining room.

He sounded almost angry. What did he have to be angry about? She thought she was giving him a way to get out of what he didn't want to do. There was no way to understand that man. She didn't know why in the world she even tried. When they returned home, she'd probably seldom see him, and that was fine with her.

When she and Daniel went out the front door, Collin stood beside an open carriage with only one seat. The three of them would have to share the same bench, and they would have to sit very close to each other.

Catherine wondered why Daniel chose to use this conveyance when she knew he had a different one that would be more comfortable for her. Maybe he hadn't even thought about her comfort. She had no desire to sit close to either of these men.

They reached the end of the stone walkway. Daniel climbed up on the seat first. Before she realized what he was about to do, Collin's hands spanned her waist, and she floated through the air and onto the seat. She had a hard time catching her breath. Why hadn't he told her what he planned to do instead of just...doing it? For the second time, the man had put his hands on her person, and that was totally unacceptable. The warmth from his strong fingers remained imprinted on her waist, and she had a hard time ignoring the feeling. If her father knew how Collin man-handled her, he might change his mind about sending the man everywhere she went....At least, she hoped he would.

Catherine wished for a telephone. She could have a discussion with her father without the telegraph operator reading every word. But instead, she'd just have to wait until they were back in San Francisco to tell her father what she thought about all of this. She huffed out an unladylike breath and tried to find a comfortable way to sit without touching either of the men.

Soon they were out of town and rolling along at a fast clip on a country road. Every time the buggy ran over a rough place, Collin's thigh bumped against hers. She could feel it even through the layers of petticoats under her skirt. Warmth spread up and down her leg. Funny how that didn't happen with her other limb. She sat just as close to Daniel as she did Collin. And occasionally they accidentally touched. Strange.

Turning her gaze toward the bothersome man, she tried to snag his attention. She wanted to get him to move over at least an inch or two, but she didn't want to just blurt out the words. Instead, she tried to scrunch herself into the least amount of space possible. All that accomplished was giving Collin more space to spread out.

"See that white wooden fence?" Daniel nodded toward a field coming up on the right side of the road.

She shaded her eyes from the sun with her hand. "Yes."

"That's the start of the Murray farm." Daniel studied the field as they passed by.

Collin started whistling a tune she'd heard before, but couldn't think of the name of the song. Didn't he know how rude that was? Would he even care? The man was really getting on her nerves.

"I don't see the farmhouse." She peered ahead, trying to peek between the branches of the trees.

"You won't for a little while. The farm is quite substantial."

Somehow Catherine had envisioned something small and squatty, since Daniel talked about all the hardships Mary had endured. This farm looked to be very successful, and everything was well taken care of.

"Mr. Murray wanted this farm to be an inheritance for the boys, so we're overseeing it for them."

"It looks...quite nice." She scooted a tiny bit farther away from Collin.

"It is." Daniel held the reins in one hand and gestured with the other one, pointing to some spot way down the road ahead. "And there's another farm a few miles away that also belongs to the Murray children."

Catherine hadn't been on a farm before, but if the Murrays owned two farms, Mary should be fairly wealthy. Somehow she didn't feel quite as sorry for her sister as she had before.

Collin leaned forward and looked past her toward Daniel. "Two farms? Wasn't that a lot of work?"

"Actually, one of the farms hasn't been worked for over six years. It's the place where Mary's mother and two older sisters died of diphtheria. It belonged to Mary's aunt and uncle, who had just brought their family west. All of them caught the dreaded disease. Since Mary's mother was their only relative, the farm was inherited by the Murrays. Mary didn't know about it until she found the deed with her father's other important papers after he died." Daniel slowed the horse. "We're coming to a curve in the road. After we round the curve, you'll be able to see the house off to the right."

While Catherine mulled the information he'd just shared with them, she kept her eyes wide open, hoping to catch the first glimpse of the place where Mary spent most of her life.

"What are you going to do with the farm?" Collin wouldn't let the subject drop. Why didn't he keep his nose out of things? He didn't need to know everything.

"Mary and I have all that worked out. Because we don't want to uproot the other children at the same time as our wedding, we'll live at the farm at first. Her hired hand Tony Chan is getting married in January. He and his wife will live at this farm and manage it for us. This will allow Mary time to find the furniture and other furnishings she really wants in our home before we move into town."

Catherine was impressed with the way Daniel treated Mary. Not every man would let the woman have that much control over things. She felt sure Mr. Elliott wouldn't.

The horse nosed around the curve, and Catherine saw a picturesque farm with a white house and a red barn. Most of the fields looked as if they had recently been harvested.

She sighed. "It's really beautiful in a country kind of way."

"Yes, it is. Kenneth took great pride in caring for the property. Tony and I have continued since his death." He slowed the horse even more to allow them a leisurely look. "Tony's family moved to the other farm soon after the large hotel fire a while ago. Other buildings were also burned, including his father's laundry.

Instead of rebuilding that business in town, they're going to sharecrop on the farm, hoping to save enough money so they can buy their own property when the Murray boys are old enough to take over their own farms. This will work out well for all our families."

"Sounds like a good deal to me." Collin leaned back, taking him a little farther away from Catherine.

Finally, she could take a breath without worrying if she would brush against the man. And she was tired of holding her back so straight without a place to lean against.

"I see them!" Childish shouts from the direction of the farmhouse drew Catherine's attention.

Two boys jumped up and down on the roof of the front porch. Wasn't Mary afraid they would get hurt? Just as that thought flitted through her mind, one boy lost his footing and started sliding toward the edge of the porch roof.

# CHAPTER 17

*H*oping neither of them would fall and hurt themselves, Collin watched the boys scramble down from the roof. He held his breath while the smaller one slid, then dangled for a moment before dropping to the ground and rolling into a ball. Immediately, the dark-headed child jumped up and brushed himself off. The kid had guts. Just as Collin had when he climbed the rigging of the ship his father captained, like a monkey in a South American jungle. More than once, he fell to the deck. He felt an affinity with the boy when not much around him was familiar...or comfortable.

By the time the buggy turned down the short lane leading to the farmhouse, the boys had been joined on the front porch by Mary and another girl. Mary appeared to be giving them a stern lecture. Maybe she saw the boy take his fall. A low chuckle escaped Collin's lips.

Daniel stopped the buggy in front of the house then helped Catherine down from the conveyance. Mary ran toward Catherine and pulled her into a tight embrace. Collin's attention was drawn to the tears slipping down each sister's cheeks. Quickly, he averted his gaze and noticed the three children trailing after Mary.

They all had dark hair and eyes the shade of a warm spring sky. So different from their older sister. For just a moment, he wondered if she had felt out of place or different because of this. Then he dismissed the thought. Mary probably didn't notice, since she grew up as a member of this family.

He climbed out of the buggy and glanced around. So much chattering and laughter clamored for his attention, but he moved away from all the noise. He wasn't a part of this family reunion and never would be. In fact, he wasn't part of any family and hadn't been for an exceedingly long time. His memories of the time before his mother died were fleeting snatches of events frozen in time. Soft words. A hug. A smile....and they quickly evaporated like fog on a sunny morning.

A young Chinese man, dressed in denim trousers and a plaid shirt with the sleeves rolled up on his forearms, hurried up the lane from the large barn, a wide smile spread across his face. Must be the Tony Chan Daniel told them about.

"Mr. Daniel." The Chinese man stopped, and Daniel turned toward him. "Old farmer down road say he sell bull to us if we want it."

Now Daniel smiled. "Good. With a strong bull, we should be able to increase the herd more quickly. Good work, Tony."

Daniel shifted position to include Collin in the conversation. "Tony, this is Collin Elliott. He's here with Mary's sister, Catherine."

Collin thrust out his hand, and the Chinese man pumped it vigorously.

"Mary happy sister come." Tony stared at the two women still standing close together. "Hard to tell which...which." He studied one of the women, then the other. "I see now. Mary have braid. Sister not."

His declaration surprised Collin. Was that the only way the man could tell them apart? What would happen when their hairstyles changed?

"Tony." Mary pulled Catherine toward where the men stood. "This is my sister, Catherine McKenna. Tony was a lifesaver when my father was so ill. I don't know what we would have done out here without him." She whispered the last two sentences into Catherine's ear, but loud enough for those nearby to understand.

"How about if I take Collin with Tony and me? We'll head down to Leland Bradford's farm before he changes his mind about the bull." Daniel dropped a quick kiss on Mary's cheek.

Her face glowed pink as she stared up at him, adoration shining like the sunlight. "Don't be late for lunch. Frances is cooking a special meal to welcome Catherine...and Collin."

Something about the look that passed between Daniel and Mary made Collin feel uncomfortable, almost as if he were intruding on a private moment. He turned away and studied the large field that looked like a garden that had gone to seed. Dry and broken stalks were strewn about. It looked as dead as his life had been before Mr. McKenna showed his trust by raising him to prominence in the company. He couldn't help being thankful for that. He just wished he were back at the office, instead of here watching over Catherine.

The words "Catherine and Collin" kept repeating in his mind. Somehow they sounded right together. But then again there was no hidden meaning in them.

The three men jumped aboard the buggy, and they headed farther down the road.

"This is a nice area." Collin continued to take in the landscape. He hadn't spent much time in the country before. Lots of trees grew in clusters all around the cultivated fields. And cows and horses grazed in some paddocks, while sheep dotted others. The autumn grass was green, but a duller green from what he usually saw in the spring.

"It really is." Daniel held the reins in one hand and gestured with the other. "The Murray farm is quite large. When they settled here, Mary's father chose their property well. Good source of water and fertile soil, but still not very far from town."

They turned onto a crossroad and headed north. At least Collin had a good sense of direction. "How far to the other farm the Murrays own?"

"Over five miles." Daniel turned the buggy onto another dirt road. "We're not going that far today."

When they reached the Bradford farm, it wasn't quite as well taken care of as the Murray farm. He wondered how much of the work had been done before Mr. Murray died, and how much Daniel had done. When they met two days ago, he pegged Daniel as a businessman who probably didn't get his hands dirty with manual labor. Perhaps he'd been wrong. He was glad he had kept his counsel to himself, so no one would know he had misjudged Mary's fiancé.

While he observed Daniel making the deal for the bull, Collin realized he was an astute businessman who knew how to talk to people from all walks of life. Finally, the men shook hands to seal the deal and from the expressions on both their faces, each one was happy with the final result. Realizing there were many things he still had to learn about doing business, Collin vowed to remember some of the gentle maneuvers Daniel used.

While they returned to the Murray farm, Daniel and Tony Chan discussed more changes they wanted to make there. Collin listened with interest. They arrived back about the right time for the noon meal.

George and Bobby waited for them on the front porch. They ran down the stone walkway to the front gate. When Daniel stopped the buggy, he and Collin stepped down, but Tony Chan stayed in the conveyance.

"I take care of horses, Mr. Daniel." The Chinese man headed toward the barn.

"Bobby, you stop swinging on that gate." Mary came through the front door and crossed her arms over her chest. "You're too heavy to be doing that now. You're going to break it again." She turned her attention toward the man driving away. "Tony, come on back to the house and have lunch with us."

He gave her a quick wave and kept going.

Catherine stood under the shade of the porch and watched the interactions between Mary, her brothers, and Daniel. Her expression was as wistful as Collin's thoughts had been most of the day.

~

Now that the men were back, Frances had sent Catherine to call everyone to the meal. Standing on the porch, Catherine watched the interaction between Mary and her siblings and wondered how her own life would've been different if she'd had some brothers and sisters in their home. Would they laugh and talk so much, almost stumbling over each other's words?

All the conversations in her home had been stilted

by comparison. She had been taught proper etiquette and how to carry on formal conversations. Yes, she, Aunt Kirstin, and her father had times of laughter and fun, but never like this. She crossed her arms and imagined the hugs Mary had been blessed with. Her sister's life had been more unstructured...and free.

*Daddy, why did you keep me from my sisters?* The question brought a deeper ache into her heart. After the talk she and her father had, she understood his thinking, but she knew even he questioned the wisdom of his decisions.

Of course, she didn't have to share her father's attention with anyone else, but that might not have been a bad thing. Especially if she could've had a taste of this family comradery.

"Frances said to tell you lunch is about to be served." Using her usual well-modulated voice didn't gain anyone's attention, except Collin's. Perhaps she should speak louder.

"That's a good thing." Collin's deep voice carried much farther than hers had. "I'm starved."

Now the other people must have noticed what was going on, and Mary started herding the young boys toward the house. The men followed behind.

Catherine didn't think she would be very hungry for lunch after that large breakfast, but the enticing aromas permeating the house while Frances cooked made her stomach growl. At least, it was soft enough so no one else heard the rude noises. She went into the large, homey kitchen to see if she could help Mary's sister with anything.

"You're a special guest. You've made Mary so happy." Using a large fork, Frances picked up pieces of fried chicken out of the skillet and placed them on a large platter. That had to be more than one chicken. "I want to show you my appreciation."

Catherine looked at the table covered with a lovely, embroidered tablecloth. Each place setting was as neat as those she was used to at home. She wondered if the Murrays always had such a fancy table, but she doubted they did. During her visit this morning with Mary, she came to understand some of what they had gone through this year. The convalescence and death of Mr. Murray had been hard on the whole family.

George and Bobby pushed around her and headed toward the table.

"Boys, go out and wash your hands in the mud room before you sit down." Mary sounded the way Catherine imagined a mother would.

"Oh, Mary, do we have to?" Bobby's voice carried a whine.

"Yes, you do. Just as you have to every day before you eat." Mary's stern look made the boys scamper out the back door into the mud room.

Her sister was much more mature in some ways than she was. Catherine couldn't imagine having to run a household right now, let alone when she was eleven years old. But that's what Mary did. Her sister was more prepared than she to start a new life with her husband. And she was glad to keep having the responsibility for her siblings. Catherine could learn plenty from her.

Daniel stood behind Mary with his hands resting on her shoulders. "Francie, it looks to me as if you went to a lot of trouble for this wonderful meal."

A blush crept up the girl's cheeks, and she kept her eyes averted. "Thank you."

"And thank you for helping Mary this way."

Finally, Frances gave him a timid smile. Then a special look passed between them. Not the same kind as he had for Mary, but Catherine knew it carried some kind of special message to the younger girl. Special approval. Perhaps there was a story to explain this exchange too. Maybe she'd ask Mary when she had a chance.

After everyone was seated at the table, Daniel bowed his head. The others followed suit. His prayer of blessing touched Catherine's heart. Most of the blessings for meals she had ever heard were sort of rote recitations that didn't carry much meaning. Daniel's tone and the words he used revealed that he had a dynamic, living relationship with God. Catherine liked that in a man.

For some strange reason, she lifted her head slightly and slid a glance in Collin's direction. She wondered what a prayer of blessing for a meal would sound like coming from his lips.

While Frances served them, they passed around the

platter of fried chicken, fried potatoes, and green peas. When Catherine tasted the peas, they were lightly seasoned with butter.

"Where did you get these? They're delicious." She took another quick bite.

"We grew them this summer, and Mary and I canned those we didn't use or sell in town." Frances seemed to welcome the interest in her cooking.

"How did it go at Mr. Bradford's farm?" Mary looked up at Daniel.

"Really well. We found a price that both of us could agree with. So we'll be picking up the bull next week when I come out with the money for him."

So Mary took part in the plans and working of the farm. An interesting concept to Catherine. Neither she nor Aunt Kirstin knew anything about her father's business.

Mary turned toward Collin. "How did you enjoy the trip to the Bradford's?"

He put down the chicken drumstick he had just taken a bite of and chewed it before answering. "Fine."

"One thing about Elliott." Daniel gestured toward him with his chicken bone. "He's a man of few words."

"It's a wonder he could get a word in edgewise, the way you and Tony Chan talk so much when you're together." Mary laughed.

Catherine thought Collin seemed out of his element here on the farm. She knew he had grown up on ships before his father died. Then he was a crewman on other ships before her father made him a captain. She wondered if he had ever been on a farm before.

Actually, she knew very little about the man, and she didn't think she wanted to know any more than she already did.

# CHAPTER 18

*A*fter lunch, the men headed out to the barn, with the boys trailing behind them. Catherine started to gather the plates.

Frances reached for them just as she began. "Catherine, please let me take care of the dishes."

"But you cooked the whole meal." Catherine shook her head. "I can help with the cleaning up."

Of course, she had never washed a dish in her life, but she had watched their cook and housemaid in the kitchen plenty of times while she was growing up. How hard could it be?

"I'm learning to like all the housework." Mary's sister leaned over and added two more plates to the stack. "Someday, I'll want to get married like Mary is, and what I'm learning now will help me be a good wife and mother."

Without giving it a thought, Catherine threw her

arms around the younger girl and gave her a quick hug. "I know Mary's glad to have you to help her."

A cloud slipped over the eagerness in Frances's face. "I haven't always been helpful." She headed toward the cabinet with the dishes. "But Mary's helping me learn now."

Mary watched the two of them with a smile. "We've been through a lot of hard times together, and all the trouble has made each of us stronger."

Catherine knew that losing their mother and sisters at the same time, then losing their father this past summer had to be hard. Somehow, Mary sounded as if there was a lot more to it. She hoped that sometime Mary would tell her what got her through the hard times.

Frances turned back around. "Catherine, I'm so glad you found Mary. I know what it's like to lose your sisters."

Her words left Catherine with nothing to say. She had only experienced the loss of her sisters for a short time. Frances and Mary had carried the grief of losing theirs for years, and they wouldn't be reunited until they were in heaven. Suddenly, she felt blessed that she hadn't known about her own loss before now. And when she found out about her sisters, they weren't dead, just missing. With God's help, she found Mary, and she had a hope of finding Margaret, the sooner, the better...for her and for Mary.

Frances wiped her hands on her apron then fisted

them against her hips. "You and Mary go out on the porch and visit. It's such a pretty day." She sounded very bossy. "After a while, I'll bring you some tea and cookies." Her last comment softened her tone.

The siren call of time alone with her sister was irresistible. Catherine followed Mary outside. Just as they sat in the swing, a gentle rain began to fall, bringing the smell of freshness to the air.

"I hope the men don't get wet." Since they were on the front porch, Catherine couldn't see the barn from here.

Mary started the swing gently swaying. "There's plenty of space for them to stay in out of the rain. And it might not last long. Sometimes these showers are short."

Catherine didn't know what to say to her sister. Her head was full of all kinds of questions, but she didn't want to bring sadness to Mary's eyes. Just sitting and looking at her was special.

"How did you feel growing up alone?" Mary started the conversation with a question that reminded Catherine of her longings through the years.

She stared through the moisture that gave the farm the feel of one of those soft-focus Impressionist paintings her art tutor had loved so much. How could she describe to Mary what she had felt without revealing too much pain? She needed to use her words the same way the Impressionists used their paint. Not too many fine details.

Mary's eyes held compassion. Tears sprang to Catherine's, and she swiped at them with her fingertips.

"I always felt a little lonely."

Actually, she ached with loneliness much of her life. With only grown-ups around her most of the time, and with the feeling that part of herself was missing, the ache was always in the background.

Yes, they went to church, and she had friends there, but they were casual friends. When she got older, Daddy hired tutors, so she had a fine education, but she wanted a really good friend more than anything. Maybe Mary could be that kind of friend for her. *Sisters could be friends, couldn't they?* This experience was so new, she really didn't know for sure.

"I didn't have time to be lonely." Mary sounded wistful.

Catherine knew Mary didn't know what she was wishing for. Isolation was a dark place in the heart. A silent chamber without the echo of meaningful conversation. But she couldn't tell Mary that.

"Around this farm, there was so much noise...and so much work to do." Mary gave a little laugh. "Being alone sounds like heaven on earth."

"You wouldn't think that if you had to live with it most of your life." Catherine held tight to the chain holding up the swing. "I like the laughter and noise you have in your home."

If Mary would come to San Francisco with her to meet their father, the house on Nob Hill could be filled with happiness as well. But Catherine knew she couldn't bring that up right now. The time was not yet right.

~

C ollin stood outside the huge barn and surveyed the landscape. So different from anything he had ever known, but it held a serenity he'd like to have in his life. When the rain started, he ducked inside and joined the other men as they talked about farming. The two younger boys whooped and hollered in the hayloft, scattering the dry stalks and raising clouds of dust.

"How soon you bring money for Mr. Bradford?" Tony Chan picked up a pitchfork and started moving soiled hay into a wheelbarrow.

Collin had heard about mucking out the stalls, but he'd never seen it done before. *Nasty job.* Far worse than swabbing a deck.

"I'll get it from the bank on Monday. We can pick the bull up then. When we get him back here, we'll need to put him in the smaller paddock closest to the barn until he gets used to his new home. It has the strongest fence."

Collin couldn't stay out of the conversation. "How do you transport a bull from farm to farm?"

"Very carefully." Daniel laughed, and Tony Chan joined him.

"Bull very big, not friendly." Tony scrunched up his face.

"Did you notice the ring in the bull's nose?" Daniel must have realized that Collin was serious when he asked the question.

"Sure. What's it for?"

"We'll tie a strong rope to a chain. Then we run the chain through the ring and up around the base of his horns and pull him behind the wagon." Daniel pulled a thick rope from a hook on the wall. "Strong, like this one."

The Chinese man nodded. "Good plan, boss."

"How in the world did you get the ring in his nose if he's not friendly?" Collin couldn't even imagine.

"The farmer puts the ring in the nose before the bull is grown." Daniel started inspecting the rope. "I don't think anyone could do that after his muscles are fully developed."

Collin grimaced. "I didn't realize farming was so dangerous."

"It can be." Daniel hung the rope back on the wall and turned toward Collin while Tony Chan headed outside into the rain with the mess in his wheelbarrow. "I wanted to continue our conversation from yesterday, but if you're not comfortable with that, I won't."

The man didn't beat around the bush. He came straight to the point. Usually, Collin liked that in a man, but he wasn't sure he did this time.

Collin stood and stared at him a long moment. He

didn't seem to have any hidden meaning behind his words. "I'm sorry I reacted the way I did." He rubbed the back of his neck. Then he pulled his hand away and shoved both into the front pockets of his trousers. "You caught me off guard."

Daniel's eyes widened a moment. "I didn't mean any disrespect. And at the time, I didn't realize you were the captain." He leaned his arms on the top of an empty stall. "I only heard good things about you."

Collin shuffled his feet, disturbing the fresh straw. "Mr. McKenna doesn't hold me responsible for the wreck."

Silence lengthened between them, and Tony Chan returned to continue his project.

Daniel ambled down the middle aisle of the large barn toward the other end. Collin followed. They sat on a wooden bench underneath a window.

"But you do, don't you?" Daniel's tone held no condemnation.

"I was in charge of the ship. It wrecked, so I do take my responsibility seriously." He gripped his hands together between his knees.

"The way I heard it, a storm blew up quickly." Still no blame in Daniel's voice. "And you saved every crew member. That's all anyone could do."

The remembered feeling of the water closing over his head brought momentary panic. He huffed out a harsh breath and stared at the rain out the open barn door.

"That's what Mr. McKenna said."

"Then you should believe him."

A shrill scream rang out. Daniel glanced toward the hayloft at the other end of the barn. Collin did too. Both men jumped up and ran.

Bobby hung from the edge of the hayloft floor, and George was holding onto his arms trying to pull him up.

Bobby had started crying. "My...arms...hurt."

Daniel stopped below him. "Let go, Bobby. I'll catch you."

George looked down at him with a frown furrowing his brow. "What if you miss?"

"Trust me." Daniel used a soothing tone. "I promised Mary I would take care of all of you...and I won't disappoint any of you now."

Two pairs of fear-filled eyes stared down at him. Collin couldn't believe this was the little daredevil he watched slide off the roof of the porch. Of course, the floor of the hayloft was much higher off the ground than the edge of the porch. Then George's attention skipped to the pile of straw on the floor beneath Bobby.

When Collin looked to see what he was staring at, he saw a pitchfork with the tines pointed up and almost covered with the hay. He quickly grabbed the tool and leaned it against the wall.

George looked relieved. He leaned toward his younger brother and whispered something to him. Bobby glanced down and then around until his gaze rested on the handle of the farm implement. George whispered again, then very slowly released his hold on each of Bobby's wrists.

Daniel held his arms wide, and Bobby slid his fingers off the edge. Collin hoped he didn't pick up a lot of splinters when he did.

A wild-Indian scream nearly broke Collin's eardrums as the boy sailed through the air. Collin shifted a little closer to Daniel in case he didn't catch the boy. Maybe he could break his fall and keep him from being hurt.

Bobby's impact knocked Daniel onto his backside. George scrambled down the wooden ladder nailed to the wall, almost falling himself a couple of times. When he was about a yard from the barn floor, he let go and dropped, landing on his feet. Then he scurried toward the fallen man and boy.

He dropped to his knees and reached for his brother. "Are you okay, Bobby?"

The younger brother burst into tears, then swiped them on his shirt sleeve. He puffed out his chest. "Sure am."

Daniel slowly sat up.

"Are you all right, Mr. Daniel?" George still held on to Bobby. "Thank you for saving my brother."

Daniel stood up and started brushing the straw off his trousers. "I told you I'd take care of you. I meant every word." His hand encountered a smear of something on the back of one of his legs. Pulling his hand away, he took a sniff. "Whew. Your sister won't want me sitting on any of the furniture with this mess on me."

They all started laughing, even Collin. He didn't know why he was laughing, but it felt almost as if he belonged with this group. Something he'd missed for a very long time.

Tony Chan stood in the open doorway. "Anybody hurt?"

Daniel glanced up at him. "Not hurt, but I'm a mess."

"You smell bad." Tony frowned. "Miss Mary not like. Mr. Murray keep extra clothes in tack room. Some still there."

Daniel smiled. "He and I were about the same size. I'll see if there are some trousers that'll fit me."

"He clean up here. Soap, towels, razor." Tony led the way through the door, and Daniel followed.

Bobby stood beside George and watched them go. His brother studied Collin.

"You helped save my brother. Thank you." The boy pushed his hands into the back pockets of his overalls. "That pitchfork was the reason I was trying to keep him from falling. He didn't realize how much farther it was to the ground than it was from the porch roof. And that pitchfork could've killed him."

It felt good to help someone else. Collin hadn't really felt useful on this trip. More like a nanny for Mr. McKenna's daughter.

George hung his head. "It's my fault really."

"How do you figure that?" Collin knew how that felt.

"I was s'pposed to put the pitchfork back where it was s'pposed to be. Instead, I just dropped it when Bobby wanted to climb in the hayloft." He dug his toe through the straw on dirt floor. "I could've killed my brother."

Collin didn't want this boy to carry the weight of guilt. He hunkered down beside him. "We all make mistakes. What you did to try to save Bobby far outweighs your mistake."

"You really think so?" George stared him straight in the eyes as if daring him to deny his assertion.

"Yeah, I really do."

A smile slowly crept across the boy's face. "Thanks, Mr. Elliott." He went to get the pitchfork and carried it to the rack where other tools hung on the wall.

Collin walked to the doorway. The rain had stopped, leaving everything looking clean and fresh, even though it was autumn. The words he's just said to George haunted his thoughts. If what the boy did to save his brother outweighed his carelessness, then his saving the crew from certain death after the shipwreck would also outweigh any mistake he might have made during the storm. Why hadn't he realized that before? Angus McKenna had tried to tell him, but his words hadn't hit home the way his own did. He would have to figure a way to start believing them for himself.

# CHAPTER 19

*C*atherine had never been involved with anyone's wedding, so she hadn't anticipated how much work it would entail. For two weeks, she and Mary had spent part of every day, except Sunday, with Daniel's mother working on things for the special day. She'd been grateful that her father had given permission for her to stay till the end of the month. She knew what a sacrifice that must have been for him.

Today, they would go to meet the dressmaker, who was creating Mary's wedding dress. They needed to find a style and choose the fabric for the dress Catherine would wear. When she packed for the journey, she hadn't realized she would be participating in a wedding, so she didn't bring any of her formal gowns.

Mr. Henry, the driver, brought the brougham around to the front of the house. Mrs. Winthrop, Mary, and Catherine were going alone. When she said goodbye to Julie, her maid looked wistful. Maybe she missed being included in everything as she was when they pretended she was a friend. Catherine was sorry Julie was disappointed, but she couldn't have it both ways.

Pulling her gloves on, Daniel's mother led the way out the door. "This will be a good day for us to take care of several errands. Maybe even show Catherine some of the sights in the area."

Mary followed her. "That'll be fun."

The driver headed a different direction from the way Catherine had arrived at the Winthrop house. Soon they were surrounded by farmland instead of houses. She was amazed at how green everything still looked, almost as if it were spring instead of autumn.

She stared out between the pulled-back velvet draperies that surrounded the carriage windows. "Where are we going? This doesn't look like any part of Oregon City that I've seen."

Mrs. Winthrop laughed. "There's a good reason for that. We're going to Portland instead. A few years ago, a French dressmaker who creates the most exquisite dresses settled there. Mary's gown will be white Chantilly lace, and Yvette's design will be like no other seen in this area."

"I showed you our mother and father's wedding photograph that I found after my adoptive father died." Mary leaned closer to Catherine. "The reason I chose to wear lace was because our mother's wedding dress was lace. And the dressmaker had several lovely European lace designs for us to choose from. My silk veil will be edged with some of it as well."

"That sounds beautiful." Catherine had always loved lace. In her opinion, the tiny flowers and leaves woven into the fine netting made any kind of dress look elegant.

"It is. You'll see." Happiness shone from Mary's eyes.

"I'm sure you'll look wonderful in it."

She watched a blush creep up along Mary's neck and cheeks. She knew exactly what her sister was feeling. The same thing had happened to her on plenty of occasions. Catherine felt their connection to each other grow stronger every day, and more of her loneliness faded away. If only Oregon City wasn't so far from San Francisco. But at least the railroad connected the cities, so travel between was easier than it had been only a few years ago.

During their many hours together, Mary had opened up and revealed many things about her life. Finally, Catherine really understood how hard circumstances had been for her. Evidently, Mary had become a stronger person through all her trials. Catherine wanted Mary's life to be as wonderful as hers had been, and maybe now it would be. Father's telegram had expressed his joy when he found out that she had connected with Mary. It would break their father's heart if he found out what Mary had gone through. Somehow, Catherine had to bring the two of them together, so he could see for himself that Mary's life was now happy and fulfilled.

"Our Mary will be breathtaking." Mrs. Winthrop drew an embroidered handkerchief from her handbag and patted her brow.

Catherine hadn't realized how warm it was until the woman did that. The sunlight streaming through the windows heated the small space very quickly.

"We must find just the right dress design and fabric for you to wear, too, dear." Mrs. Winthrop dropped the hanky back into the bag. "There are a number of superstitions about weddings. An old one was that often bad luck tried to ruin a wedding. The bride and her bridesmaid wore the same exact same clothes, so bad luck wouldn't know which one to bother. Of course, that's silly, but since you and Mary look so much alike, maybe we could have Yvette make you a dress using the same design, but in a different color."

Catherine didn't want to take away from the specialness of the day for Mary. She glanced toward her sister and found her smiling.

"That sounds like a good idea—" Mary stopped abruptly. "Unless you find something else you like better."

"But it's your special day. I want whatever you want."

Mrs. Winthrop gave her hand a quick squeeze. "Why don't we wait until we see the suggestions Yvette has for us?"

Catherine wished they were in the open carriage,

but perhaps, Mrs. Winthrop didn't want them to risk getting wet if it started to rain as it often had since Catherine arrived in Oregon City. Conversation between the three women flowed freely, and she felt more at home with these two women than she had ever felt, even with Aunt Kirstin. Daniel's mother didn't treat her like a child as her aunt had.

She realized she had given Aunt Kirstin no reason to treat her like an adult, but with Mrs. Winthrop, she didn't have to earn the right to be accepted that way. Mary being her sister pulled her into the middle of this family. All of which was new and exhilarating. For a moment she felt almost lightheaded.

As they approached Portland, the farmland gave way to houses, then businesses. Portland appeared much larger than Oregon City. Expecting them to stop near one of the many stores they passed, she was surprised when they pulled into the drive beside a modest-looking house. Nothing indicated it might be a business.

After they alit from the carriage, Mrs. Winthrop swept up the stepping stones to the tiny front stoop. She didn't knock on the door. Instead she opened it and walked in, accompanied by the tinkling sound of the bell suspended above the door.

Catherine's eyes explored the cluttered area they entered. Even though a cluster of furniture on one side was an inviting sitting room, the rest of the space had shelves overflowing with bolts of fabric and all kinds of buttons, lace, and other trims. The only empty wall was practically papered with overlapping sketches of all styles of clothing—dresses, skirts, waists, cloaks, capes, jackets, and long coats. She wanted to go over and study them, but a spritely woman of indeterminate age caught her attention as she entered from the middle of the curtained-off doorway at the back.

Her hair was swept into a style on the top of her head that probably was neat earlier in the day, but now looked wilted. But her stylish dress fit her like a dream. If she made that gown, Catherine knew she would love whatever the French woman came up with for her.

"Meez Winthrop." The woman's accent sounded authentic to Catherine, but she had only been around a few people from France. "Your beautiful daughter-in-law will be so lovely at the wedding. The dress is even ready for a final fitting." Her eyes darted back to where Catherine stood close to Mary. "Oh, my! There are *deux jeunes femmes!* My eyes, they are seeing things. They are so alike."

Mary laughed, and Catherine couldn't keep from joining in her mirth. With the woman's surprise and excitement filling the room, even Mrs. Winthrop laughed.

"This is Mary's identical sister, Catherine."

She was glad when Daniel's mother didn't give any other information. She still didn't feel comfortable discussing their situation with strangers.

"Will she be the *demoiselle d'honneur?* How do you

say? ...Bridesmaid, *oui?*" She clapped her hands. "This is splendid!"

"Yes." Mary put her arm around Catherine's waist and pulled her forward. "We want to order a gown for her to wear to the wedding."

Yvette walked around the two younger women, studying everything about them. "They are exactly alike. That will be beautiful. I have a new shipment of silk." The longer and faster she talked, the less pronounced her accent became. "And I can use the same dress design with only a few changes, so they will look very much alike still."

A smile spread across Mrs. Winthrop's face. She turned to Mary. "What would you think about that, dear?"

Catherine was glad Daniel's mother was letting her sister make the decision.

"What changes did you have in mind, Yvette?" Mary moved over toward a table Catherine hadn't even noticed, because it had so many things piled on it. "Is my design over here?"

Catherine wondered how the designer could find anything in all that jumble, but the French woman quickly extracted a drawing and laid it on the only empty space on the tabletop.

"Here it is."

The skillful sketch had simple, but elegant, lines covered with a lace pattern that pooled slightly on the floor under the model. It appeared to be a lined sleeveless dress with a scooped neckline and princess seams, and a long-sleeved bolero jacket made from the same lace covered the woman's shoulders and gave the outfit the appearance of a high neckline. Just imagining Mary wearing such an exquisite dress brought a wide smile to Catherine's face. Her sister would be a beautiful bride.

Yvette picked up another sheet of drawing paper and a pencil and placed it over the first design. Her pencil flew across the page, and a new design rapidly appeared. The same lines, and even a jacket, but this dress was a solid fabric and only the jacket was lace. And the skirt wasn't quite as long as the wedding gown.

"What do you think? You like it?"

The designer looked only at Mary for an opinion, and Catherine agreed. Her sister should be the one to decide.

"Would the jacket be the same lace as mine?"

"It can be, if that's what you want."

Mary nodded. "I do. Now let's see this silk you were talking about."

Catherine followed Mary and Yvette as they went through the curtained doorway. In this room, the shelves had bolts upon bolts in a rainbow of colors and various finer fabrics than the ones displayed in the front room. The dressmaker led the way to a stack of several colors of watered silk.

Yvette lifted the edge of one bolt. "See how the richness of the color changes as the fabric moves. It will be beautiful without taking the focus from the bride as the most important woman in the room."

Once again Mary blushed. Evidently, she wasn't used to being the focus of attention. Catherine would do all she could to make sure Mary's day was a dream come true for her.

"What color do you want her to wear, Mary?"

Catherine respected this businesswoman's astute attention to her sister. She stood back and waited for Mary to speak. No matter what color her sister chose, Catherine would agree. Suddenly, she realized she liked giving the center of attention to Mary.

What a revelation. When had she become thoughtful of other people? She hadn't realized she wasn't until that very moment. Satisfaction crept through her. Perhaps she had matured on this trip. Or maybe it was just because Mary was her sister. Whatever the reason, Catherine decided to explore other ways to reach out to others, make them feel special. Warmth spread inside her, fanning out from her heart.

Her life was poised to change more than ever before.

# CHAPTER 20

$C$ollin found Mrs. Winthrop, though kind and gentle, to be a force to be reckoned with, and he hardly ever swayed her opinion. The woman had finally convinced him she was sure Angus McKenna wouldn't mind him trusting Catherine to her care. This had allowed him to spend more time with Daniel and Tony Chan at the farm. He'd learned a lot about all the work needed to keep the farm running. He'd always figured farmers had time off after all the crops were harvested for the year. That was as far from the truth as people thinking all the captain of a ship did was stand on the bridge and give orders.

He enjoyed the physical labor and felt himself grow stronger, even his damaged leg. Most of the time now, his limp was almost gone. Something he was thankful for. If only he could do something about the ugly scars. Looking at them sickened him. He was sure the sight of them would be enough to make a woman run from him in horror.

Today Catherine had gone with Mary and Mrs. Winthrop to the dressmaker's. Only after they left did he find out the place was in Portland instead of Oregon City. He was having a hard time keeping his mind on what they were doing, because he did worry about Catherine being that far away. Garrett Henry drove them, and the man was strong enough to protect them, but somehow Collin couldn't stop worrying about her.

At least, he, Daniel, and Tony Chan were hauling hay today. Something that didn't need him to concentrate too much on what was happening. Tony Chan had backed the piled-high hay wagon into the barn and parked it beneath the edge of the hayloft.

"How about if you and Tony pitch the hay up here, and I'll stack it where it needs to go?" Daniel headed toward the boards nailed on the wall to form steps. He quickly scaled them and grabbed a pitchfork that was already up there.

"All right." Collin pulled one of the pitchforks from under the seat of the wagon.

Lifting the hay, one forkful at a time, and throwing it high enough to reach the hayloft took a lot more energy than loading the stuff from the haystack in the field onto the wagon.

Daniel's shoes sounded like a drum beating on the wooden floor above them while he moved the hay they threw up there and stacked it so they could get even more into the limited space. Although the men had visited some while they were in the field, inside the barn they remained quiet. Without wind to blow it away, the air became thick with dust and debris. No one wanted to breathe that in, and talking took too much effort. The only sounds were the scraping of the pitchforks and his own heavy breathing. The other two men didn't seem to be bothered by the strenuous feat.

This left Collin plenty of time to think. He was becoming very comfortable with these people, even though their backgrounds were hugely different. Besides learning about Catherine's sister and her fiancé, for the first time in his life, he experienced what it meant to have a normal family life. They treated him as though he really belonged.

But he didn't, and he knew it. He couldn't forget that fact.

Going back to his solitary life of work and living in the boardinghouse would be hard. Before this trip, he hadn't realized he was lonely. But just imagining life without these people around revealed the bleakness he'd considered normal.

He would be glad to relinquish the responsibility of Miss Catherine McKenna back to her father. And he looked forward to returning to his new position at McKenna Shipping. But now that he'd experienced family life from the inside, he wasn't sure he would be as content as he was before.

Besides that, the two weekends they had been in Oregon City, he had gone to church with all of them. The only preaching Collin had ever heard had been itinerant preachers, shouting on the street corners in various cities where the ships he was on docked. These men talked about hellfire and brimstone. He never put much stock in all those scare tactics. He'd seen enough of the seamy side of life here on earth. He didn't want to even think about anything after death. Death was final, wasn't it?

Reverend Horton told a different story. Instead of scaring people with the threat of hell, his sermons had been about God's love and His grace. He talked about God wanting to be a part of a person's life here on earth, so when he or she died, going to live with Him in heaven wouldn't be a drastic change. And he talked about Jesus. Not just about Him being born in a manger and dying on a cross, but as a Lord who wanted to not only save a person, but also took an active part in people's lives right now. That sounded pretty good to Collin. But so many questions were running through his thoughts he almost missed the hayloft with his last pitch.

"Hey, guys." Daniel smiled down at them. "Isn't it about lunch time? I'm eager to dig into that picnic basket that Mrs. Winthrop had Mrs. Shelton prepare for us. What do you say? Shall we go eat?"

Collin's stomach let out a roar loud enough for Daniel to hear it all the way up there.

"I'd say that's my answer." With a chuckle, Daniel headed toward the ladder.

Tony Chan and Collin burst into laughter.

"Sounds good to me." Collin wanted a long cool drink of water, too, to clear this dust from his throat. The spring water that was piped to the house tasted so clean and fresh. His throat felt drier just thinking about the refreshment.

"Me too." The Chinese man jumped down from the wagon.

Collin had seen many Chinese workers both in San Francisco and on the ships he'd sailed on. They all worked hard, but this man might be the hardest worker he'd ever encountered. He respected him for it.

All three men washed up in the mud room, then headed into the kitchen. When Daniel opened the basket, the enticing aroma of fried chicken wafted through the air. Collin did love fried chicken, even when it wasn't still hot. His landlady cooked plain fare, mostly roasts, stew, and soups. And she didn't use anything to season the food except salt. The cooking coming from the Winthrop kitchen whetted his appetite. He'd miss this as well when he went back to San Francisco.

Along with the chicken, they found buttered biscuits and potato salad. Even an apple pie. They dove into the food with a minimum of conversation. What had looked like enough food for the whole family soon disappeared.

A few minutes later, Collin leaned back in his chair, feeling stuffed. A meal like this might make him want a nap, but there was no time for that. Or they wouldn't finish moving the hay.

After loading the basket up with the dirty dishes and napkins, Daniel patted his stomach too. "We can take a break from the hard work for awhile."

"Sounds good to me." He was glad Daniel had made that suggestion.

Tony Chan stood. "I go finish rest of hay in wagon. When finish break, we get next load." He headed out the back door.

Daniel watched him go. "I've told him it's all right to take breaks, but he never does."

He nodded. "I've been around a lot of Chinese workers. They are diligent."

"We can sit out on the front porch and enjoy the breeze." Daniel led the way through the house. He sprawled on the swing, and Collin dropped into one of the rocking chairs. The cushions felt good against his sore back.

"Why are you going to live out here on the farm when you have that house in town?" Collin felt they knew each other well enough so he could ask this question that had been on his mind.

"I told you about not wanting to change too much in the lives of Mary's siblings all at once, but there's more to it." Daniel appeared to be deep in thought. "I need to prove to Mary that anywhere she is will always be home to me."

"I'm not sure I understand." He had never consider what made relationships work before.

"I've always loved sitting out here." Daniel looked around at the countryside. "I did a lot of my courting right here."

Collin laughed. "No wonder you like it."

Daniel leaned forward with his hands on his knees. "Not everything that happened out here was good."

*What does he mean by that?*

"All you've seen is the good part of our relationship." Daniel stopped and stared at him. "I must confess I almost lost Mary by being stubborn. Pretty full of myself. Thought I should run everything in the relationship. You know, be the head of the household and all that."

*Interesting.* That painted a different picture from the man Collin thought Daniel was.

"We quarreled while her father was ill. I'd promised Mary I would always love her and take care of her, but when she needed me most, I ran away. Went up to Washington Territory to help my uncle on his sheep ranch. I was running away from the possibility I couldn't handle everything that might come with Mary. Maybe having to care for her father because he could no longer work the farm. Being responsible for the younger children. Things like that. I wanted us to be unencumbered."

Because Collin had watched his warm interactions with Mary's family, that admission came as a surprise. "So what changed your mind?"

"My uncle told me point-blank that I shouldn't be and didn't need to be Mary's savior. Mary already had a Savior, who cared more for her than I ever could. He needed to be the one in control in our marriage."

"You mean Jesus, don't you?" Everything in these people's lives always seemed to come back around to that.

"Yes."

The wind blew through the trees, clicking the bare branches together. Collin stared at them, wondering why Jesus made a difference.

"When I came back, Mary didn't believe I wouldn't run out on her again. I had to show her my faithfulness through serving her the way the Lord would have served her."

"I have to admit, I never attended church before we came here. My father believed in God, but didn't teach me any of the things your pastor has been preaching about. Been thinking a lot about what he said."

"I'll tell you this much. God does much better with running my life and my relationship with Mary than I ever did. I don't want to live in complete control of my life ever again."

Collin stared down at the wooden floor that squeaked under the rocker when it moved. "I don't think I understand completely, but I look forward to hearing more from the Reverend Horton."

A wide smile split Daniel's face, but he didn't push Collin about this religious thing. Collin was glad. He'd heard some people actually fight over their beliefs, and he'd not wanted anything to do with that.

"How about us heading back out to help Tony?" Daniel stood and stretched his back, which made a popping sound. "I really want to get all the hay into the barn while we have a bright, sunny day." He stepped off the porch and rounded the house. "You never know when it'll decide to rain again."

Collin smiled. Maybe he would have to ask Daniel more about all this, but he was glad today wasn't the day. He was a lot like his father, mostly keeping his own counsel. People thought Collin was stuck-up, but that wasn't it at all. He just liked to think things through without making rash decisions he'd later regret.

## CHAPTER 21

The night before the wedding, Catherine stayed with Mary and her siblings at the farm. After the other three were in bed, she and Mary sat on the swing on the front porch in the moonlight. Because of a chilly wind, they each wrapped up in a quilt and stared at the moon and stars.

Often she knew what Mary was going to say before the words left her mouth, but she hadn't ever experienced what her sister was going through right now. "Are you excited about tomorrow?"

"More excited than I've ever been in my life. That's why I wanted to sit out here even though it's late." Mary smiled at her. "I don't think I'll be able to sleep a wink tonight."

"But won't you be tired tomorrow?"

"I doubt it." Mary pulled her feet up and tucked them under her quilt. "The anticipation is intoxicating.

All I can think about is the fact that Daniel and I will get to live together after the ceremony."

A blush crept up Catherine's cheeks. Since she hadn't experienced romantic love yet, she hadn't even thought about what the living together would mean. But she didn't want to ask Mary. She might not know either.

"Aren't you a little scared?" She shivered.

Mary shivered, too, but hers didn't seem to come from cold or being scared. "All I've dreamed about is being married to Daniel. But I hate to think that you'll be going back to San Francisco day after tomorrow. Our time together has been far too short."

Catherine totally agreed. She didn't want to leave Mary, but Daniel's claim on her was much stronger than Catherine's. "Maybe you and your family can come visit Father and me soon."

Even though Mary's face was masked by the moonlight, Catherine saw her brow pucker. "I don't think I'm ready for that. That's why I couldn't invite him to the wedding when you asked about it."

"Why not? He loves you...and so do I." She infused her words with the whole weight of her affection.

"I'm not sure." Mary's expression turned pensive. "We'll need to adjust to being married, and besides...he gave me away." The last words were barely discernable.

Catherine reached for her hand. So *that* was what had bothered her sister so much. "And he has regretted it most of the rest of his life."

"Since you found me so quickly, I know he could have, too, if he had ever tried." Tears glistened on Mary's eyelashes.

She didn't really want to upset her sister right before her wedding, so she didn't point out that their father had not tried because he was keeping his word not to.

"Do you think you'll be able to find Margaret Lenora?" Mary deftly changed the subject.

"I had hoped I could find her as quickly as I did you. However, even though your mother introduced me to all the people who still live here that came on the same wagon train, no one had any information about the Caine family. She even took me to meet the people who bought the Caine's house here in Oregon City when they left. Every lead came up empty. I don't know where else to look." She stared up at the moon that had a sliver missing from one side. "Only God knows where they could be."

"Then we must pray for Him to reveal to you where you should look next." Mary squeezed her hand and bowed her head.

Catherine followed suit. She waited for Mary to start...if she would.

After a moment of silence, Mary's sweet voice lifted in prayer. "Dear heavenly Father, we know you love us, and we know you love Margaret. Everything inside my heart believes our sister is alive and well. Catherine and I don't know where to go from here to find her. Jesus, we ask for divine wisdom to know where to go."

They continued to beseech the Father about their sister, then Catherine finished with a prayer of blessing for Daniel and Mary's married life. This spiritual connection was an extra blessing the two sisters shared, and Catherine would miss it when she left. Just thinking about going back to the lonely mansion in San Francisco after being with all these people was dispiriting.

She had lived such a selfish life, because she hadn't known anything else. Now she would try to find ways to reach out to others. Daniel's mother helped at an orphanage. And according to Mary, Mrs. Winthrop and other women at the church had helped the Murray family when her father was ill. Catherine had never looked outside her life to see if there was anyone to whom she could give aid. When she returned home she hoped to find a way.

The breeze turned colder and a few clouds blew across the sky, playing hide and seek with the stars. The simple beauty of this area touched a place in her heart. Perhaps there was just as much quiet beauty around San Francisco. For a moment, she wished Collin Elliott would help her find it. Over the last month, he had seemed to soften toward her...at least a little, but she had no indication that he would spend any time with her after they returned home. So why did she keep thinking about him so much?

She shivered.

Mary turned toward her. "You're cold."

"A little. And I really need to get some sleep. I don't have as much excitement to carry me through the day tomorrow."

They went into the house, and for the last time in their short life together, they would share a bed. When she was in the dark room with her sister breathing beside her, an odd feeling crept over her of a long distant past when they shared a space before, in their mother's womb. How she wished their mother could be here now, to see her daughter happily married.

~

The next morning, Catherine was awakened by the sound of a horse coming down the lane from the road. The other side of the bed was empty. She ran her hand over the mattress and could still feel the warmth where Mary had been.

She slipped into her robe and went to the parlor. After peeking out and seeing Mrs. Winthrop in the brougham driven by Garrett Henry, she opened the door. "You're out here pretty early."

"Please wait here, Garrett." Daniel's mother lifted a basket from the floor and hurried up the stone walkway to the porch. "Mr. Henry is ready to take Frances and the boys to town. They can dress at our house."

Frances came out of her bedroom, stretching and yawning.

"How long will it take for you and your brothers to gather up your things? Garrett will drive you to our house as soon as you're ready. Mrs. Shelton and dear Edward are looking forward to helping you get ready for the wedding. You will go to the church with them."

Catherine hurried and helped Frances and the boys. Last night, they had packed their bags for the time they would be staying with Daniel's parents. Soon all their wedding attire was also added.

Mrs. Winthrop helped them get it all to the carriage. She stood on the porch and waved while they drove away. She picked up the basket she had set on the table in the parlor. Enticing aromas followed Mrs. Winthrop down the hallway, and Catherine was right behind her.

Drying her hands on a towel, Mary came into the kitchen through the mud room. She must have made a trip to the necessary and missed all the excitement.

"I brought breakfast. I didn't want you girls to have to worry about cooking. Mrs. Shelton got up early to fix everything. I knew neither you nor Mary would be able to sleep very late. The day I married Edward, I awoke before dawn." Daniel's mother set the basket on the kitchen table.

"What is that I smell?" Mary peeked into the basket. She lifted the edge of the towel covering the food. "Looks delicious, but I don't think I could hold a single bite. My stomach is a little jumpy this morning."

Mrs. Winthrop pulled Mary into a hug. "I know you think that, but the day will be long and exciting. You need to eat a good breakfast. With everything that will be happening, your stomach may be even jumpier later. So let's pray together, then sit down and relax. Eat leisurely. Later Garrett will bring the brougham for us, and Julie is coming with him. She'll help with fixing your hair. Yours and Catherine's."

Mary looked as if she were going to disagree.

"She's right." Catherine started taking the food out of the basket. It even contained all the cutlery and plates they would need. "Do you have milk in the spring house, Mary? Maybe that would be better than trying to drink coffee."

"I did bring my favorite tea and the teapot. We can have whichever you want." Mrs. Winthrop helped set the table.

"Tea will be fine with me." Mary dropped into the closest chair. "Perhaps I *should* eat something. I don't want to feel weak later."

Mrs. Winthrop dipped hot water from the reservoir in the wood-burning stove and poured it into the teapot. Then she put the leaves in the tea ball infuser and hung it in the pot to steep.

While they waited, Catherine removed the food from the basket. Biscuits wrapped in towels to keep them warm, a pot of honey, a dish of butter, fresh fruit, scrambled eggs, and bacon. The table looked very festive with the china plates and silverware.

The women sat down and started eating. While they talked, Catherine watched Mary, hoping she would eat enough to keep her going. She seemed to be completely involved in the discussion. Without thinking about it, Mary ate quite a bit of the delicious food. Catherine relaxed and enjoyed her own meal as well.

"How are Frances and the boys? I saw Mr. Henry drive away with them."

Mrs. Winthrop patted Mary's hand. "They'll settle in just fine. I think it's an adventure for them to be in town with us for the next week while you and Daniel are gone on your wedding trip. It'll be good for them. Don't you think so, Catherine?"

Catherine nodded. "They probably think of you and Mr. Winthrop as sort of grandparents. They haven't had any nearby, have they?"

"That's right, and we'll love spoiling them."

Mary rolled her eyes. "I hope they aren't too spoiled when we get back."

"You might want to think about letting them stay a little longer while you and Daniel get settled in here with some time alone." Mrs. Winthrop winked at Mary. "You'll be newlyweds, you know."

A blush rushed up Mary's neck and into her cheeks.

Catherine understood why. She had never heard an older woman talk to a younger woman quite so openly about private things. This was a new side of Daniel's mother. Maybe women did discuss things in the family when they were alone. Not having a mother, she didn't know what other women actually did.

When she and Mary were dressed in their wedding clothing, they stood side by side and stared into the tall cheval glass. Their dresses were so much alike. Only the color set her apart from Mary. Instead of the white lining most of Mary's lace dress, Catherine wore a dress made from the peacock blue that was so fashionable this year. The watered silk shimmered from blue to green and back every time she moved. And the only lace on her outfit was the white lace jacket. Julie had arranged both of their hair in a similar style. She had tamed some of it into long curls that rested on their left shoulders. They would wait to put Mary's veil over her hair until they arrived at the church.

They walked into the parlor together.

Mrs. Winthrop clasped her hands against her waist and sighed. "You look so beautiful. The only way I can tell you apart is by the dresses you're wearing."

She leaned to plant a quick kiss on Mary's cheek. "I'm so glad to welcome you into my family. You'll be a good wife for my son."

For a fleeting moment, Catherine wondered if she would ever hear those words spoken to her. Surely, she would...someday.

Mrs. Winthrop helped Mary out to the brougham. She held up the bottom of her skirt while Mr. Henry helped Mary into the conveyance. Then she climbed up beside her and arranged the skirt, so it wouldn't get soiled. Then Garrett helped Catherine in, and Julie sat beside her.

When they arrived at the church, everyone had already entered. Two ushers waited by the doorway to help them. The anteroom was small, but large enough that the two men standing near the preacher couldn't see the women. One of the ushers went into the sanctuary and returned with Mr. Winthrop.

He stopped in front of Mary and watched Julie drape the silk veil over her hair with the front edge barely reaching the top of her forehead. Then she used hairpins to anchor it to her style. When she finished, he took Mary's hand in his. "My dear, thank you for asking me to walk you down the aisle. You've been so good for Daniel. And I love you and your sisters and brothers. Our family is blessed to have you."

The strains of "The Wedding Chorus" on the organ signaled the time for them to enter. Catherine walked down the aisle before Mary and her soon-to-be father-in-law. As she neared the end of the aisle, she glanced to the side and noticed Collin staring at her. For the first time, she read admiration in his gaze. Her uncontrollable blush made a quick appearance, and her breathing became rapid as warmth spread down her body as well. When she took her place, she could feel his gaze on her back. Something inside her wondered why he was watching her so intently. She hoped she wouldn't stumble or take a misstep, and her heart beat like a caged hummingbird in her chest.

# CHAPTER 22

*C*ollin had never been to a wedding before. People started looking over their shoulders soon after the organist began to play some kind of high-brow music. Wondering what was wrong, he shifted so he could see back up the aisle. His breath caught in his throat. The woman walking toward the front was the most beautiful woman he'd ever seen. It took him only a moment to realize it was Catherine, not her sister.

The skirt of her dress looked like water swirling around her body, and the lace jacket reminded him of the foam that topped gentle waves. Everything about her radiated warmth, as if he were in a tropical ocean. He could almost feel the floor of the church rock gently. Or was that him. He was caught in a maelstrom of unfamiliar emotions. Finally, he was able to take a deep breath, and the feeling slipped away like a wave pulling back from the sand.

The rest of the wedding passed in a blur, with him wishing that someday he could get married. His bum leg twitched, then took aching to a deeper level. A firm reminder of what his future would be. And it didn't contain a wedding or family, no matter how much he wanted those things.

The members of the church rallied around the newlyweds, many of the ladies helping provide a lavish wedding meal. And the pile of presents from them was equally impressive. *Is this the way normal people do things?* He hadn't realized his life experiences were so limited until this time in Oregon City.

After Daniel and Mary left the Winthrop mansion, the rest of both families gathered in the parlor along with Catherine and him. She even brought Julie with her. Bobby and George were restless, fidgeting and picking up knickknacks on scattered tables around the room.

Mrs. Winthrop kept watching their progress as they moved about. "George, would you and Bobby like to go out and enjoy the sunshine? Tomorrow might not be as pleasant of a day."

They both returned the things they were holding to the proper places.

"Yes, ma'am." George's enthusiastic reply came quickly.

"Please go change out of your Sunday clothes first." Her voice contained no tone of reproof for the boys.

Maybe she didn't worry about them breaking any of the fragile-looking, porcelain doodads.

"Yes, ma'am." Bobby echoed his brother's previous reply, and they walked out of the room.

When they reached the staircase, their steps quickened until they were almost running.

Daniel's mother smiled. "Mary has done such a good job teaching those boys to be polite."

"Yes, she has," Catherine agreed. "I hope I'm as good a mother as she has been to all three of them."

The thought of Catherine as a mother stuck in Collin's mind, and he couldn't rid himself of the picture of her holding a baby close to her heart and rocking while humming a soft tune. A flash of a memory from the dim past brought to mind a faded moment of himself being rocked by his mother, and she hummed the same tune to him. He hadn't pictured his mother for a long, long time. His gut clenched, and he quickly jumped to his feet, regretting the action when his injured leg almost gave way.

"I think I'll go outside with the boys."

"That sounds like a good idea." Frances smiled up at him. "They do get into places where they shouldn't sometimes."

He chuckled. "Wouldn't want them to try to climb up on this housetop."

Horror covered Catherine's face. "I was scared for them when we saw Bobby slipping down the slope of the roof. I was sure he would be seriously injured from the fall."

Frances huffed out a deep breath. "Mary told them to stay off the roof of the porch, but they climbed up there many more times than she knew about. I finally quit reminding them what she said. It did no good."

When Collin walked out of the room, Catherine and Mrs. Winthrop were trying to convince Frances that she'd been a big help to her sister, even though the boys didn't always mind her.

He hurried to change his clothes and met the boys at the top of the stairs. "I'll go with you."

"Yea!" Bobby jumped up and down. "We can show you where everything is in the stable. It's even a lot bigger than our barn."

He enjoyed every minute spent with the curious little scamps. As they enjoyed exploring together, Collin wondered if his life would've been like this if his mother had lived, and he'd had brothers.

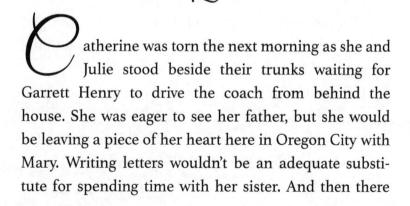

Catherine was torn the next morning as she and Julie stood beside their trunks waiting for Garrett Henry to drive the coach from behind the house. She was eager to see her father, but she would be leaving a piece of her heart here in Oregon City with Mary. Writing letters wouldn't be an adequate substitute for spending time with her sister. And then there was the matter of Margaret Lenora Caine. Where could she have gone? This western part of the United States was such a large area. Catherine couldn't just strike out and hope to find her somewhere...sometime. But how could she give up her quest?

Collin came down the stairs carrying his Gladstone bag and a carpetbag. If she remembered correctly, he only had the one bag when they came to the Winthrop's lovely home. How could a man travel so far with such a small amount of luggage?

She glanced at the two trunks and two carpetbags she and Julie had arrived with. Two more pieces of luggage had been added because of all the things she had purchased and the gifts from Mary's new family. Tucked between the folds of some of her clothing, she also had presents for her father.

"I hear the carriage." Collin stuck the carpetbag under his arm and picked up the Gladstone with the same hand. Then he lifted Catherine's carpetbag with the other. "I'll help Garrett carry the luggage."

Her maid opened the door for him.

"Thank you, Julie."

"You're welcome." Her voice followed him down the stone walkway.

They arrived at the train station just as the southbound train stopped by the platform. Catherine was glad Collin bought their tickets earlier in the week. He had also sent her father a telegram telling him when to expect them in San Francisco.

With no other passengers getting on the train at this station, they quickly boarded while the station master, Garrett, and Collin made sure their luggage was safely stowed in the baggage car. Catherine watched Collin as he bid farewell to the Winthrop driver. From the looks of the conversation, the two men must have become friends in the month they had stayed in the Winthrop home. She didn't know why she found that strange, but she did somehow.

After the conductor's final boarding call, Catherine watched Collin grab the handrail and swing up on the steps of their railcar. Remembering all the trouble on the journey to Oregon City, she sighed, hoping nothing would go awry on this trip. If so, they could get to San Francisco by dawn tomorrow. She dreaded the long boring trip.

Collin came and sat in the seat facing her and Julie. "Will you be glad to get back home?"

"Yes. But I'm disappointed we didn't find any clue to where our sister Margaret might live." She stared out the window at the passing scenery, occasionally catching a glimpse of the ocean far to the west.

"Don't give up hope." He sounded as if he really cared.

She looked back toward him. "I'll never give up hope, but right now I don't know where to start looking. But Mary and I will be praying for something to happen to give one of us a clue."

"Do you pray about a lot of things?" He stared at her as if looking for something specific.

"Yes. We've always prayed in our family." She didn't know why he would ask such a thing. "Don't you?"

Julie bumped her knee with her own. Catherine peeked out of the corner of her eye at her maid, and Julie gave a barely perceptible shake of her head. Maybe she didn't want Catherine to pry too much into Collin's life. Hadn't they spent enough time together so it would be all right to really get to know each other?

"My father believed in God, and I do too. But we didn't go to church or read the Bible." He sounded almost regretful. "But we did pray over our meals."

What a revelation! How could anyone know God if he never went to church? A lot of her family's social life and friendships were grounded in the church as well.

Collin attended the Sundays they were with the Winthrops. He looked as if he was really listening to every word Reverend Horton said when he preached.

"Mary and I had so many things to talk about that I forgot to ask her why they got married on a Wednesday, instead of Friday night or Saturday. I've never known anyone who got married in the middle of the week, especially in the daytime." Catherine dug into her handbag to find her hanky. Her hands were already soiled from the train.

"I know why." Collin grinned at her. "One day, Daniel and I were talking about the wedding. He said both his parents and his grandparents had gotten married on the twenty-eighth of October. He and Mary decided to carry on the tradition, especially since she didn't know the traditions in her parents' families."

Catherine wiped her palms with the hanky. "I think that's sweet. Actually, I don't know what traditions my parents had either." She stopped and dropped her hands into her lap. "If they had special traditions, they would be Mary's family too. I had hoped I could get her and Daniel to come meet my father soon."

"Maybe they'll consider it once they get back from their wedding trip." Collin started rubbing his knee.

Catherine wondered why he did that. She'd noticed him doing it unobtrusively at other times while they were in Oregon City. Maybe he had an ache in one of his limbs.

Since they settled into their seats in the railcar, she felt a letdown from all the frantic activity of the last few days. She hoped she could get some rest on the journey. She took off her hat, leaned her head against the back of the seat, and closed her eyes. Later they would enjoy a sleeping coach, but for now, her seat would have to suffice.

~

Soon after dawn, the train finally chugged to a stop in San Francisco, accompanied by the screeching of the brakes and hissing steam. Catherine, who had roused herself early to dress, quickly placed her hat on her head and thrust the hatpin through it to attach it to her head. When the cloud of moisture started dissipating, her father appeared through the mist. Her heart leapt at the sight of him. She hadn't realized just how much she had missed him. Without waiting for Julie or Collin, she grabbed her reticule and hurried to the door closest to where he stood. By the time she reached the steps, he stood at the bottom with his arms open wide.

She hadn't been entirely sure how he would receive her. After all, she had willfully run away. But his eyes held only love...and a hint of relief. She took his hand and stepped down into his arms. The tight embrace felt like heaven. She was home.

"I'm so glad to see you." He whispered against her head, almost knocking her hat off.

"And I am too." She reached up and kissed his wrinkled cheek. "I have so much to tell you."

"I can hardly wait." He held her against his side while he looked toward where Collin was helping Julie down from the train.

She felt like the prodigal son returning to his father. She wouldn't be surprised if there wasn't a feast with a fatted calf waiting for her, even though she didn't deserve it.

# CHAPTER 23

"*D*inner at seven." This was the last thing Angus said to Collin when he dropped him off at his boardinghouse after leaving the train station. They rang through his mind like a ship's bell chiming. Angus also gave him the day off to rest from the journey. He could hardly believe his good fortune. Since he had been unable to sleep on the train, he knew how he'd spend his day.

He'd been dreading his first evening alone. But more than that, knowing he probably wouldn't see Catherine often, if at all, made his future look bleak. And to think about eating the bland food Mrs. Molloy served for years to come, until he could afford a place of his own, upset his stomach. At least that's what the knot in his belly felt like.

He'd stripped off his clothes and left them in the middle of the floor, then climbed into bed without another thought. Instead of falling quickly to sleep as was his custom, restlessness haunted his slumber. When he awoke in the middle of the afternoon, he got up to bathe and shave. Anticipation danced in his mind, more about Catherine than about the good food he would have. But he knew his drab existence, when compared to his last month, would commence soon enough.

Almost stumbling over his clothing piled on the floor, he separated the clothing he wore and brought back from the trip into things to send out for cleaning and what he could just hang up or pack into his trunk. Not knowing what kind of dress Angus expected for the evening meal, he decided to err on the side of dressing too well. He pulled one of his newer suits, that he wore to the office, from the trunk where he stored most of his clothing. He'd learned while on the ship how to pack things to keep them from wrinkling.

After he finished dressing, he glanced out the window to check the weather. The McKenna coach sat in the street in front of the boardinghouse. Angus hadn't said anything about sending his driver for him, but that took care of one of his quandaries. He wouldn't have to try to find a hansom cab. With his bum leg, walking all the way to the mansion on Nob Hill was out of the question.

Instead of a butler this time, Angus answered the door and welcomed him. While Collin was hanging his coat on the carved hall tree near the front door, he heard quiet footsteps on the stairs behind him. Looking up, he watched Catherine descend. The muscles in his stomach tightened and his eyes widened. He fought hard to keep from revealing how glad he was to see her.

Lovelier than ever, she wore her hair pulled back the same way she had at the Murray farm, but her dress was of finer material than anything she wore on the trip, except at the wedding. Like the dress for the wedding, the lines hugged her curves and swept into a wide loose skirt. But this one was a rich, dark green. The color enhanced both her flaming curls and her green eyes. She glided across the entrance hall toward him.

"So glad to see you, Collin." She held out her dainty hand.

The chandelier shining above intensified the tiny flecks of gold in her eyes and the way her eyelashes curled up, framing them. He was caught in her gaze. He swallowed, his Adam's apple almost choking him. Why did this woman affect him so strongly? Without a doubt he would never have a future with a woman like Catherine McKenna. He would never want to see the horror on her face if she ever caught sight of his hideous leg. That degree of rejection was more than he could handle.

"You look lovely tonight, Catherine." Without thinking, he lifted her hand and pressed his lips against the backs of her fingers.

He'd never done anything like that in his life. He

caught himself before he did anything else. What must Angus think of him now?

Glancing toward his employer, he caught a sincere smile on his face.

"Right on time. That's one of the things I like about you, Elliott. I can always depend on you." Angus held out his arm toward his daughter. "Let's go into the dining room. Cook is prepared to start serving our meal."

Bemused, Collin followed them. Soon he was seated across from Catherine with her father sitting between them at the head of the long table. Immediately, a young maid entered, carrying in a tray and setting it on the sideboard. She quickly served the three bowls of steaming soup.

Angus bowed his head, and Catherine followed suit, so Collin bowed his as well.

"Dear heavenly Father, thank you for protecting Collin, Catherine, and Julie on their long journey. And thank you for helping them find my Mary so quickly. Bless Mary and Daniel on their wedding trip."

He paused for a long moment. Collin wondered if he was finished with his prayer, so he glanced up. Both the other people had their heads down, so he bowed again.

"And, Lord, bless this food to the nourishment of our bodies and us to Your service. In Jesus' name. Amen."

Figuring that was the end of the prayer, Collin

looked up. Something about the words Angus said picked at Collin, making him uneasy. Why did he say "and us to Your service"? Yes, Collin had been listening to Reverend Horton, and a lot of what the man said made more sense to him than any other preacher had, but he didn't consider himself in the service of God. He wasn't even sure what that meant. And he didn't know if he really wanted to know. Right now, that part of his life was in total confusion. But would it make any difference to the way Angus felt about him if he revealed that fact? For now, he'd keep the information to himself.

Angus picked up his spoon and dipped a taste of the soup. "Sophie." He glanced at the maid waiting by the door. "Tell Cook this is delicious as usual." Then he laid his spoon on the plate under the soup bowl and turned to Collin. "I asked you to dinner so the three of us could discuss your journey. Not the business part of it, but the rest."

Collin quickly swallowed his spoonful of soup. "What did you want to know about it?"

"You sent me updates, but telegrams are so short and impersonal."

Collin knew that during the whole meal, they would probably be discussing this, so he decided to take a bite whenever he could. After his long nap, he was ravenous.

"What did you think of Oregon City?"

"It's a nice place and very progressive for a small town." Collin glanced at Catherine, and she nodded her agreement. "Of course, it has all these elements—industries, nice hotels, a fairly large area of homes, and all kinds of businesses and city services. One of the big things this year was the bank installing a large round vault. It's supposed to be able to keep the money safer somehow. Daniel told me about the special event they had the day it was delivered." He wasn't sure exactly what else Angus wanted to know.

Catherine frowned. "Oregon City also has some of the bad elements of cities too."

"I'm sure your father doesn't want to hear about that." At least Collin hoped he didn't. All that happened before he found Catherine.

"Of course, I do." Angus laid his spoon down again and signaled the maid to pick up the empty soup bowls.

Catherine looked regretful, as if she realized she shouldn't have mentioned what happened. "It was nothing, really."

"Then why did you mention it, Katie?"

A storm cloud dropped over her smile. "I don't know."

"Actually, if you hadn't gotten lost and ended up near that saloon, I wouldn't have found you so soon, and we wouldn't have learned the details that helped us find Mary." Collin hoped she understood that he didn't mind revealing what went on that day.

She looked startled. "But you had been at the bar ..."

Collin glanced at Angus. He didn't look disturbed, just interested.

"Yes." He was going to lay his cards on the table and take whatever trouble it might bring. "And I had ordered a drink. But I didn't take a single sip. My leg was giving me a lot of pain from walking all over the town, trying to find you. I stopped for a drink, the same way I used to do when I was first got out of the hospital after the shipwreck. But I finally decided not to indulge."

Angus cleared his throat. "That had to take a lot of willpower, Elliott. I don't like a man who's given to alcohol, but I'd say you proved you're not."

Catherine squinted her eyes and studied Collin as if to see if he were lying.

He stared right back at her. "If I hadn't been there, that drunkard Gary what's-his-name might have done some damage when he accosted you."

Angus rose up a ways from his chair. "Now see here." He settled back into it. "Why didn't either of you tell me my Catherine was accosted by a drunk?"

Catherine leaned forward and huffed out an exasperated breath. "I don't think he would really have hurt me. He thought I was Mary and I was being stuck up or something like that. That's the only reason we found out about her and Daniel. We could still be in Oregon City trying to find my sister." She leaned back in her chair.

Angus studied each of them in turn, then a smile curled his lips. "I'm sure someone else would have mistaken you for her by now, anyway. No harm done."

The maid and the cook entered carrying plates heaped with savory food. The delicious aromas told Collin he wasn't mistaken about the quality of the meal to come.

The rest of the meal passed in comfortable conversation, and soon after, Collin took his leave. Riding home in the coach, he mulled over the whole evening. He wondered how different his life could have been if his ship hadn't wrecked in the storm. He pushed away the pictures that invaded his thought as quickly as they came. Letting them stay was just too painful.

～

*C*atherine looked at her father after Collin left. He put his arm around her waist and accompanied her to the parlor. They sat in the two wingback chairs beside the fireplace. Even though her gown was made of heavier fabric, the coolness of evening had invaded the house and made her feel chilled. The fire was just right, warming her clear through. Much more comfortable than the train, which often had a chill in it.

"I didn't see Aunt Kirstin when I got home or after I awoke early this afternoon. Is she doing something with her ladies' circle today?" Sometimes those ladies had teas or some other sort of get-together. And they'd been known to attend an opera or ballet when one was in town.

"I forgot to tell you she isn't here. I was so glad to

have you back. Her brother, your uncle Malcolm, died last week. Since you were gone, I told her to go home to North Carolina for a visit. She'll be gone for two or three weeks. I've missed her."

Catherine knew Uncle Malcolm was Aunt Kirstin's favorite brother. Her aunt tried not to reveal this information, but every time she received a letter from him, she beamed for several days. "She hasn't gone back since she came to live with us. It's time for her to see her family." Catherine now knew how it felt to miss a sister or brother who was close to her.

"I haven't asked yet, but I can't wait any longer. Did you invite Mary to come here to meet me?" The hope that shone from his eyes broke her heart. She didn't want to destroy it.

"Yes...I did." She was trying to decide how to tell him the rest.

He stared straight at her. "You sound a little hesitant to talk about it."

"Oh, Daddy." She wove her fingers together and gripped them tight. "Mary wanted to see me, and she wants us to find Margaret, but she...didn't want to come meet you...yet."

He got that faraway look in his eyes he had when he was thinking about a serious subject. "What did she say exactly?"

Catherine didn't want to say the words. She sighed. "She said you gave her away. I think the thought of that hurts her."

"I'm so sorry. It hurts me as well." He looked almost defeated.

"I explained that, but all the information was really new to her. She only found out what happened a few months ago. I'm hoping she'll change her mind. We'll be writing each other letters." Catherine decided right then to write a letter that could be waiting for Mary when she and Daniel returned from their wedding trip.

Her father nodded, then leaned forward, holding his hands out toward the flames. "I felt a lot better about you being gone after I heard from Elliott that he had found you." Her father had done that before often enough. Changed the subject when the one they were discussing became too uncomfortable. "I hope he made you feel safe."

She had to think about that a minute. Even though she resented his presence when she first found out he was following her, having him around had been a good thing.

"He did." Her conscience pricked her. "I have to admit that I wasn't happy when we first met in Oregon City. I actually thought he had been drinking as Gary Bowen insinuated. I told him you wouldn't like what he was doing. Tonight was the first time he told me he didn't drink in that saloon."

"He shouldn't have ordered the drink. But he showed a great amount of integrity and strength by not consuming it."

She couldn't believe her father would say such a thing.

"Even Christian men make mistakes, Katie. If the Lord Jesus forgives him, I have no right to condemn him. He's forgiven me for many similar shortcomings." Sorrow dimmed his eyes with tears that trembled on his lashes, but didn't fall.

Her father hadn't told her anything like this before. Maybe he finally realized she had grown up. And she had in so many ways. Hopefully, over the next few weeks, he'd see even more evidence of that.

One thing bothered her, and she didn't know if she should mention it. But her relationship with her father needed to develop on levels of maturity and truth.

"I'm not sure Collin actually knows God the way we do. From things he said around me and in conversations I overheard, I got the impression that he hadn't attended church before he went with us in Oregon City."

Her father steepled his fingers and leaned his pursed lips against the tip. He appeared to be deep in thought. Maybe he was even praying. She knew he often did in the middle of conversations.

"So how were the services in the church where Mary's family attends?"

"Both the Murray family and the Winthrop family go to the same church. They have an organ, so the music was really good. Everyone sang as if they meant every word. I liked that." She glanced down at her hands into her lap. "And Reverend Horton preached very good sermons. They were interesting too. He didn't drone on and on like some of the preachers who have visited in our church."

Her father perked up at that. "Did Collin go to church every Sunday?"

"Yes, we all did." She straightened the crocheted doily on the arm of her chair.

"Did you notice whether he was listening to the sermons?"

She nodded. "Yes, he did. Nothing that happened in the sanctuary distracted him, even when a baby cried."

Her father got up and stared into the fire, watching the dancing flames as if they were revealing something to him. "I'm glad you went on your pursuit, even if you left without telling me."

"I was so afraid you'd be angry with me." She released a relieved sigh.

"I'll admit I was upset at first. But the Bible tells us God can take even things we plan for evil and made good come out of them. I'm not saying you had evil plans, but He took what you did and I think He worked through it to reach Collin Elliott in a way he had never been reached before." He turned his back to the fire and clasped his hands behind him.

Catherine stared up at her father. Could he be right? Did God use her to reach Collin? "I hope so."

"Just the fact that he had the ability to stare at an alcoholic beverage and choose not to drink it, even before he heard a sermon, shows he has strength of character. I believe God is drawing that young man toward Him."

Catherine stood up. "Yes, I can see that. He revealed his good character a number of times while we were on the journey."

Her father took her hand in his. "Would you like to join me in prayer before we retire for the night? We should pray that you discover a way to find Margaret Lenora and that God will continue wooing Collin toward Him.... Also that Mary will decide to meet me."

While they stood before the fire praying, Catherine felt a new closeness to both her earthly father and her heavenly Father. And new hope coursed through her for Collin Elliott's salvation as well as her chances of finding her other sister. She would not give up on either thing.

# CHAPTER 24

*S*itting before the dressing table in her bedchamber, Catherine looked forward to dinner tonight. Collin would be coming to eat with them again. In the more than two weeks they had been back in San Francisco, her father had invited him several times. And he'd asked Collin if he wanted to go to church with them. Surprising Catherine, he agreed both Sundays. She was sure Daddy had invited him for tomorrow as well.

The trip to Oregon City had changed both Collin and her. She knew he hadn't liked her very much when they first met. And she hadn't liked him either, but now they had settled into a comfortable friendship. She enjoyed the time she and her father spent with him.

Although Daddy saw Collin at the office, she recognized that he liked having the young man in the more relaxed environment of their home. All three of them liked to read, and they discussed various books they had read. After that first night back from the trip, they dined more informally in the kitchen, instead of the large dining room. And they laughed a lot together. Catherine was happier than she ever remembered being in this house.

A soft knock at her door was accompanied by Julie's voice. "Catherine, you have a letter from your sister today."

She jumped up and hurried to open the door. "I'm so glad. She and Daniel have been back from their wedding trip for over a week. I know she's been busy, but I was anxious to have her answer my letter." She took the proffered envelope and quickly opened it. She went to her balloon chair and dropped into it to read the missive. Enclosed in the familiar comfort, she could feel almost as if she and Mary were sitting together talking.

"Do you want me to help you with your hair this evening?" Julie's words interrupted her daydream.

"I don't think so. Thank you, anyway."

Julie left and closed the door behind her. A lot had changed in the time they had been back in California. Catherine tried not to be as demanding as she had been before. She gave Julie more time off, and she asked her father not to cut her wages to compensate for the extra time off. Julie had done enough for her over the years, and especially while they were in Oregon, to deserve more personal time.

Turning back to the letter, Catherine unfolded the two sheets of paper. At least Mary had written a substantial letter, not just a quick note, with some details of their wedding trip to Portland. Mary had loved going to Portland, so Daniel took her to stay in a hotel there. They didn't want to go very far away, but he wanted them to be able to explore the beautiful city and stay in luxury so Mary wouldn't have to worry about a thing. They truly were on a honeymoon where they wouldn't have any outside distractions and could enjoy concentrating on each other. Once they returned home, they would both have plenty of distractions.

How romantic. Catherine wanted something like that someday. A man who would love her for who she was, and one who would think of what was in the best interest of them as a married couple. Not someone who only saw her as the daughter of a very wealthy man. It would take a special kind of man to move beyond all that and really get to know her. Since she hadn't even had a gentleman caller, she didn't have any idea when something like that could happen for her.

In a tiny way, she was jealous, but she wouldn't deny her sister this kind of happiness. She'd had enough sorrow to last a lifetime. Now Catherine hoped Mary's joy would continue for the rest of her life, and happiness like that would soon come into her own life as well.

As her eyes traveled down the first page, then continued to the second, she chuckled and enjoyed all the things Mary was sharing. Suddenly, she encountered a change of subject.

*My dear sister, now that we are home, I miss you terribly.*

Tears filled Catherine's eyes. Even though they had met less than two months ago, she felt as if she knew Mary always. And she sorely missed her as well.

*Daniel and I discussed this, and he agrees. Our families celebrate Thanksgiving Day later this month. We're not sure what they do in California, but we try to have a day of feasting and praising God for our blessings. Getting to know you is one of the major blessings of my life. Of course, so is getting married to Daniel.*

*We want you to come visit during this time. Mrs. Winthrop said she would love to have you stay at their house again. And we all know your father won't want you to travel without a man to protect you, so Collin will also have a place with us. And Julie as well. You can't think about traveling with a man who isn't kin to you without a chaperone. Julie made such a good one before.*

*Say you'll come by November 23 and stay at least two weeks. Please!*

No mention of their father. For a moment, Catherine felt hurt and even angry on his behalf. If Mary could not forgive him on his own account, why could she not accept him on Catherine's behalf? Besides, was it fair to ask her to come for Thanksgiving, knowing full well that would leave her father alone during a holiday?

Still, despite her misgivings, a larger part of her longed to go. They would only have been back in San Francisco less than four weeks by then. What would her father say to this invitation? She hoped he would agree. After all, he'd had over eighteen years with her. Surely, he could lend her to her sister for this long.

She quickly finished reading the letter then returned it to its envelope. She and her father had been praying for Mary ever since that first night after they arrived home. Maybe this was part of the answer. If their father allowed her to visit Mary again this soon, maybe she would see that he was a good man who was only trying to keep his word, as declared on the adoption contract. She bowed her head and began to pray.

Her father had gone into town for something, and he returned to the house soon after she finished praying. She hurried down the stairs carrying the letter.

Glancing at her, he noticed the envelope clutched in her hand. "Who did you get a letter from? Kirstin?"

"No, it's from Mary. I had written her a letter that was waiting for her when she returned home from her honeymoon. I wondered how long it would take her to answer." She smiled at him.

"So what did she say?" He waited quietly, staring down at the marble floor of the entrance hall.

Catherine told her father about much of the information in the letter. Then she opened it and read the three most important paragraphs, surreptitiously glancing at him to catch his reaction. He didn't frown. That was a good sign, wasn't it?

"I didn't expect anything like this." He didn't sound very happy about it, but neither did he sound upset.

"I didn't either." She shrugged. "But I do miss her. We've lost so much of our life together." She hoped he wouldn't take offense at her words.

"Give me a chance to think about it. All right?" He sounded almost choked up.

*He didn't say no.* And if he said he would think about it, she knew some of that thinking would be spent in prayer. *Oh, please, God, help him agree.*

"Of course. What time will Collin be here tonight?" She could change the subject as he often did.

"We're eating at seven, and will probably make an early night of it. I want to be fresh at church tomorrow." He walked away, and she watched him go, his feet tapping a staccato on the marble tiles.

Catherine knew she would have to wait until he decided what should be done. And she was fine with that. She knew her father to be a fair man. She was sure that wasn't going to change.

As usual, Collin arrived right on time. When he walked in the door, warmth started in the pit of her stomach and spread all the way to her toes. More and more she had grown to enjoy his company. Both her life and her father's had been changed for the better because of him. He was beginning to feel like...family.

Cook had made a Scottish broth with lamb, which was her father's favorite soup. Served with hot scones and butter, they feasted on their traditions. And the shortbread was such a good dessert. This plain fare tasted like a banquet to Catherine.

Collin dug right in, eating as much as both her and her father combined. A man that size really needed a lot of sustenance. She liked watching him enjoy the good food.

"Angus, this is delicious." He took another bite of the shortbread. "When I'm finally able to get a house, I might try to entice your cook away from you."

The woman was beside the sink on the other side of the large kitchen. Catherine could see her from where she sat at the table. A broad smile split her face and she turned back to drying the dishes. "Oh, git on with ya, Mr. Elliott. Tis nothin'."

Collin didn't turn around to look at her, but Catherine was sure he heard the smile in her voice.

"I meant every word, Mrs. Campbell." He polished off the cookie and reached for another.

The cook's merry laugh rang out, and the others joined her.

"I'm going to my room now, Mr. McKenna. Just leave the rest of the dishes on the table. I'll be back to take care of them later." Then the woman hung up the tea towel and left the kitchen.

"Elliott, did you enjoy your time in Oregon City?" Her father had finished eating and sat watching Collin.

Catherine wondered why he asked that question. And from his puzzled expression, Collin did too.

He stared at her father a minute before answering. "Yes, for the most part. After the first day or two, everything went well. I like both the Winthrops and the Murrays."

"What do you think of Daniel?" Her father leaned forward with his arms resting on the table.

"A good man." Collin evidently didn't have to think about that answer. "He has good business sense, and I enjoyed the time we were together. I even worked on the farm with him and his hired hand, Tony Chan."

Catherine kept glancing from one to the other of the men. Something was brewing. She hoped it was in relationship to the letter she had received from Mary. Perhaps Father was considering letting them go again.

"Glad to hear that." Father wiped one hand across his chin, then started tapping the fingers of his other hand on the table.

Something was agitating him, but he didn't look angry. So maybe this was a good thing.

He turned toward her. "Katie, tell him about your letter."

She explained what Mary had asked, all the time watching Collin's expression. He didn't appear surprised.

"What would you think about taking that trip with

Catherine and Julie?" Her father scooted his chair back from the table and crossed one leg over the other.

This time Collin took his time considering the question. She waited with bated breath. Was it really going to happen? *She could actually see Mary again soon.* The excitement was hard to contain.

"Do you think you will need me during that time?"

Catherine knew if anyone asked her a question about taking a trip, she would be thinking about what she wanted, instead of what her father needed. Collin's answer told her he was a good man in more ways than one. One her father could trust implicitly...and so could she.

"Having you in the office has been such a help to me. Everything is in better shape than ever before." Her father finally smiled. "I'm sure we'll be fine while you're gone. I've been thinking about having you do some more traveling for the company. However, this isn't a business trip. It's for my family. We stayed in touch just fine last time, and I know we can again."

Catherine didn't want to appear too eager to hear Collin's response, so she got up and started removing their dishes, taking them to the sink and stacking them there. But her ears were tuned to every word spoken on the other side of the room.

After a brief pause, Collin cleared his throat. "I'll be more than happy to accompany the women on the trip."

"Good." Her father arose from the table. "We can work out the details tomorrow."

The two men headed toward the front of the house. Catherine didn't follow them. She didn't want them to see how excited she was. She giggled, then covered her lips with her fingertips. *I'm going to see Mary again.* She wondered if her sister's marriage would have changed their relationship in any way. Soon she would find out.

# CHAPTER 25

*W*hen the train pulled up to the station platform in Oregon City, Catherine spied a group of people gathered, waiting for the train to stop. At first she thought several people were waiting to board the train when it left, but then as each person became recognizable, she knew. All the members of the Winthrop and Murray families were there to greet their arrival. A smile slid across her lips and her heart expanded to include all of them.

She had been reading in First Chronicles last night. In chapter 4, verse 10, Jabez prayed for God to enlarge his coast. Seeing all these people waiting at the station, she knew that God was expanding her world, just as he expanded Jabez's coast. And the added people didn't take away from her. Instead, each one had become a blessing that enriched her life.

By the time the train was completely stopped, she

was standing. She started to reach for her carpetbag, but Collin picked it up instead.

He leaned toward her and whispered in her ear. "I'll get it. You go to your sister." Almost as if he knew what her heart was feeling.

She nodded, wishing she could give him a sisterly kiss on the cheek, and was startled by her next thought. She didn't want to be a sister to this handsome man with such a big heart. She wanted much more. Where had that idea come from? When she was alone later, she'd take it out and examine it more leisurely.

Rushing down the steps, she fell into Mary's arms, both sisters crying tears of joy. Daniel stood behind Mary, waiting until they were finished with their monumental hug. Catherine glanced at him, and his wide smile warmed her heart. These people were her family too. For so many years, she had felt lonely, but now when she had a feeling of melancholy trying to steal her joy, she could just remind herself that she had a large, loving family. It didn't matter that they were scattered across the country. They were connected. And someday, Margaret Lenora would be part of this group. She didn't know how or when, but she knew in her heart it would happen.

She and Mary walked over to the rest of the family while Collin and Julie went to check on the luggage in the baggage car. Each member of both families took turns giving Catherine a hug, and she felt her spirits rise even higher with every warm greeting.

"Catherine..." Bobby pulled on her skirt to get her attention. "Me and George are sure glad you came back."

She bent over to give him another embrace. "I am too." She straightened and studied the boys. "I believe you have both grown an inch since I was here."

"Aw, Miss Catherine..." A blush spread across George's face. "You was here less than a month ago."

She could sense Collin's presence behind her. She didn't know how, but over time she had become attuned to him.

George pushed past her. "Mr. Collin, you gonna come out to the farm while you're here?"

Catherine turned and glanced up at him. He was the most handsome man on the platform. Tall, with that wavy, nut-brown hair, his dark eyes that sometimes took on the hue of hot chocolate, and his wide shoulders. Just thinking about him made her feel flustered, and her palms became moist. She didn't want to rub them on her skirt or pull out her hanky to wipe them, so she removed her gloves from her reticule and slipped them on her fingers. Maybe no one would notice her sweaty palms.

Bobby stood looking up at Collin. "Are you and Miss Catherine betrothed like Daniel and Mary was before they got married?"

A hush fell on the group, and Catherine discovered that Collin could blush too. Even his ears turned red, but the bottom of his hair covered half of his ears.

Maybe no one besides her noticed. Unfortunately, the possibility of that was deflated when everyone in the group started laughing...except the two of them.

Collin cleared his throat. "No, Bobby, we're not."

Catherine was glad he didn't brush off the young boy's question. That showed a lot of character.

"Why not?" Bobby looked from Collin to her, then back. "She's really pretty. She looks just like Mary."

Her sister had been trying to keep from laughing again, but she removed her fingers from covering her mouth and leaned down toward her younger brother. "Bobby, it's not polite to ask these kinds of questions to adults."

"Why not?" The boy actually looked confused. "I just wanted to know."

Mary took Bobby's hand. "Come on. Let's take Catherine to the carriage." She slipped her other arm through Catherine's, and they quickly left the group behind.

After they were seated in the conveyance, Mary tried to explain to her brother what she meant, but Catherine didn't think Bobby understood. Finally, Mary just said, "It's because I told you it's not polite. So don't ask again."

Just as she had been when they were here before, Mary was a good mother for her brother. Catherine hoped she and Daniel would have children of their own, because she was such a good parent.

Mary pulled Bobby down on the seat beside her

and put her arm around him. "I want to talk to Catherine now, so please sit quietly until we get home. Okay?"

He nodded and leaned his head against her side.

"When I sent the letter, I really didn't know if your father would let you come back so soon." She took a deep breath and let it out slowly.

Catherine fingered the lacy ruffle on the skirt of her traveling suit. He was Mary's father as much as he was hers. Couldn't Mary see that? Didn't she even want to get to know him, now that she had no parents of her own? But Catherine quelled her own indignation. "When I first read the letter to him, he didn't act as though he would let us come. But after he thought about it almost all day, he agreed. When he says he'll think about something, I know it means he'll not only consider it, but he will also pray about it. I didn't think he would allow me to come. We were gone so long last time. But I think he understands why we want to spend time together."

Mary nodded. "And he wants me to agree to come meet him sometime, doesn't he?"

Catherine didn't want to answer this question but she must. She mulled over what to say before she spoke. "He didn't say that was part of the agreement...but I know he aches to see you and Margaret. Even more than that, he is willing to wait until you want to meet him. That's a strong indication of how much he loves each of us."

Mary nodded soberly. But the tightness in her face told Catherine she was not ready...not yet.

~

*C*ollin hadn't spent a holiday time with so many people before, but he enjoyed every minute. Good food, fellowship that made him feel almost as if he were a part of the family, and getting to spend more time with Daniel on the farm had been highlights for him.

He even enjoyed attending the church in Oregon City again. The church Angus and Catherine attended in San Francisco was different in many ways. The services were more formal, and the music sounded like it might be in an expensive music hall where professional singers gave performances. Even though the music in Oregon City occasionally had an off-key note, the voices seemed to be more spirited. As if they were singing from their hearts instead of trying to make it sound perfect.

Both pastors preached sermons straight from the Bible. He listened to each one and learned more about this faith. He didn't become distracted in either service, but the words from Reverend Horton felt more like arrows aimed straight at his heart. Collin still didn't know what to do about what he heard, but he was opening his heart a little more each week.

After the first service they attended in Oregon City

this time, Collin followed Daniel out to the stable when they'd finished the noon meal. "I went to church with Angus and Catherine when we returned to San Francisco. He started asking me every week, and I really wanted to go."

Crossing his arms, Daniel leaned against the stall where Sultan was usually stabled. "How was it?"

"I wouldn't have accepted the second time if I hadn't liked the service the first time."

Daniel smiled. "I wondered if there was another reason you went?"

"You're thinking about what Bobby said, aren't you?"

"Maybe a little."

Collin dropped down on a bench beside the tack room nearby. "I can't allow myself to become involved with any woman, even if I wanted to."

That raised Daniel's eyebrows. He came to sit beside him. "And why not? You're not bad looking, and you're a fairly likeable guy."

They shared a laugh at his facetious comments.

"Okay." At first, he hesitated to mention his real reason, but Daniel was the closest thing to a good friend that he had. And he trusted the man. "I wouldn't tell this to just anyone, but I know you can keep a confidence. First, I don't have much to offer any woman, but more than that, my bum leg is a mass of atrocious scars. Really hideous looking. They make me sick, and I can't imagine any woman not being repelled by them."

"I think you're wrong, man. Believe me, the right woman won't be put off by them."

Collin shook his head. "You haven't seen them." This conversation was getting more uncomfortable by the minute.

"We were talking about going to church." Daniel clapped him on the shoulder.

"You're right. I like what I'm hearing, but I'm not sure where all this is taking me. I just know I like what I see in your family and the McKennas. I understand the difference is tied to going to church somehow." He sure wasn't doing a very good job of explaining himself.

Daniel leaned his forearms on his thighs and looked down at the floor for a minute. "It's simple really. God loves you. He wants a relationship with you. The only way for that to happen is for you to believe that Jesus died for your sins and rose from the dead so you can have a relationship with Him."

"That does sound easy enough. But how do I do that?"

"You talk to Him just the way I'm talking to you."

Collin nodded. "So I pray....silently or out loud?"

"Whatever you want to do. I can pray for you first. Then you start talking to Him."

"I'd like that."

The two men bowed their heads.

"Lord God, I bring my friend Collin to You. He wants to know You the way I do. Please accept Him as You did me. In Jesus' name. Amen."

Collin waited, trying to formulate his words. Then he decided to just begin and let them pour out however they came. "Lord God. I know You came to take care of my sins, and Lord, I've committed plenty of them. I'm truly sorry for the way I lived for so long. I was bitter toward You for taking my family members from me. I blamed You for my accident and injury. And I wasted too much time and money on trying to drown my problems in a bottle. Lord, please forgive me. Make me Your own. I want to follow You the way I see Angus, Catherine, and Daniel follow You."

When his words ran out, he just sat there and waited. At first nothing happened. Just about the time he started to tell Daniel it hadn't worked, a strange feeling of someone standing close to him overcame him. He raised his head and looked around. Nothing. So he closed his eyes and waited again. Soon he felt as if strong arms had enveloped him, and warmth flowed over him from the top of his head to the bottom of his feet. He just sat there and basked in the presence of God.

Finally, he raised his head, and Daniel followed suit.

Collin stared at him. "That was awesome. What do I do now?"

"Now you learn to walk with God, day by day, minute by minute." He stood. "And you learn more by reading the Bible. I suggest starting with the gospel of John, then read the rest of the New Testament. After you're finished with that, read the Old Testament.

That will give you the history from the beginning of time."

"All right. I'll get me a Bible." Now he got up and stretched to get the kinks out of his back and legs. For some reason, his future looked brighter already.

Near the end of the second week they were there, Daniel came to Collin, out in the barn at the farm, with a proposition. "Do you think you could get Mr. McKenna to agree with the three of you traveling to Seattle with Mary and me before you go home? You would still be home in plenty of time for Christmas."

Collin shook his head. "I don't know. He looked like it was hard for him to let Catherine go this long. Why would you want us to go to Seattle with you?"

"Mary likes having Catherine around." Daniel picked up the pitchfork and hefted some hay into his stallion's stall. Then he stuck the tines in the dirt floor and leaned his forearm across the end of the handle. "Tony Chan will be getting married in January, and they'll be moving into the house here on the farm. I want to take Mary to Seattle to see if she would like some of the furniture manufactured by Stanton Furniture Company. I heard about this company quite a while ago from one of our customers who had bought furniture from them. He said it is the finest furniture on the west coast."

"I can understand that." He thought he knew where this conversation was heading.

"The man invited me to his house to see what they

bought, and he was right. I thought about just ordering furniture from their printed catalogue, but it has no pictures in it, just prices and descriptions. Besides, I want Mary to pick out what she wants. The trip would allow the girls to spend more time together, and if need be, the three of you could return to San Francisco from there."

Collin stared out the door at the gentle rainfall. Today, Mary and her siblings were spending the day in town with Catherine and the Winthrops. They were trying to get as much visiting in as they could before Catherine, Julie, and he would return to San Francisco. He understood their strong desire to be together.

The air had a chill in it this late in the year. He crossed his arms over his chest. His injured leg was reacting to the cold weather, and the throbbing ache interfered with his concentration.

He turned back toward Daniel. "All I know to do is to send a telegram to Mr. McKenna and await his decision. It'll be a hard one for him to make." He stared straight into the other man's eyes. "He wants to see Mary, and it hurt him that she won't come."

Daniel shook his head. "I know. I've tried to talk to her about Mr. McKenna, but she refuses to discuss it. Perhaps it's all too much to handle right now—losing her father last summer, getting married, meeting Catherine. So much emotion, so many changes."

Collin nodded. "I understand. And thankfully Mr.

McKenna is not a man to hold a grudge. I can send the message as soon as we get back to town."

At least the rain stopped by the time the two men were ready to ride the horses to town. Instead of going straight to the house, they rode to the telegraph office. Collin sent as succinct a message as he could, but he didn't expect an answer very soon. This late in the day, Mr. McKenna might not receive it until tomorrow morning. And he knew Mr. McKenna would take a while to make a decision.

Soon after they arrived home and cleaned up, the evening meal was ready to be served. Watching the interaction between Daniel and Mary made Collin kind of hope that Catherine's father would want them to go back to San Francisco as planned. He was only human, and while they were with the other couple, Collin had a hard time controlling his desires for things he could never have. Spending so much informal time with Catherine filled his dreams every night with scenes of the two of them being married. Having a forever kind of future. The fact that it was impossible frustrated him, but all he had to do was imagine her face if she were to ever catch a glimpse of his scars. Revulsion. Rejection. Maybe derision. He could not risk that.

About the time they finished eating, a loud knock sounded on the front door. Mr. Winthrop went to see who was there. He returned to the dining room holding a telegram.

"This is for you, Collin."

Collin accepted the envelope and went into the foyer to read it.

RECEIVED MESSAGE. STOP.
GO TO SEATTLE WITH THEM. STOP.
NEW SHIP LENORA SHOULD BE THERE. STOP.
MAY NEED HELP. STOP.
CONTACT ME FROM SEATTLE. STOP.

*Interesting.*

# CHAPTER 26

*W*hen the train pulled into Seattle late in the afternoon, a cold rain was falling. Catherine huddled close to Mary so they could see out the same window. The station was situated by the Puget Sound, and a railway bridge crossed the water. Various kinds of boats were also anchored nearby, from small fishing vessels to ocean steamships

"Washington is still a territory instead of a state like California and Oregon, so I didn't expect Seattle to be quite this large, even though it is the capital." Catherine leaned back in her seat.

"I heard they are working toward becoming a state too." Collin glanced out the window as well. He and Daniel stepped into the aisle.

"The conductor told us the train will stop here for half an hour." Daniel's gaze kept returning to Mary while he talked to both of the women. "We want you to stay here a few minutes while we check to see what kind of conveyances are available. We'd prefer a closed coach with enough room for all five of us and our luggage."

Collin added, "We don't want you to get wet if we can help it."

The men headed out into the rain and ran across the platform into the station. By the time they returned with a coach and driver, the rain had stopped. Catherine, Mary, and Julie already had the conductor and station master unload their luggage and put it inside the station. The brisk breeze blowing across the water kept them indoors as well.

Daniel took off his hat and dropped a kiss on Mary's cheek. Catherine watched her sister's face redden. After spending all this time with Mary, Catherine could easily imagine how she herself looked when a blush stained her own cheeks.

Collin smiled at Catherine. "You ladies were busy while we were gone."

"We're not exactly helpless, you know." She enjoyed the way they had gradually moved from a feeling of antipathy to a place where they could share banter. She felt more at home with him than with any other man besides her father.

Collin helped get the ladies settled into the coach while Daniel talked to the driver. Then he returned and pulled the door closed behind him. He dropped into the seat beside Mary, while Collin shared the seat with her and Julie. The way they were crowded together, all the way from her shoulders to her knees was pressed against both of her seat mates. She was thankful she hadn't worn a traveling suit with a wider skirt or bustle. They wouldn't have all fit. This close, they didn't have to worry about being too chilly.

"There are several hotels in downtown Seattle. We've decided to stay at the Arlington House Hotel. It's near the middle of the business district." He started filling them in on all the details. "Our driver told me that the older Mr. Stanton passed away late last year, and his grandson inherited the store. The furniture store was in the same building with an emporium. The two owners have formed a partnership and combined the two stores. Our hotel isn't far from the building. The driver seemed proud of the fact that Seattle finally has this new department store. First one in the territory."

Catherine looked at her new brother-in-law with admiration. "You leave no stone unturned when you find information, do you?"

Mary snuggled closer to her husband. "He's very astute."

"I asked the driver to go there first, so we can just check it out before we settle in at the hotel."

As soon as Daniel finished this statement, the coach stopped and the driver hopped down to open the door.

"Julie, if you're tired, you don't have to come in with us. We shan't be long." Catherine knew the extra trip was taking some of her maid's usual time off away from her.

"Thank you." Julie smiled. "I think I'll just sit here and read my new copy of *Harper's Bazar*."

The large open space of the store didn't look as cluttered as many stores did. Merchandise was displayed in appealing ways. Catherine drifted farther into the soft goods section of the store, while Mary and Daniel headed toward the furniture. She wandered between several display aisles with Collin following her. When she arrived at the sewing notions section, he stayed back at the end of the aisle with his hands shoved into his front pockets. A woman came from the other direction and stopped to look at the spools of ribbon. Catherine started to go around her, and the woman glanced up at her.

"Miss Margaret, I heard you were back from Arkansas. How was your trip?" The woman gave her a wide, sincere smile.

Catherine stood still a minute. "I beg your pardon. What did you call me?"

A strange look of confusion settled on the older woman's face as her gaze darted past Catherine, only to return immediately. "What's going on here? You can't both be...Margaret Caine."

Catherine glanced behind her to find Mary and Daniel approaching, with Collin behind them. She quickly returned her attention to the flustered woman. "Did you just call me Margaret Caine?"

The woman turned as white as a sun-bleached sheet. She started patting her chest and breathing faster.

"Ma'am, are you going to be all right? We can get someone to help you." Catherine didn't want to upset the woman any more than she already was, so she would wait to question her further.

Before Catherine could take the woman's arm, a man hurried toward the group clustered near her. "I'm the store manager. Do you need any help, Mrs. Murdock?" His gaze landed on Catherine's hand reaching toward his regular customer. "What seems to be the prob—"

His eyes widened as he looked at them. His gaze slid from Catherine to Mary. Then he turned his attention back toward the other woman. "Come with me, Mrs. Murdock. We'll get you a glass of cold water, and you can rest in my office." He shot a stern look at the rest of them. "Please remain where you are until I return. I must take care of her."

"Of course, you must." Catherine felt sorry for the two of them, but she was also quaking on the inside. The woman called her Margaret Caine. Their sister must be in or near Seattle. Nothing would entice her to move an inch until the man came back. She had to find out where Margaret was.

In a very short amount of time, another man hurried toward them. "Praise the Lord. Our prayers are answered." This man was almost as tall as Collin, and he didn't seem the least surprised to see the two of them. He had to be in his late forties or early fifties, but he was still hale and hearty. He stopped right in front of Catherine.

Her knees felt weak. Before she could reach for something to hold onto, Collin's arm slipped across her back and his hand settled on her waist.

"Just lean against me," he whispered. "I'll support you."

The man thrust out his hand. "I'm Joshua Caine. Maggie's father. Which one of you is Catherine, and which one is Mary?"

Mary slipped to the other side of Catherine and took hold of her hand. "I'm Mary, and this is Catherine. Margaret Lenora goes by Maggie?"

"Most of the time with family." He chuckled. "She thought of herself that way long before the rest of us caught on." The smile on his face looked like sunshine on a hot summer day. "Come, let's go up to my office."

"Sir?" Daniel intervened, then shook the proffered hand. "We've come by train from Oregon City today, and we're fatigued. We were just going to check into the Arlington House Hotel. Could we do that and meet later this evening? I'm sure all three girls want to be rested when they first get to spend time together."

"Of course..." Mr. Caine appeared to be studying the ceiling a moment. "Of course. But there's no need to check into the hotel. Neither Maggie nor Florence would want that. We have a large house with plenty of room for all of you. You must come home with me."

Catherine took a deep breath and felt less shaky. "There are actually five of us. My lady's maid is traveling with us."

"That's fine. We have plenty of room." He gave a hearty laugh. "This is too wonderful. So how did you get here from the train?"

"We have a coach waiting outside for us. The luggage and Catherine's maid are in the coach." Daniel shifted toward the door.

"Come, come." Joshua Caine walked between and led the way. "I'll have a word with the driver."

They all trooped out of the store through a crowd that had gathered at the end of the aisle. Catherine hadn't noticed when that happened. She glanced back wondering if that Mrs. Murdock would be all right. She whispered a prayer under her breath for the woman.

While the men helped them climb into the coach, Mr. Caine gave the driver directions. Then he came back to the open door of the conveyance. "He knows where to take you to our home on Beacon Hill."

"Won't your wife be surprised?" Catherine felt a little uncomfortable about barging in on them.

"Of course, she will. So will Maggie, but I'll borrow a horse to ride and beat you there. We'll be waiting with open arms. Too bad Charles Stanton is out of town on business. He and Maggie are engaged to be married." He shut the door and strode away.

When the driver started the coach moving, the tension broke apart. Mary leaned toward Catherine. "This is the answer to our prayers!"

"It certainly is. God is so good." Catherine leaned her head against the padded back of the bench seat and closed her eyes. "There were no more clues for us to follow to help us find Margaret...and now this." She had never experienced as much happiness as this in her whole lifetime.

The ride to the Caine home didn't take long, but they were able to see some of Seattle. They drove up several hills, by a university and a hospital as well as a large number of houses, before stopping in front of a house that reminded Catherine of the Winthrop home in Oregon City. Three stories with well-cared-for gardens surrounding it. The coach had taken a turn off the street onto a semicircular driveway.

Before they could all get out of the coach, the front door flew open and Maggie hastened down the steps toward Mary and her. Everyone moved out of their way so the sisters could reach each other quickly.

For the first time in her life, a feeling of completeness and contentment enveloped Catherine. The last piece missing from her heart clicked solidly into place. She threw her arms around her sisters and they clung together, all talking at once. Catherine didn't know one word the others were saying, but it didn't matter. They were together as they were meant to be from the moment they were conceived in their mother's womb.

Clapping started near the coach, and soon was joined by Mr. Caine and two women waiting on the wide front porch. No one seemed to care that they were making a spectacle in the front yard. Finally, the sisters eased back and just stared at each other.

"Maggie." A gentle, feminine voice called from the porch. "Bring your sisters in, and we can all get settled. We'll have plenty of time for you to catch up with what has been going on in your lives."

"Yes, Mother." Maggie linked her arms with a sister on each side, and they walked to the house together.

"I'll have Erik come get the luggage so your coachman can leave." Mr. Caine went out to the street. Catherine noticed that Maggie's father insisted on paying for the coach ride.

Catherine knew she, Collin, and Julie would need to leave for San Francisco in a few days, so she wanted to spend as much time as she could with her sisters while they were here.

Tonight would be an amazing experience. The very thought stole her breath away.

# CHAPTER 27

*C*ollin arose early, but he didn't beat Daniel to breakfast. A buffet of chafing dishes containing scrambled eggs, ham, biscuits, and sausages were sitting on the sideboard in the dining room. Small dishes contained butter, honey, some kind of jam, and a fruit compote. And a carafe of hot coffee. What a spread. His stomach rumbled, even though he'd had plenty to eat at the feast last night.

"Couldn't sleep late?" Daniel glanced over the rim of a china cup.

"No." Collin put a goodly portion of food on his plate and sat down across from his friend. "I really need to send Mr. McKenna a telegram to let him know we arrived safely...and to catch him up on what we found out after we got here."

"I know the sisters will want to spend today

together. We're kind of superfluous. I'd like to accompany you, if I might." He took the last bite of his ham.

"Sure. But I need to check to see if the *Lenora* is in port. Mr. McKenna indicated there might be a problem with her." Wiping his mouth, he laid his napkin beside his plate. "This is good food, but I've had enough. I need to see if we can get a ride down to the docks." He arose and headed toward the entrance hall.

Daniel followed. "We could check out back to see if the stable is there."

"Sounds good to me."

Just as they turned to go, Joshua came out of his study. "You men are up early after our late night."

"Yes, sir." Collin grabbed his coat and hat from the hall tree. So did Daniel.

"Where are you going?" Joshua studied each man.

"I need to send a telegram to Mr. McKenna." Collin started buttoning his coat. "And I have to check to see if a McKenna Lines ship is in the harbor."

"Follow me."

Soon the Caine brougham stopped to let Joshua out at the store. He turned toward the driver. "Erik, you are at these men's disposal today. Take them wherever they need to go and wait for them."

"Yes, sir, Mr. Caine." The driver started whistling as he drove them toward the telegraph office.

After sending the longest telegram he'd ever written, Collin returned to the carriage with Daniel. When they reached the docks, Collin checked with the harbor master. He pointed out where the large ship was at the far end of the docks with its gangplank lowered, but no activity to be seen.

This one looked a lot different from any of the other McKenna Line ships. More modern and not exactly like a freighter. He'd seen the drawings of the vessel, but having the real thing in front of him was altogether different. They hailed the ship and started up the gangplank. A crew member in the uniform of a first mate met them at the end.

"I'm Collin Elliott, Mr. McKenna's assistant. I'd like to talk to the captain." He thrust out his hand.

The seaman pumped it, then stood as if at attention. "I'm afraid that's not possible. He's not here."

Collin's gaze swept across the clean deck. Everything looked shipshape. "And where, pray tell, is he? According to the harbor master, the *Lenora* was scheduled to depart early this morning." The captain should be ready to take the helm.

"Yes, sir. She was." The man frowned. "But Captain Harvey is in the hospital."

"Why? What's wrong with him?" Collin wondered what had caused Angus to be worried about the ship.

"Well, sir, he was visiting with his sister in Seattle several days ago, and he collapsed. He was taken to Providence Hospital. It may be his heart." The expression on the seaman's face revealed his concern. "He's a good man. I've served under him for over two years."

Collin stared across the water. The slight movement

of the ship at rest felt natural to him, even after all the time away. He would have to send another telegram to Angus right away.

After a trip to the hospital to check on Captain Harvey, Collin and Daniel went back to the telegraph office. He sent another message letting Angus know that Captain Harvey might not be able to ever come back to work. His sister was going to take care of him until he recovered, and according to how well he recovered, then they would decide about his future.

Collin wanted to go back to where the *Lenora* was docked. He and Daniel stood on the dock and took in the sleek lines. One of the newest type of steamships, the *Lenora* had a number of first-class cabins above the main deck of the ship in addition to the large cargo holds below. Angus planned to carry passengers to ports along the west coast of North America, as well as haul freight. The area where the cabins were also contained a dining saloon and a passenger lounge. Officers' quarters, the bridge, and the wheelhouse were above this level. Collin crossed his arms and imagined her out on the open water.

Daniel stuck his hands in the front pockets of his trousers. "That's really a special ship, isn't it?"

"Yes, she is. We could take a tour this afternoon if you've a mind to."

"Sounds good to me." Daniel glanced back to where the Caine coach waited for them to return. "Where do you want to go for lunch?"

Collin turned and started toward Mr. Caine's driver, who stood looking across the water. "Perhaps Erik can make a recommendation."

He took the men to a café across the street from the train station and telegraph office. From the number of people crowded into the small room, and the enticing aromas, Collin figured Erik had steered them in the right direction. Within a few minutes, they found a table, ordered, and had steaming bowls of a hearty fish stew in front of them,

Right after they started eating, a young man came through the door. "Is there a Mr. Collin Elliott in here?" He had to raise his voice to be heard over the general hubbub.

Collin stood and raised his hand, signaling the young man. The youth hurried toward them and thrust a telegram toward him. Collin took it and dropped a couple of coins in his hand. The boy thanked him and hurried away.

"How did he know you were here?" Daniel picked up his cornbread and took a large bite, butter running down the side of his mouth. He used his napkin to wipe it off.

Erik looked up from his bowl of stew. "Mr. Caine's coach is a familiar sight in Seattle. I'm sure the telegraph operator recognized it."

Collin tore open the envelope and scanned the page. He almost dropped it in his food. Surely, Mr. McKenna didn't mean what he said. He could not captain a ship...ever again. Besides, at this time of year, there was more of a chance for a storm, and he couldn't face one.

The memory of the rolling and pitching of the ship stole his hunger like a homeless beggar. The sound of the ship breaking apart...water closing over his head and him sinking, unable to breathe before he pushed his way back to the surface...the cries of his crew. So many of them, like him, couldn't swim. His frantic efforts to save them, all the while clinging to pieces of the shipwreck to keep himself afloat. Being too intent to even realize how bad his injuries were until he saw the dorsal fins begin to circle the area where the parts of the ship dipped and bucked with each wave. Then realizing his own blood probably drew the sharks to the spot. Believing that all of them were goners. The reality of what happened crashed in on him, and he began to tremble.

"Are you all right, man?" Daniel leaned close to him. "You're white as a sheet, and you look as if you've seen a ghost."

Taking a deep breath, Collin tried to shake off the memories. "Maybe I have."

Erik looked up from his meal. "Do we need to get you back to the house, sir?"

"No. I must send Mr. McKenna another telegram." He stuffed the papers in his pocket, dropped some money on the table, and rushed out the door.

He took a deep breath of the fresh air. The sun

shone bright and a gentle breeze blew from across Puget Sound. He had to escape from the memories, but getting on a ship to captain her wasn't the way. He huffed out a long breath and jogged across the street and down the block to the telegraph office, his injured leg aching from the exertion.

After sending another message to Angus telling him he couldn't captain the ship and that he'd await an answer, he went outside where Daniel stood talking to Erik. "I need to stay here until I hear back from Mr. McKenna. If you want to go somewhere, I'll understand."

Daniel smiled. "We're in this together today. If you wait, I will too."

Collin turned toward Erik. "If you need to run any errands or anything, go ahead. You can come back by here every so often and see if we're ready to go."

Daniel and Collin walked along the platform of the train station until they came to a bench. The area was deserted for now, so they sat down and watched the gently moving water.

"Listen, I know something really upset you. I'd like to help you if I can." Daniel studied his face.

"There's not anything anyone can do."

"Maybe it'll help just to talk about it. I know it helps me sometimes. You know whatever you say will be just between the two of us."

Collin hadn't ever really shared his innermost thoughts with anyone. But this wasn't just anyone.

Daniel had prayed for him and helped him to understand how much God loved him. He knew he could trust him. Daniel could be his port in the storm.

Maybe now was the right time to unburden himself.

"I hate to even tell anyone, but maybe I should. It goes back to the shipwreck." Haltingly, in the privacy of the great outdoors, he began to tell the awful truth about his failure and deep fears.

Instead of derision, Collin read understanding in the expressions on Daniel's face. Compassion and even a supernatural kind of love, like the one he felt when he asked Jesus into his life. Daniel didn't interrupt or comment. He just listened intently until Collin finished the telling.

After all the words poured out of him, he felt as if a huge weight had been lifted from his heart, the same way God had lifted the weight from his soul.

"And so, I told Mr. McKenna that I can't captain the *Lenora* back to San Francisco. I don't know what he'll do now."

"Fear is an ugly companion." Daniel spoke with the conviction of someone who had experienced something similar. "The Bible tells us that God didn't give us a spirit of fear, but of love and power and a sound mind. That fear isn't coming from Him. Yes, you've been through a lot, but God can take you through anything. And maybe this is something you need to face."

Collin stood and thrust his hands into his pockets.

"It would mean taking Catherine and Julie on the ship as well. I don't want anything to happen to her."

"Which 'her,' Julie or Catherine?" Daniel's voice held a note of humor.

Collin stared at him. How should he answer? Hedge a bit, or truthfully? "Catherine."

"I thought so." Daniel got up and stood beside him. "Does she know you're in love with her?"

"No." He shook his head. He'd only recently admitted it to himself. "We could never have a future together. She's...and I'm not..."

Daniel's laugh rang out and a couple of men on a fishing boat stared across the water at them. "Listen. Mr. McKenna knew what he was doing when he entrusted his daughter into your care. Twice. And he wouldn't tell you to take her on a ship he thought was in danger. Right?"

His words made a lot of sense.

"So what are you going to do? Run away, or go in the strength of the Lord? Just look at what He's been doing in all our lives. He brought Catherine and Mary together, then when there was no clues to find Maggie, He made a way. Don't you think He can take all of you back to San Francisco safely? Besides, I'll be praying for you all the way. So will Mary. You don't need to be fearful about captaining a ship again, and you don't need to be fearful about the way Catherine will react to your scars."

Daniel's word settled inside Collin, immediately

taking root and growing. He could believe that God would go with them. He didn't have anything to fear.

~

*C*atherine awoke early in the morning when someone's arm dropped across her face. She gently moved it and stared lovingly at the two girls sharing the same bed with her. Although Mrs. Caine assigned each of them a room nearby, they quickly migrated to Maggie's room.

Even Mary left her husband alone to visit with her sisters. She said her new husband totally understood her need to be with her long-lost sisters. Catherine already liked Daniel a great deal, but this decision of his put him over the top in her estimation.

After they came together none of the girls wanted to go back. So they spent the night talking until they all finally fell asleep sprawled across Maggie's bed. Looking at her sisters made Catherine realize why other people had mistaken her for them. Yes, they dressed a little differently from each other, but evidently they liked many of the same colors as evidenced by their wardrobes.

And they all had those unruly curls. Both Maggie and Catherine had worked hard most of their lives to try to tame them into an acceptable style, while for the most part Mary had just done whatever she could with hers.

Someone said the eyes were the windows of the soul. If that was really true, she and her sisters shared similar souls. Looking into their eyes was like looking into the cheval glass every morning.

Mary rolled over and opened her eyes. She sat up and stretched her arms above her head. "Did you sleep much last night?"

"Actually, I did. Being with the two of you felt so natural, as if I had come home."

Catherine slipped from the bed and padded across the rug to the window. In the distance she could see the Puget Sound, with the light of dawn painting the clouds in pastel hues. Everything outside looked as beautiful as life felt right now.

She had wanted to find her sisters so much. Now she had. Instead of merely a happy ending, it felt like the joyous beginning of a new day in their lives. Last night had been spent catching up on each other's lives, but the road ahead would be even more exciting.

A lock of her hair fell across her cheek. She tucked it behind her ear.

Mary came to stand beside her. "You know, all three of us do that...tuck our curls behind our ears. I noticed one time last night when we all three did it at exactly the same time. It felt really strange watching the two of you."

A groan issued from the bed, and Maggie rolled over. "I never have liked getting up too early in the morning." She came to stand beside her sisters. "I asked for the room on this side of the house, because I like to watch the movement of the water in Puget Sound."

Catherine nodded. "Our house is on Nob Hill in San Francisco. I often went into the ballroom so I could watch the water in San Francisco Bay."

Mary stared out the window. "I really haven't been around any body of water except the Willamette River. But I do enjoy the falls."

"Well, you can enjoy San Francisco Bay when you come to visit us." Catherine smiled just thinking about introducing them to their father. She glanced toward her sisters and was surprised. Neither one looked at all interested in her suggestion.

She walked over and sat on the side of the bed. "What's going on?"

Mary turned back toward the window. "I told you before that I don't think I'm ready to meet...Angus McKenna."

Maggie put her arm around Mary. "I understand. I'm not totally ready either."

Catherine felt like crying. "What are you talking about? I've worked so hard to find both of you. I had a clue about where to start looking for you, Mary, but we couldn't find any idea about where to start looking for you, Maggie. I believe this meeting was God's will for us."

"As soon as I found out I had sisters, I decided to find you," Maggie agreed.

"And I did too. That's one thing I told Daniel. I had

to find my sisters. And he agreed to help me." Mary ducked her head. "But I never really thought about finding...him."

"Why wouldn't you want to meet our father?" When she said the word "father" both of her sisters almost flinched.

"He chose to...give me away." Each of Mary's words was sharp as a dagger.

Maggie nodded. "And even more than that. He promised never to try to find us. That really hurt, Catherine. Why did he choose you and not me? Or Mary?"

Catherine had never thought about it in those terms. "He told me that it was because I was the oldest. He only gave you away because he knew he couldn't care for all three of us."

Her sisters both looked skeptical. What could she say to help them get over their pain?

"I understand your hurt. I really do. But I need to tell you something. Then I won't bring it up again. Our father has regretted his decision for most of our lives." She glanced at Mary. "You showed me a daguerreotype of our parents in their wedding attire. They were a handsome couple, full of life. Now Daddy looks as if he were our grandfather. He has aged so much more than most men his age. After I found out about having sisters, he finally told me how he has carried the burden of his decision for almost two decades.

"Think of his predicament. Three babies. How

could he have possibly fed us, cared for all of us? His decision very likely saved our lives."

Mary wilted somewhat under Catherine's gaze. "Having brought up small children, I have a taste of what work a child can be. But why has he not sought us out now?"

Catherine's mouth dropped open. "Mary, did you show any interest? Did you write to him? Did you invite him to visit, or to attend your wedding? He knows you don't want to see him, and he is grieved all over again."

She turned to Margaret. "Maggie...?"

Both her sisters stared at the floor, seemingly ashamed, but also unwilling to make the first step. Catherine looked from one to the other and sighed. "I love our father and hope you both will come to love him too. But I don't want to carry this burden anymore. I will be praying for each of you when I go home."

Only God could make a difference in their lives now. She would make the most of her time with her sisters before they left for home, knowing she might not ever see them together again.

Maggie came back to sit beside her. "Remember, we'll get to be together again when Charles and I get married. I want the two of you to be my attendants."

That was something to look forward to, but Catherine knew she wanted much, much more.

# CHAPTER 28

*Two whole days.* Catherine had only two days with her sisters before they boarded this ship to head back to San Francisco. Her father's new ship, the *Lenora*. She knew he named the steamship after her mother, but he chose the one name that all her daughters also shared. So actually, it was a tribute to all of them.

Maggie and her betrothed and Mary and her husband saw them off at the dock. She hoped and prayed her sisters recognized the significance of the name. If so, they should change their minds and come to meet their father. She longed for the day when her family would all be together.

Catherine ambled along the deck, stopping occasionally to stand by the railing and watch the water. She was fascinated with the way the ship made the water look much like the dirt as it turned over when plowed.

Only the water was a dark grayish-blue with a lot of foam churned with it. And when she was at the back of the ship, that foam left a trail in the wake of the ship.

Even though her father had owned ocean-going vessels almost as long as she could remember, he had never taken her far from land. She loved the invigorating breeze that held the tang of salt water. Gulls and other birds soared overhead among the scattered clouds. Soon after they left Puget Sound, they reached the open water and headed what she assumed was south. At first, it felt strange not being able to see any land, but now she was used to it. She could hardly wait until she could watch the sun set over the western horizon. Having read about the beauty, she knew the experience had to be even more awesome than words could reveal.

Just when she started to go back inside the lounge, Julie joined her, and they decided to take another turn around the deck.

"Have you been on a ship before?" She noticed her maid looked a little pale.

"No, ma'am. And I'm afraid I've been a little seasick." That explained Julie's pasty-looking complexion.

"How are you now?"

"I'm better. The steward gave me some soda crackers, and they helped settle my stomach." Julie grabbed hold of the railing with both hands and hung on tight.

"He told me the fresh air would be good for me. It is lovely out here."

Catherine leaned against the metal railing with her back to the waves. "Yes, I like it. However, it did take me a bit to get my sea legs. Now the movement is soothing."

"I hope it soon is for me." Julie gave her a weak smile. "I almost wish there were other passengers besides us. Have you talked to Mr., uh...I mean, Captain Elliott since we boarded?"

"No, I haven't." Catherine stared up at the windows above the passenger cabins. "I only caught a glimpse of him on the bridge once. I'm sure he's busy." Even she heard the wistful tone in her own voice.

Over the last two and a half months, she had gotten used to having Collin Elliott nearby. Sometimes, she thought he liked her a lot. Other times, not so much. And he'd been on edge ever since he knew he was going to captain the ship back to San Francisco.

If she understood it right, this was the *Lenora*'s maiden voyage. Perhaps that was why there were no other passengers. She knew her father hoped this passenger deck would increase their revenue while they hauled a lot of cargo. Of course, she only heard snatches of their conversations about work, not all of them. Perhaps she had it all wrong.

"I like Mr. Elliott." Julie let go of the railing with one hand and swept an errant lock of hair back and tucked it under the bun at the nape of her neck. "I feel much safer when he is around. Ever since he saved us in Oregon City."

"I feel that way too." And Catherine had started comparing him to every other man they met on their journeys. He was by far the most handsome. Tall and strong, he had an impressive presence. And with his strong chin and rugged features, he exemplified masculinity at its best. At least she thought so. Of course, Maggie and Mary wouldn't agree with her. They had their own handsome heroes in their lives. But theirs were a permanent part, and Catherine knew Collin Elliott could walk out of her life at any time. Just the thought dampened her day.

Someday, he could fall in love with some woman who also recognized what a wonderful catch the man would be. A man of honor and integrity. Just what every woman needed. Especially her. She needed someone who was more interested in her as a person than the fact that she would be an heiress.

The ship's bell pealed once across the deck. Since the sun was almost straight above them, Catherine decided maybe it was calling them to lunch. All her walking on the deck had worked up an appetite.

"Let's check out the dining saloon and see if our meal is ready for us."

When they entered the large room with floor-to-ceiling windows on three sides, Catherine's gaze was captured by their captain. A blush started up her cheeks, even though the man wouldn't know she had been thinking about him a lot today. Hopefully, he would merely think her cheeks were rosy because of the cool breeze.

Collin arose from his seat. "Would you ladies join me?" He pulled two other chairs out from the table.

After they were seated, Catherine unfolded her napkin and arranged it on her lap. Collin glanced at Julie, then turned his attention toward Catherine. "Are you enjoying yourself?"

"Immensely."

Collin turned to Julie. "Not really," she admitted.

"What seems to be the problem? Maybe we can take care of it."

"I don't think so, Captain. I just found out today that I get seasick."

Collin frowned.

"But your steward helped me. I'm not as indisposed as I was earlier." She took a sip of water from the crystal goblet.

As if he had been called by her comment, the steward came through the swinging door to the kitchen area and stopped beside their table. "What can I get you to eat?"

Collin smiled at the man. "Please bring Miss Myers some broth for her soup course."

Julie smiled and nodded. "That sounds good."

After they ordered, they discussed the ship and how long it would take them to get to San Francisco. Catherine hadn't realized they would probably arrive before they would have if they'd taken the train. That was welcome news.

"We don't have the stops and possible damaged tracks when we're out here on the water. The only thing that might slow us down is a storm, but the skies have been mostly clear so far. I'm hoping that lasts until we reach our destination."

Catherine had to agree with him on that.

After they finished their meal, Julie excused herself and headed back to her cabin. Collin asked Catherine if he could stroll the deck with her.

"Who will be steering the ship?"

His merry laugh pealed through the room. "The first mate and I take shifts manning the wheel. I have a while before I need to go back." He offered her his arm.

Catherine slipped her hand through the crook of his elbow, and they promenaded around the deck. Their steps developed a rhythm that coincided with the gentle rocking of the ship. Somehow, it felt as if they were connected.

Their conversation ebbed and flowed like the waves on a sandy shore. Catherine enjoyed the tone and cadence of his words, no matter what he was talking about. And when they laughed together, she felt almost giddy. That would never do...to lose her head over a man who was such a good friend. She didn't want them to lose their easy comradery, and they just might if she let him know that she was drawn to him.

When he needed to return to the bridge, he walked

her to the door of her cabin. "Thank you, Catherine, for a most pleasant afternoon."

"You're welcome, Collin." When she shut her door and went to sit on her bed, she couldn't stop herself from wishing they would have many more times like this one.

The invigorating air and good exercise lulled her to sleep. Her dreams were filled with her sisters, and although she pleaded with them to come home with her, they were adamant about not ever wanting to meet their father. The words of rejection they'd spoken echoed through those dreams, and her father cried because his daughters hadn't come home.

When she finally awoke, she had missed the sunset, and it was far past the time for the evening meal. Catherine changed into warmer clothing, pinned her hair into some semblance of order, and went out to walk the deck. The memory of her dreams lingered, making her heart heavy. Finally, she stopped beside the railing that was closest to the front of the ship. While the wind blew in her face, she looked at the bright stars.

The crescent moon was close to a half-moon shape. The missing part of the orb was an additional reminder that her family was broken in half, and she didn't know how to bring it back together. A tear dropped from her eyelashes and made its way down her cheek. Soon a deluge followed. She had nothing to wipe them off with, except her palms. Why hadn't she carried her hanky with her?

~

*W*hile Collin was in charge of the wheel, he also watched Catherine walk the deck. He had missed her at dinner but decided not to disturb her, figuring that the excitement and sleeplessness of the last few nights had finally taken their toll. And there was nothing like the gentle rocking of a ship to put one to sleep.

As he continued to watch, she leaned against the fore railing, and her shoulders slumped. Could it be? She looked...dejected. His first mate arrived right on time a few minutes later, so he hurried down the ladder and walked briskly toward where she stood. Before he reached her, he saw the tears glistening on her face.

"Here. Use mine." He held out his handkerchief, glad he hadn't needed to use it anytime today.

Catherine jumped as if startled.

He slipped his arm around her waist to steady her. "I'm sorry. I thought you heard me coming."

After swiping at her tears, she turned toward him. "I was so deep in thought I wasn't aware of anything else."

He smiled at her. "That could be dangerous, especially when you're standing by the railing. If the ship had hit a trough between waves, you could've been thrown over the barrier to the deck below."

For a moment, fear entered her eyes, but then she turned them up toward him. "You make me feel safe."

No one had ever said anything like that to him. Of

its own volition, his chest expanded. With praise like that in his ears, he'd have to be careful to keep pride from taking over.

He walked with her toward the wall of the lounge, trying to get them out of the wind. "Do you want to tell me why you're so sad?"

Her wide eyes studied him in the moonlight, her gaze roving over his features feeling like a caress. What if this woman had as deep of feelings for him as he did for her? Could he trust those feelings? Would she be repulsed by his disfigurement?

Remembering Daniel's words about this not bothering the right woman, he was almost ready to find out, but he held back. He drew her down to a bench attached to the wall, then sat beside her.

He stared down into that beautiful face that was so like her sisters'. Still, he knew he'd be able to pick her out from the trio even if they were dressed alike. Something about her drew him, and the others did nothing for him. Yes, he could be their friend, but that was all. But this woman sitting beside him had the potential to be the world to him. Could he risk it?

"Please tell me what brought on those tears." He tried to sound soothing. Perhaps he did, because she gave him a watery smile.

She twisted his sodden handkerchief in her nervous hands. "My family is still apart. Yes, I've met my sisters, but they aren't willing to come meet our father. And he made a vow not to go to them. The only way they can meet is if Maggie and Mary give their permission."

Now he understood. He knew this news would come as a blow to Angus. He dreaded the time when the older man would have to hear it.

"I'll have to tell him, and I don't want to hurt him." Her last word ended on a sob.

"I know. It won't be easy. I'll tell him if you want me to." Anything to keep her from hurting even more.

"You'd do that for me?" She seemed surprised.

"Yes." He slipped his arms around her and pulled her against his chest, resting his chin on the top of her head. Those glorious red curls tickled his cheeks, but he didn't pull away. It was exquisite torture. The light scent of lilacs mesmerized him.

"No." Her words were muffled against his jacket. "I can't let you do that. The information has to come from me."

He leaned his head back so he could look her in the eyes. Right now they had a look as if a storm were brewing. "Then wait until I'm there with you. OK?"

She stared straight at him, with the moon outlining her delicate features giving them a silvery glow. Somehow, because of the way she had lifted her head, their lips were only a breath away from each other. A slight movement would connect them. And he wanted to kiss her more than anything in the world. Now he realized he'd wanted to press his lips to hers for a very long time.

Catherine sighed, and he breathed in the essence of

her. He waited for her to pull back, but she didn't. Instead her gaze dropped to his lips, then her eyes slowly closed. He didn't know if she moved, if he did, or if they both did, but their lips connected. Such a gentle touch, yet so powerful.

He felt her hands creep up and across his shoulders then her fingers touched his hair. Nothing could have kept him from burrowing his fingers into her hair as well, even though her pins slipped out, releasing the abundant curls into his hands. The kiss that started so softly soon rose to a new crescendo, opening emotions he had never bared before. The sweet taste was seasoned by the slight saltiness of the tears she had shed. He wanted to take every pain from this woman and shield her for the rest of her life. All he dared to do was funnel all the emotions she raised into that kiss, trying to show her just how profoundly his emotions were engaged in this exchange.

# CHAPTER 29

*C*ollin was behind the wheel when the *Lenora* entered San Francisco Bay and headed toward the docks. He'd had to force himself to concentrate the rest of the journey after that fateful kiss. Why had he taken such liberties with Angus's daughter? The man had trusted him to protect her, and instead, he'd stolen a kiss. More than just a kiss...and it felt so right.

Yes, he'd been trying to comfort her. And yes, she had welcomed the caress. But he should have respected her enough to talk to her father before anything like this happened.

Daniel's words must have convinced him not to fear rejection from the right woman. But was he the right man for her? She was an heiress. Her father was his employer. Even though Angus had expressed his interest in making him a partner in his business empire, he was just an employee. What did he have to give to this special woman?

*Love.*

The word whispered deep in his soul. Did he love her? If this wasn't love, he couldn't imagine how much more love could be. Watching her glide across the floor like a graceful swan on a hidden lake made him want to be by her side, always. The twinkle in her green eyes that sparkled like emeralds. And that hair. He'd seen only two other women with hair that seemed to come from an inner fire—her two sisters. Of course, they didn't make his heart pound in his chest like a blacksmith with his anvil.

He had been so wrong about her. Judging her before he really knew her. He had watched her grow in these last two and a half months from a self-centered girl into a woman with a heart for others. And now that Jesus had become a part of his life, he recognized the ways her life was touched by God's hand.

Collin knew he couldn't continue to work for Angus without confessing his indiscretion to him. He was willing to face whatever punishment the man would mete out. But he would not regret one second of the powerful kiss that changed his perception of the world.

Angus and his sister-in-law waited near the McKenna coach.

Collin watched Catherine and her maid make their way down the gangplank. Angus drew his daughter into his arms and held her tight. Even from where he stood, he read the disappointment in his employer's face as he looked over her shoulder. When they pulled back from the embrace, Catherine's aunt hurried her toward the coach.

After directing two men to unload the women's baggage, Collin strode down the gangplank as well.

"Collin, my boy. You did a fine job of bringing the *Lenora* home." Angus shook his hand and clapped him on his shoulder. "I've sent the women on home to rest. Come to the office, and we'll talk."

Collin decided it might be better for the two men to discuss what happened with the family in Seattle. That way, Catherine wouldn't be burdened to share all the bad news. She and her father could discuss the details, but Angus would be prepared when they were able to discuss the events.

After they were seated in Angus's office, his employer leaned his elbows on his desk and leaned forward. "So tell me about how you found Margaret."

"She likes to be called Maggie."

Angus laughed. "I know I'll love her. Catherine never likes me to call her Katie. But I do, anyway." He picked up a pencil and started tapping it on the ink blotter pad on his desktop.

Collin described their visit to the Caine Emporium and Stanton Fine Furniture department store. "I thought the customer was going to faint when she saw Mary walking up behind Catherine."

"I wish I could have been a fly on the wall." Angus

relaxed into his chair. "Did my daughters mention when they might come to see me? I had kind of hoped they might be on the ship with Katie."

Collin studied the large painting of a schooner with all the sails unfurled that hung behind Angus's desk. A storm approached in the distant background. Until today, he hadn't wanted to look at it because of his past experience with a storm, but today he welcomed anything to keep him from seeing Angus's disappointment.

"I know Catherine will tell you more about it, but neither of your other daughters wanted to come yet. It might have been because it's so close to Christmas." He crossed his scarred leg across his other knee and kept his eyes trained on his own shoe. "They all three look alike, but I can easily pick out Catherine from the others."

He dared a glance up at the older man and caught a smile on his face.

"Oh, you can, can you?" Once again the older man started tapping with his pencil. "Just what makes her unique?"

Collin scratched his head. "Well...it's not something I can describe. She's just different somehow."

Angus got up and came around the desk, then leaned back against the edge. "Don't think I didn't realize you really didn't want to go traipsing off after Katie when she left without telling me. But I knew I could trust you. That's why I sent you."

Collin had to really steel his nerves to keep himself from flinching. He didn't deserve that trust. The memory of that kiss invaded his thoughts again.

"And I can tell something happened on this last journey." Angus crossed his arms. "Want to tell me about it?"

How could he say *no* gracefully? "Several interesting things happened."

"I'm interested in what happened to you personally."

Then it hit him. "You know I'd been going to church with you. When we were in Oregon City, I attended that church again as well." He shifted in his seat then stood up, thrusting his hands in the front pockets of his trousers. "Daniel Winthrop explained some things to me...and I asked Jesus for forgiveness." He whirled around and started pacing the office. "That was a big change. Later Daniel helped me understand that I didn't need to fear captaining the *Lenora*." He stopped abruptly and turned toward Angus.

A smile lit the older man's face, and he dropped his arms to his sides, resting his hands on the edge of the desktop. "That makes me very happy, Collin."

"Me, too, sir." And it did. Nothing in his life had ever given him so much happiness except...

"Mr. McKenna, I need to confess something to you." He had a hard time forcing those words out.

"You are in love with Katie, aren't you?" Angus had a

twinkle in his eye. He might not if he knew the whole truth.

"How did you know?"

The older man gave a wry smile. "I'm not so old I don't remember when I met my Lenora. It didn't take me long to fall for her either.... Besides, I saw the way you watched her as she left the ship. Does she know?"

Did she? Or did she think he'd overstepped the bounds of acceptable behavior?

He shook his head. "No...maybe...but I don't think so."

Again Angus laughed. "What are you going to do about it?"

"Well, I haven't...made any plans." This was not the response he expected. But maybe he should just keep the information to himself about...that kiss.

"Sit down, and let's discuss this." Angus returned to his chair behind the desk. "What do you really want long term?"

Collin dropped into the chair. What did he want? "I want to be married and have a family."

"With Katie?"

Collin nodded. "I'd like to court her...with your permission."

"Permission granted. Why don't you come over to the house for dinner tonight?"

Collin walked out the door of the office not believing what just happened. Now if he could only convince Catherine they belong together.

*C*atherine couldn't get the kiss out of her mind. The tender touch of his lips. The depth of emotions that overwhelmed her. How she wanted to stay in his arms forever. She wished her sisters were here, so she'd have someone to ask about the way she felt. Was it normal? She hadn't wanted the kiss to stop. The caress stopped as gently as it started, with each of them moving back. Nothing more was said about it. And she wanted more from Collin, but she wasn't exactly sure what that more would entail.

When Collin arrived at the house the evening they got home, he brought her a silk scarf that reflected the colors of the watered-silk dress she had worn to Mary's wedding. After dinner, she and Collin talked for hours, even after her father and Aunt Kirstin retired. Julie had sat in the parlor, working on her embroidery and ignoring them. If she didn't know better, she'd think Julie was their chaperone, just so they could visit.

They had talked over everything that happened on the journey. Then moved on to a number of personal subjects. Almost everything, but the kiss. They never mentioned it. She wondered if he even remembered.

He had returned every evening, and each time he brought a small gift for her. A box of French chocolates. A porcelain figure of a woman, who had red hair, standing at the railing of a ship. A book of poetry. A hand-painted china cup and saucer. Ribbons for her hair. It almost became a game, with her wondering what he would bring next.

Today, he was going to accompany her and Aunt Kirstin on a Christmas shopping trip downtown. She had a hard time choosing what to wear, but finally chose a holly green, woolen suit, which matched one of the ribbons he had given her. Julie wove the shiny strip through her hairstyle.

A knock sounded on her door.

"Come in."

Aunt Kirstin stuck her head in. "Your young man is waiting downstairs."

"Thank you." Was Collin her young man?

He hadn't made any kind of overture to her except to treat her with the utmost respect. Was he coming mainly to see her? She certainly hoped so.

When the two women arrived at the foot of the stairs, Collin met them, but his eyes homed in on her. "You look lovely, Catherine."

"Thank you." Those words warmed her clear through, but she still donned her coat. There would be a chill wind when they walked to the coach.

Collin helped both women into the conveyance before giving the driver directions.

When they reached the emporium, Catherine noted all the newer merchandise she hadn't seen before. Soon she had several parcels wrapped in paper and tied with twine. Collin offered to take the load to store in the boot of the coach. The driver could guard the bundles.

Catherine hoped the man was dressed warmly enough while he sat on the driver's seat.

"So, Catherine, are you about finished with your shopping?" Aunt Kirstin added two bundles to the ones waiting for Collin to fetch.

"Yes, I have all the gifts I was looking for except I want to buy something for Collin, since he's been so helpful to me." Catherine stared around the large store. "I'm just not sure what would be appropriate to give him."

"Since he likes to read, maybe a new book, or maybe he could use a muffler or gloves. Those wouldn't be too personal."

Collin returned and picked up the other parcels. "I'll be back in a bit, ladies. Maybe we can go somewhere close for lunch."

"That sounds nice." Catherine flashed him her sweetest smile.

After he turned away, she walked into the men's department, and Aunt Kirstin followed behind her. One counter held matching leather gloves and woolen knitted muffler scarves packaged together. Catherine chose a set that was the deep brown of the hot chocolate she liked to sip in the evening. The color would really complement the color of his eyes. She urged the sales clerk to quickly wrap the purchase for her.

"Aunt Kirstin, would you wait for this package. I want to find something for each of my sisters. I don't want to say anything to Daddy about it, but I'm hoping and praying they'll decide to come by Christmas. Maybe I should buy something for Charles and Daniel as well."

Her aunt glanced toward the front door. "Collin is coming in. I'll purchase two more of these sets. Maybe he'll think we're getting them for someone else, and that's why we're in the men's department. What colors should they be?"

"Buy one of the navy blue and one of the forest green. I'll go to shop for Maggie and Mary."

With only a few days until Christmas, Catherine's excitement for the holiday began to bubble within her. Only one more thing would make her life complete—if her sisters would come to San Francisco for Christmas.

# CHAPTER 30

*A* sense of excitement pulled Catherine from her slumber on Christmas morning. She stretched, reveling in the feeling. Something momentous would happen today, she could feel it. Would it be the arrival of Maggie and Mary?

She and Aunt Kirstin spent much of the morning helping Mrs. Campbell and Sophie the kitchen maid prepare Christmas dinner. They had bought a large goose. After stuffing the bird with a mixture of bread cubes, raisins, chopped apples, onions, and spices, they put it in the oven to bake slowly enough so all the stuffing would be thoroughly cooked. Then they started the side dishes—glazed carrots, mashed potatoes, and green beans. Hot rolls and pies would complete the meal.

Catherine loved all the smells of Christmas. She went into the parlor to enjoy the pungent tang of the evergreen tree. She and Kirstin hung popcorn chains and red ribbons on the boughs, interspersed with a few blown glass ornaments. Then they attached the candle holders to various branches. The tree stood waiting until the evening when they would light the candles.

Father had invited Collin to spend the holiday with them. Of course, the handsome man had been here every day or evening since they returned from Seattle, almost as if he were family. But when Catherine was with Collin, she didn't think of him as an almost brother, and she didn't know what to do with her runaway emotions. She had a hard time controlling them whenever he was near. Her heart often beat erratically enough to make her breathless. His presence filled the room and surrounded her with conflicting emotions.

Aunt Kirstin hadn't talked to her about the ways of a woman with a man. She didn't know what to make of that wonderful kiss on the *Lenora*. Did every woman lose herself in the wonder as she did when Collin first kissed her? Would those feelings continue in a relationship, or was it an anomaly? She wanted more than anything to experience those delicious tingles again. Just thinking about it caused her heart to pulse double-time.

In the early afternoon, the doorbell rang. When Father answered the door, Catherine heard the deep melodious sound of Collin Elliott's voice. She knew he was coming for the late afternoon dinner, but he was far earlier than she expected him to be. After wiping her hands on her apron, she removed the protective garment and took a tea tray into the parlor, anticipating the moment she would first see him.

"Collin?" She set the tray on the low table in front of the sofa and tried not to be too obvious as she caught glimpses of him from head to toe. "How nice to see you. I'm helping with the finishing touches on the meal."

He arose from the wingback where he was sitting. "Catherine."

The sound of her name coming from those chiseled lips sent a delicious shiver up and down her spine. Something about the man totally mesmerized her. "I didn't know to expect you this early."

His dark eyebrows quirked a question.

Father crossed one leg over the other. "Collin and I can enjoy a friendly chat while you women finish working on the meal. In the office, we're always discussing the business, but none of that today."

Catherine had considered staying in the parlor with them, but her father definitely dismissed her. She glanced back at Collin and found him studying her. After flashing him a smile, she left the room accompanied by the swish of her silken skirt and petticoats. She felt his eyes follow her progress. She forced herself to maintain decorum when what she wanted to do was throw herself into his arms. She had to banish thoughts like that, so they could all enjoy the day.

How could one event, that probably meant nothing

to him, have totally turned her world upside down? The man was only comforting her because she was crying. For sure, he had forgotten all about it.

Finally, Aunt Kirstin went to tell the men the meal was ready to be served. Collin hurried into the dining room and pulled out the chair where Catherine usually sat. She smiled up at him before she settled onto the chair. "Thank you, Collin."

The twinkle in his eyes was almost her undoing. She hoped she would be able to eat, because the flutters in her stomach wouldn't settle down.

He helped Aunt Kirstin into her chair as well. Catherine shouldn't allow her imagination to run away with her. He had been nothing except a gentleman when he assisted both of them.

With the pleasant conversation flowing around the table, she relaxed and forgot about her earlier discomfort.

"This bird is delicious. I don't think I've eaten anything like it before." Collin took another bite.

"Aunt Kirstin really knows how to pick the goose." Catherine smiled at him. "She likes one that is large, but without too much fat. The flavor is better."

Collin set his fork on the edge of his plate. "In all the times I've eaten here, the food has been excellent. But this is the best of all."

The way he looked at Kirstin made Catherine wonder if the man was interested in her. The very idea was preposterous. Her aunt was nearly as old as her mother would have been if she had lived. That thought reminded her that her sisters hadn't arrived as she was sure they would today. Did they still hold a grudge against their father?

She set her own fork down with enough food on her plate for a complete meal. Why had she ever taken so much? She couldn't force another bite down her throat.

"You aren't giving up now, are you, Katie?" Why had her father noticed so quickly?

"If I eat all this, I won't have a bit of room for the pumpkin pie." Even though there was a grain of truth in her statement, it felt like a complete lie.

Collin studied her while he continued to enjoy his own food. "I like pumpkin pie."

"My favorite is apple," her father interjected.

"Don't worry." Aunt Kirstin patted his arm. "We have both apple and pumpkin."

"Today…" Her father patted his stomach. "…I'm going to have a slice of each kind. Won't you, Collin?"

"I wouldn't miss it for all the tea in China."

They quickly finished the meal. Father stood. "Collin, would you like to help me light the Christmas tree?"

"Yes, sir." The men went into the parlor.

Mrs. Campbell quickly entered the dining room.

Catherine took a deep breath. "The food was wonderful. Thank you so much."

When she arrived in the parlor, the tree looked wonderful, even better than last year. She stood and stared at the ornaments reflecting the glittering light of the candles. "It's beautiful."

Her father came and put his arm around her. "Not as beautiful as my wonderful daughter." He pressed a kiss to her cheek, and she reveled in his love.

Collin stood to the side of the room, studying her with a speculative gleam in his eyes. Whatever could that mean?

Soon they had all exchanged their gifts. Catherine enjoyed the things her family bought her, but she was surprised by the gift from Collin. A book of poetry by Emily Dickinson.

She turned her attention toward him. "Thank you so much. I love poetry. How did you know?"

His gaze traveled over her features, leaving a warm trail across her face. Then he settled on her eyes. "It was only a guess, but I thought you might...after spending so much time with you..." His voice trailed off, but not his focus.

"I shall treasure it." Her fingers moved across the soft leather cover, then opened the pages. She loved the smell of a new book. Seeing the first poem, she read the words, "In a Library... A precious, mouldering pleasure 'tis... To meet an antique book, ...In just the dress his century wore;...A privilege, I think." She glanced up at him. "I know I shall enjoy this for a long time."

A smile spread across his handsome features.

Her father cleared his throat. Everyone turned to look at him.

"I've had a long week. I think I'll go on upstairs." With that he walked out.

How very odd. The evening had just begun. This was so unlike Father. Maybe he did look rather tired. Catherine wondered if she should worry about his health.

Aunt Kirstin arose from the wingback chair where she sat. "I'll go check on him." She swept out of the room and up the carpeted staircase.

Catherine remained on the loveseat and clasped her hands in her lap. Should she gather up her gifts and get them ready to take upstairs? But that would be impolite to Collin. Would he want to leave now? She stared at him, remembering him striding along the deck of the *Lenora*. Tall and handsome in the captain's uniform. Very competent. With the movement of the ship, his slight limp disappeared. She couldn't think about their ocean voyage without that kiss coming to mind. A blush gravitated into her cheeks. Could he see it in the dim light from the candles?

*The candles?* She jumped up. "We need to extinguish the candles before they burn too low."

As she headed toward the tree, Collin joined her. They quickly took care of the possible fire hazard. When they finished, she glanced out the window. The moonlight glazed everything in the yard with a silver sheen, and fog rising from the bay drifted between the tree trunks. The world outside looked like a wonderland.

Without turning, she felt Collin move closer to her, almost touching her back. The warmth from his body encompassed her.

"I want to talk to you, Catherine." His voice took on a husky tone, one she'd never heard before.

She turned toward him and gazed up into his eyes. "What about?"

He stood there as if he were mute.

Something compelled her to fill the silence. "What did you and Father discuss while we were preparing the meal?"

He relaxed. "Shall we sit down?" He led her back to the loveseat.

After she was seated, he joined her instead of taking one of the wingback chairs again. With him this close, their tryst onboard ship returned to her mind, and her heartbeat accelerated.

"When we returned from Seattle, I asked your father if I could court you." He studied her eyes, holding her gaze captive. "He agreed."

"So..." She was breathless, and the word came out as a whisper. "The gifts have been courting?"

A smile spread slowly across his face. "Yes."

She nodded. "Oh."

"Tonight, he asked me why I wanted to court you."

Catherine waited for him to continue and thought he never would. "What did you tell him?"

"That I love you with all my heart."

Those words dropped into her heart like water on

desert sand, soaking into her whole being. "What did he say to that?"

Collin's large hands enclosed hers and his thumbs moved across the backs, the caress so gentle. "He told me he knew the first time he saw your mother he loved her and wanted to marry her."

*Marry her?* Even though the logs in the fireplace were dying down, Catherine felt overheated.

"He wanted to marry her as soon as they could." He released the hand closest to him and laid his arm across the back of the loveseat, close enough for her to feel his presence.

"So did they get married very soon?"

Collin leaned his head close to hers, and his warm breath brushed her forehead. "Yes, as soon as she and her parents could plan the wedding."

She relaxed against the back of the cushions.

"He gave me permission to ask you to marry me, Catherine." He let go of the hand he was holding and thrust his hand into the pocket of his jacket.

Leaning forward, he pulled out a small velvet drawstring bag. Then he opened it and emptied the contents into his hand.

She stared at the golden and glittery ring.

"Catherine, will you marry me?" He held the ring and reached for her left hand, then paused to await her answer.

"Yes...yes, Collin."

He slipped the beautiful ring onto her finger. "I

chose this emerald ring, because it reminded me of your eyes when you smile."

She stared at the large stone surrounded by tiny diamonds. "I love emeralds, and I love you even more."

He turned her face up toward him and stared into her eyes. "You've made me the happiest man on earth." Then his lips descended and settled gently on hers.

This time the emotions were even stronger than they had been when they were on the ship. Slowly, then with more intensity, they poured all their love into the kiss. Pledging their love for all time. The sweet taste was even sweeter, the connection even longer, and she knew she would never tire of sharing their love in this manner.

Catherine had gone on a journey pursuing her sisters, and at the same time the most wonderful gift in the world pursued her. True love in the person of Collin Elliott. She was the most blessed woman in the world.

# CHAPTER 31

Friday, January 1, 1886, dawned with new promise. Catherine could hardly believe how wonderful her life had become. From Christmas until this New Year's Day, Collin, Father, Aunt Kirstin, and she had experienced all that the holiday season had to offer. They attended parties and the opera together, and dined privately at home a few times.

She loved watching the way the two most important men in her life interacted. Father was looking younger and happier than he had been in a long time. Today, they were planning to spend the evening at home.

One of the ships had been delayed by bad weather. Late yesterday, they received word it would dock this morning. Father went to meet Collin early and together they would check with the captain and make sure the merchandise was unloaded and put in the warehouse. The warehouse crew could check the bills of lading tomorrow, so she expected the two of them to be home for lunch.

She finished her ablutions, and Julie helped her dress. Then Julie tried a new hairstyle on Catherine. She wanted to get downstairs and help Aunt Kirstin. All this time working with her aunt was helping her learn what she would need to know to run a household after she and Collin married.

She hurried down the stairs just as someone twisted the doorbell knob. Since she was near the door, she opened it. Her eyes widened and for a moment, she just stood and stared.

"Catherine, I didn't know you were near enough to answer the door." Aunt Kirstin came down the hallway from the kitchen. "Oh, my goodness." She stopped beside Catherine.

"Mary! Maggie!" Gathering her sisters into a huge hug, she couldn't stop the tears from running down her cheeks. "You came. You really came."

Then her sisters were talking at the same time. She couldn't distinguish one's voice from the other. And she couldn't let go of them.

"Please. Come in." Aunt Kirstin spoke over their shoulders to the other three people standing on the porch. "It's really chilly this morning."

Finally, the sisters stepped from their mutual embrace, wiping their eyes as they did. Then Catherine reached to tuck a stray curl behind her ear. All three of the girls performed the same gesture in unison.

Aunt Kirstin laughed. "So it's true." The group came into the house, and she shut the door behind them. Aunt Kirstin gazed at the three young women. "You are as alike as three peas in a pod."

Everyone joined in the mirth. Then Catherine made the introductions. After all, Kirstin was Maggie's and Mary's aunt too. She finished, "And this is Mary's husband, Daniel; Maggie's fiancé, Charles; and...?"

"My aunt, Miss Georgia Long," Maggie supplied.

After taking their wraps, Aunt Kirstin herded them into the parlor. "It's warmer in here by the fireplace than it is in the foyer."

As they stood beside the flames warming their hands, Catherine had a sudden thought. "Where is your luggage?"

Daniel turned toward the doorway. "Charles and I can retrieve our bags from the coach and release the driver. He doesn't need to sit out in the cold wind."

"While they are gone, I'll bring in something to warm you up." Aunt Kirstin glanced at each of the girls in turn, then shook her head. "This will take some getting used to. With all of you standing together, if you weren't dressed differently, I don't think I could tell you apart. We have some scones. They should carry you to lunchtime. I'll have Mrs. Campbell start preparing more food for that meal. Do you want coffee or tea?"

"The men will like coffee, but the girls love tea. If I may, I'll go with you. I'm tired of sitting so long." Georgia followed her.

Catherine hugged each sister once again. "I still can't believe you're here. Let's sit down."

She pulled one of the wingback chairs close to the loveseat where Maggie and Mary were sitting. "Now tell me all about how you decided to come."

Maggie leaned forward. "Mother heard us discussing why we wouldn't come, and she asked to speak to Mary and me in private. She told us about the night we were born."

"And how it affected..." Mary gripped her hands together. "...our father."

"She made it seem so real, as if we were truly there." Maggie took up where Mary left off.

"By the time Maggie's mother was finished, I was crying." Mary slipped a hanky out of her reticule and dabbed at her eyes. "See, it still makes me sad. I'm so sorry I couldn't forgive him sooner. I hope he'll not hold it against us."

Catherine shook her head. "He won't. He'll be so glad to see you. Just wait until he gets home."

"When will that be?" Maggie and Mary spoke in unison as if they had practiced it. Then they both laughed.

"He and Collin will be here in time for lunch. That will give all of you time to refresh yourselves from the trip."

The front door opened, and Daniel and Charles came inside, each carrying two bags. They approached the parlor and set the luggage down just outside the door.

Aunt Kirstin reached the doorway right after they did, and she carried a silver tray with plates, the scones, butter, and three kinds of jam on it. She set it on the table in front of the sofa. "Come in. After we've had some refreshments, I'll show you to your rooms. It will be so wonderful to have so many young people here. How long will you be staying?"

Georgia entered the room on the last question. "We can only be here a week."

The kitchen maid followed her, carrying a tray with the coffeepot and teapot with the cups and saucers. She curtseyed and left.

Mary took a sip of the fragrant beverage. "This is really good tea." She set her cup and saucer back down. "Catherine, have you always lived in this lovely house?"

She glanced around the room, remembering the farmhouse where Mary had grown up. "Only since I was about seven years old. Father and I lived at Placerville near the gold mines. He and Henry Marshall ran a general store to supply the miners and their families. Then Father sold his share of the store to Henry and came here. That's when Aunt Kirstin came to live with us."

"It does seem rather big for such a small family." Maggie glanced around the room. "But everything is really beautiful."

"A lot of this has been collected over the years."

Catherine's gesture encompassed the whole room. "If you want to know what I think, Daddy was probably preparing a place, hoping that someday the two of you would also be here. Now it has happened. I can't wait until he sees you."

Maggie grabbed Catherine's hand. "This is a beautiful ring."

Mary stared at it. "It's on your left hand. Does this mean…"

"Collin asked me to marry him." The excitement bubbling inside Catherine became more pronounced.

Both of her sisters started laughing and congratulating her at the same time. And they threw their arms around her in another warm hug.

Soon the conversation settled into a comfortable session of catching up on happenings since they parted a few weeks ago. After they finished their food and warm drinks, Aunt Kirstin led the way upstairs. She put Mary and Daniel in the room across from Catherine's, with Charles in the room next to them.

"Maggie." Catherine smiled at her sister. "You can have the room next to mine, or you can share my room with me. Your choice."

Of course, Maggie made the choice Catherine had hoped she would. They would spend as much time as possible together.

"Then Georgia can be in the room next to yours. I'm sure she'll want to stay close to her niece." Kristin opened each bedroom door.

Maggie grinned. "Since Kirstin is also my aunt and Mary's, I'll share my other aunt with the rest of you, if it's all right with her."

Before she finished, Georgia was nodding. "How much fun, to gain two more nieces."

~

*A*ngus McKenna led the way up the steps of his home. "This morning went better than I expected it to."

Collin hurried behind him. "Yes, sir. I was happy to see there was no damage to any of the freight or the ship."

After coming through the door, Angus removed his hat and coat, hanging them on the hall tree. A noise from the stairs drew his attention. His daughter stood at the top, her hand on the banister and her eyes wide.

"Catherine, is everything all right?"

She didn't answer. Actually, she didn't move a muscle.

"Angus, that's not Catherine."

It took a moment for Collin's declaration to sink in. He turned to stare at the younger man. "Not Catherine? How can—?"

"If I'm not mistaken, that's Maggie. I sometimes get her and Mary mixed up, but never Catherine." Collin hung up his own coat.

"Father?"

The voice that asked the breathless question sounded like Catherine, but now Angus could tell it couldn't be her. He walked to the bottom of the steps, then slowly started up. He wasn't sure how to approach Margaret Lenora. After Catherine explained why his other daughters wouldn't come to meet him, he understood their reticence. He knew he'd hurt them deeply with the decision he'd made so long ago. He stopped when he was a third of the way to the top.

"Yes, dear Margaret." He poured all the love he'd bottled up in his heart for this child into those three words.

When he started speaking, she rushed down to meet him. Tears flooded her cheeks, and he could hardly see them through the veil of his own tears. He held his arms wide, but waited for her, not wanting to rush her and take a chance of pushing her away.

When she was close enough, she jumped into his arms, almost causing him to lose his balance. After closing her into a tight embrace, he remembered that long ago day when he had held her for the last time. His dreams and prayers were finally answered. He closed his eyes and savored the moment, never wanting to let go of her.

"Oh, my precious child. Have you forgiven me for the worst mistake I made in my entire life?"

He felt her head nod as her tears soaked his shirt. He slipped his arm around her back and walked with her down the stairs. "I can't believe you came to meet me. Catherine said—"

"I know. She told you what I said." She stepped back a bit. "And I meant every word at the time. But Mother helped me understand what you went through that awful day."

"Maggie, where are you?" Catherine's voice came from above them, but when he glanced up, Angus couldn't see her.

Collin started up the stairs, taking them two at a time. When he reached the top, Catherine met him. After he gave her a hug and dropped a quick kiss on her cheek, she glanced around him.

"Maggie." She started down the stairs. "Daddy, I see you've discovered our surprise."

He slipped his arm across Margaret's shoulders. "She forgave me." He had to force the words around the lump as large as a giant gold nugget in his throat.

Catherine's smile lit her face like the summer sun, much brighter than the weak winter one outside the house today, and she stopped about halfway down. "I know." She held up a forefinger. "I'll be right back." She ran all the way to the top, as she had when she was a little girl.

He glanced down at Margaret. "I can't tell you how happy you've made me. The deepest desire of my heart has been to see you and your sister again. To tell you how much I've always loved you."

Margaret pulled a hanky from her sleeve and started patting her cheeks, mopping up the tears.

"Daddy."

Catherine's voice drew his attention away from her sister. He could hardly believe his eyes. Two gorgeous redheaded women rushed toward him.

"Mary." He held his other arm wide, and she slipped to his side.

Catherine joined them in a large familial hug. His beautiful daughters, each one the spitting image of his precious Lenora, had returned to his arms. All his heart could do was praise God for the miraculous thing He had brought to pass in their lives. After eighteen long years, they were finally together again---a large and laughing, blessed and glorious *family*.

Did you enjoy this book? We hope so!
**Would you take a quick minute to leave a review
where you purchased the book?**
It doesn't have to be long. Just a sentence or two telling
what you liked about the story!

Receive a FREE ebook and get updates when new Wild
Heart books release: https://wildheartbooks.org/
newsletter

Enjoying this series? Check out Lena's Love's Road Home Series

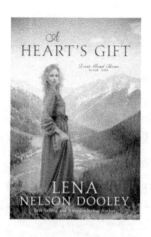

**Book 1: A Heart's Gift**

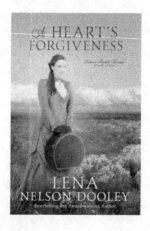

**Book 2: A Heart's Forgiveness**

Book 3: A Heart's Forever Home

Book 4: A Heart's Rescue

# ABOUT THE AUTHOR

Multi-published, award-winning author Lena Nelson Dooley has had more than 950,000 copies of her 50+ books sold. Her books have appeared on the CBA and ECPA bestseller lists, as well as Amazon bestseller lists. She is a member of American Christian Fiction Writers and the local chapter, ACFW - DFW. She's a member of Christian Authors' Network, and Gateway Church in Southlake, Texas.

Her 2010 release, *Love Finds You in Golden, New Mexico*, won the 2011 Will Rogers Medallion Award for excellence in publishing Western Fiction. Her next series, *McKenna's Daughters: Maggie's Journey* appeared on a reviewers' Top Ten Books of 2011 list. It also won the

2012 Selah award for Historical Novel. The second, *Mary's Blessing*, was a Selah Award finalist for Romance novel. *Catherine's Pursuit* released in 2013. It was the winner of the NTRWA Carolyn Reader's Choice contest, took second place in the CAN Golden Scroll Novel of the Year award, and won the Will Rogers Medallion bronze medallion. Her blog, A Christian Writer's World, received the Readers' Choice Blog of the Year Award from the Book Club Network. She also has won three Carol Award Silver pins. In 2015 and 2016, these novella collections—*A Texas Christmas, Love Is Patient, and Mountain Christmas Brides* have all appeared on the ECPA bestseller list, one of the top two bestseller lists for Christian books.

She has experience in screenwriting, acting, directing, and voice-overs. She is on the Board of Directors for Higher Ground Films and is one of the screenwriters for their upcoming film Abducted to Kill. She has been featured in articles in Christian Retailing, ACFW Journal, Charisma Magazine, and Christian Fiction Online Magazine. Her article in CFOM was the cover story.

In addition to her writing, Lena is a frequent speaker at women's groups, writers groups, and at both regional and national conferences. She has spoken in six states and internationally. The Lena Nelson Dooley Show is on the Along Came A Writer Blogtalk network.

Lena has an active web presence on Facebook, Twitter, Goodreads, Linkedin and with her internationally connected blog where she interviews other authors and promotes their books. Her blog has a reach of over 55,000.

- Website: https://lenanelsondooley.com
- Blog: http://lenanelsondooley.blogspot.com
- Blogtalk Radio: https://blogtalkradio.-com/alongcameawriter/2

facebook.com/Lena-Nelson-Dooley-42960748768

instagram.com/lenanelsondooley

pinterest.com/lenandooley

goodreads.com/lenanelsondooley

x.com/lenandooley

amazon.com/author/lenadooley

linkedin.com/in/lenanelsondooley

# WANT MORE?

## WANT MORE?

If you love historical romance, check out our other Wild Heart books!

*Lone Star Ranger by Renae Brumbaugh Green*

**Elizabeth Covington will get her man.**

And she has just a week to prove her brother isn't the murderer Texas Ranger Rett Smith accuses him of being. She'll show the good-looking lawman he's wrong, even if it means setting out on a risky race across Texas to catch the real killer.

Rett doesn't want to convict an innocent man. But he can't let the Boston beauty sway his senses to set a guilty man free. When Elizabeth follows him on a dangerous trek, the Ranger vows to keep her safe. But who will protect him from the woman whose conviction and courage leave him doubting everything—even his heart?

~

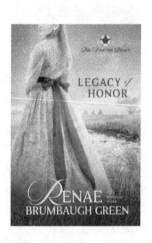

*Legacy of Honor by Renae Brumbaugh Green*

**He's been raised to carry on the legacy.**

Riley Stratton has it all, or so it seems. Growing up as the youngest son of the rich and powerful John Stratton, Riley stands to inherit a legacy of greatness in the Stratton Ranch—as long as he does things the Stratton way. On the surface, his family looks like they have it all, but manipulation, deceit, and an ever-present quest for power leave him desperate for change.

After her mother's untimely death, Emma Monroe's dreams to become a teacher are dashed. She takes a job as maid and cook at the local Stratton Ranch, where she endures humiliation and hardship in order to provide for her ailing father and younger brother. Only Riley Stratton, her childhood friend and heir to the Stratton fortune, sees her heart. When she's asked to care for Skye, the young half-Indian girl most family members refuse to claim, Emma finally finds the purpose she craves.

As Riley and Emma choose between honor, dreams, and expectations—not to mention the love they can no longer deny—their first steps prove how quickly the situation can spin into danger. When their best efforts threaten the lives and hopes of those closest to them, it becomes clear the decisions they make will change the course of their lives forever.

❧

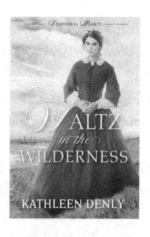

*Waltz in the Wilderness by Kathleen Denly*

**She doesn't need his help. He doesn't need another delay. But God has other plans...**

Eliza Brooks's worst nightmare has come true—her father is missing. Now she'll do anything to find him, even if it means taking a chance on who she must trust. But once aboard the steamship bound for San Diego—her father's last known whereabouts—she finds herself in far more danger than she imagined.

Daniel Clarke is a man of his word. Though he never imagined he'd be in California for four years, at least he's finally earned the money he needs to get married. Now he just has to get back to his fiancée in Massachusetts...the sooner the better. Especially since she's stopped replying to his letters.

When he boards a ship bound for San Diego, the first leg of his journey home, the last person Daniel expects to meet is his boss's niece. What could Eliza be thinking, traveling with no escort? With the lecherous captain determined to ruin her, Daniel has no choice but to offer his protection.

From shipwreck to cavalry outpost to the Southern California mountain wilderness, Daniel's entanglement with Eliza forces them—and their hearts—to face a future neither of them ever dreamed.